UNHINGED

A Chrissy McMullen Mystery

LOIS GREIMAN

Unhinged
Copyright © 2017 by Lois Greiman
ISBN-13: 978-1543174465
ISBN-10:1543174469

NYLA Publishing
350 7th Avenue, Suite 2003, NY 10001, New York.
http://www.nyliterary.com

Praise for Lois Greiman

predicaments that almost get her murdered. The chemistry between the psychologist and the police lieutenant is so hot that readers will see sparks fly off the pages. Lois Greiman, who has written over fifteen delightful romance books, appears to have a great career as a mystery writer also."
—*thebestreviews.com*

"Ms. Greiman makes a giant leap from historical fiction to this sexy and funny mystery. Bravo! Well done!"
—*Rendezvous*

"A fun mystery that will keep you interested and rooting for the characters until the last page is turned."
—*Fresh Fiction*

"Fast and fun with twists and turns that will keep you guessing. Enjoy the ride!"
—Suzanne Enoch, *USA Today* best-selling author of *Flirting with Danger*

"Lucy Ricardo meets Dr. Frasier Crane in Lois Greiman's humorous, suspenseful series. The result is a highly successful tongue-in-cheek, comical suspense guaranteed to entice and entertain."
—*Book Loons*

Dedication

To Caitlin Alexander, who has been brave enough to edit my Chrissy books since their inception and who understands the incomprehensible world of commas. Thanks for being spectaculent!

One

"If it wasn't for weird I'd be bored out of my mind."
—Christina McMullen, who is rarely bored

"You look well," I said and kept my tone clipped, my wayward hands strictly to myself. I was casually dressed in cutoff jeans and a T-shirt that had seen better days.

He smiled, just a tilt of those swoon-worthy lips. "As do you," he said, but his eyes, those burning sapphire flames, said so much more.

Heat seared my cheeks, then zipped off to less humdrum parts. But I resisted fidgeting, though I had dreamt of this moment on a hundred less . . . conscious . . . occasions. I put my hand on the countertop, making certain I was still in the here and now. The newly installed granite felt cool, smooth, and simultaneously sticky. Sure enough, I was home.

"So your business in Callatis went well?" I asked.

He shrugged. The gesture would have been oh so insignificant had he not been sans shirt. His chest, a lightly oiled work of art, was, in a word coined by a man I'd known as Thing One, *spectaculent.*

"Well enough." His voice was slightly accented. He took a step toward me.

I lifted my chin to maintain eye contact. At 5'9" plus, I'm no wilting dandelion, but no part of him appeared to be droopy. His pecs were bulging, his arms corded, his chiseled face shadowed with bristly scruff.

"Rahim was satisfied?" I asked.

He stepped closer, crowding my personal space, filling my senses. He looked like a wet dream, smelled like chocolate Bundt cake. "When have I failed to satisfy?"

I ignored the steamy suggestiveness as best I could, but honest to Pete, he was shedding sexual innuendoes like a molting lovebird. "I'm glad—" I began and turned away, but he grabbed my arm, yanking me toward him.

"Admit it!" he snarled.

His grip was steely around my biceps. My heart pounded. I should never have agreed to meet him. But he was here now, up close and personal, while my cell phone, my most reliable means of obtaining help, seemed a million miles away.

"Admit what?" My voice was raspy.

"You want me." He breathed the words into the air between us, setting it afire. "Say it."

But I couldn't. Didn't dare. Too much had happened. I straightened my spine. Raised my chin. "No. You're—"

He kissed me.

His lips seared mine, but I held strong, held steady . . . for two endless seconds, then I twisted my fingers in his hair and jumped him like a hyena on a hapless hare. He stumbled a little under my weight, then grabbed my ass, holding me astride as I wrapped my legs around his waist and dove in.

"Cut."

His torso was hard and rippled against mine, his lips full and warm and—

"Cut!"

His heart was drubbing like a kick drum. Other parts throbbed in concert. My own answered lustily. I fumbled with his belt, but his sword—the plastic one suspended from his hips—kept impeding my progress.

"Mac," Laney called.

"Ms. McMullen," he murmured.

"Christina Mary McMullen!" Laney scolded, perhaps thinking that using my full name, as the Holy Name sisters had done on a thousand ill-disciplined occasions, would somehow penetrate the fog in my brain.

Sadly, it worked. I felt reality seep in like battery acid. I unsuctioned my lips, blinked, and turned my head groggily to the right.

Brainy Laney Butterfield, aka the Amazon Queen, stood ten feet away, baby to her shoulder, TV script held loosely in one hand. "That's the end of the scene."

Sergio, more commonly known as Morab to the viewing public, stared at me, brows raised. There might have been a little WTF in his gaze.

"That was . . . " Laney paused, patted the baby. "An interesting interpretation."

"Oh . . . " I cleared my throat, carefully avoiding Sergio's bewildered gaze. "Thank you."

"You can probably . . . " She sighed but resisted rolling her eyes. Laney's kick-ass disciplined that way. "Dismount now."

"Oh, right. Right!" I said, and yet my legs failed to comply, while my fingers, nasty little sluts that they are, remained curled in Sergio's waistband like eagle's claws gone rogue.

That's when someone knocked on the door.

I gasped and jerked my attention toward the foyer. Perhaps because the arrival of visitors is generally followed by screaming, running, and subsequent death threats.

Don't ask me why people keep trying to murder me. Mysteries abound. Even for a psychologist, a PhD, and a really dynamite kisser such as myself.

"Should I get that?" Laney asked, nodding toward the door.

"What?" I was having a little trouble dragging myself from the just-interrupted scene and back into reality. Some might say I'd been employing the acting technique called the Meisner method. Others could argue that I was just really really horny.

Laney gave me one more hopeless glance and pattered toward my front door.

"*Apaixonado,*" Sergio said.

"What?" I repeated. It was the best I could do. My blood, it seems, can either supply my brain or my reproductive system. Both is beyond my ability.

"It is what we call women such as yourself in Brazil."

Our mouths were inches apart and our chests even closer. My nipples, those damn little bullets of destruction, were aimed directly at his heart. "Women . . . " Good God, he had fantastic lips, made to suck and be sucked. "Like myself?"

"Women with . . . " He shook his head as if searching his memory banks for a politically acceptable term. "Verve." His sparkling-heaven eyes bore into mine. "Women who are aflame with . . . "

"Should I call the fire department?"

4

The voice ripped my attention from Sergio's suckable lips. I snapped my head to the left, and there, sure as that bastard Murphy, with his deplorable law, would predict, stood my nemesis, protector, and ex-lover.

Lieutenant Jack Rivera.

Two

"There's no room in my life for you anymore. My trunk's pretty empty, though."
—Angela Grapier, a girl who knows when enough is enough

Rivera's voice was deadpan, but his hot mocha eyes could only be described as jaded. Or disgusted. Or annoyed. Or pissed as holy hell. Okay, there was a shitload of ways his eyes could be described, so long as none of them implied even the tiniest degree of happiness.

He raised one low-dipped brow at me.

"Oh . . . I . . . umm . . . we were just . . . " I shook my head, honestly uncertain what the hell Sergio and I had been doing. Although I was pretty damn clear on what my vervish body had been hoping for.

"Rehearsing a scene," Sergio supplied evenly.

"Were you the villain or the horse?" Rivera asked and shifted his killer gaze to my impromptu mount.

"The . . . " Sergio's tone was perplexed, but then he

chuckled heartily. "She is neither attempting to strangle nor ride me," he said. "It is a love scene between Morab the indomitable slave and Hippolyta"—he nodded toward Laney, who stood to Rivera's left, expression bland and not a bit surprised by this turn of events—"the Amazon queen. Our Christina was kind enough to act as Elaine's understudy."

"*Our* Christina?" Rivera said and stared at him in silence for half of forever.

"She is a wonder," Sergio added.

"Yeah, she's peachy," Rivera said, then moved his smoking eyes to mine. "Shall I tell them to bring the Jaws of Life?"

I scowled, but my brain cells were finally beginning to twitter back into real time. "Oh, because . . ." Rather belatedly, I realized that my thighs, recently honed by a thousand hours of not so willing physical training, were still clamped around Sergio's rock-hard waist like opinionated pliers. I exhaled carefully and loosened my death grip. Despite the lack of discernible seasons in SoCal, my legs looked winter white against the love slave's Brazilian skin.

Sergio, gentleman that he was, let his hands slide up my behind and over my waist, making sure I didn't fall on my ass as I pried my legs apart and dropped my feet to the floor.

The room was suspiciously quiet. I cleared my throat in the cricket-chirping stillness and stepped back a pace, though honest to God, I had nothing to be embarrassed about. Yes, the dark lieutenant and I shared something of a tumultuous history. We had, in fact, been caught in a similarly awkward situation not too many months before, but recent developments involving general dishonesty and an individual I referred to simply as Skank Girl had made me swear off men in general and Rivera in particular.

Men, of course, did not include Hollywood love slaves who'd been branded on their superlatively sexy loins and who tended to be oiled like Caesar salads.

"Sergio," Laney said, voice dulcet in the pulsing silence, "this is Lieutenant Rivera of the LAPD. Jack, meet Sergio Carlos Zepequeno."

"Ahh." Delight sparked in Sergio's eyes. He couldn't have looked happier if he'd spied a leprechaun toting a large pot. "You're an officer of the law? But this is *maravilhoso*. I wish to read for the part of a detective. Yet I was unsure whether I could assume such a commanding presence." He stepped forward, offered his hand. "Perhaps we could speak sometime. I would love to . . . how do you say . . . pluck your brain."

"That would be . . . what's the term?" Rivera asked, sarcasm needle sharp in his tone. "Fantastical. In fact . . . " His eyes narrowed. "We could step outside right now if you'd like to learn a few things."

"Truly? You would do that for me?" Sergio splayed artists' fingers across his Greek-god chest. But I grabbed his arm before he scampered out to his doom.

"Don't be a moron." I crushed Rivera with a glare. The dark lieutenant had been the bane of my existence for years. Maybe I'd kind of liked him at one time, but now I saw him for what he was . . . a pushy Neanderthal with a superiority complex. So what if he also had a really primo ass and a semi-endearing way of making baby talk to our love child/Great Dane on the phone?

Sergio frowned. Laney shook her head, then spoke into the confusion.

"Mac and the lieutenant are . . . " Laney paused. She's my oldest friend and very possibly the nicest person on the planet.

"What would you call your relationship, Jack?"

He shifted his gravedigger's gaze to hers. Men usually find it impossible to maintain a scowl when Laney's in the universe, but Rivera was giving it the old college try. "She was in danger," he growled, alluding, I assumed, to his supposed reason for exiling me from the city some months before. An exile that caused me an extended stay in purgatory. "She could get herself killed in the Vatican. I was trying to keep her alive."

"And I trusted you to do just that," Laney said. Her tone suggested she wasn't quite ready to absolve Rivera of his most recent FUBAR. That fact almost made it possible for *me* to do so.

"Danshov should have known better than to—" Rivera began, but she cut him off.

"Danshov?" Her voice had risen a little, causing baby Mac to squirm like a tadpole. She patted his back but kept her gaze pinned to Rivera's. Her eyes, those knock-'em-dead emerald orbs, snapped like peas. "Does it strike you as ironic that you trusted a known assassin to ensure the well-being of my best friend?"

"You are associated with an assassin?" Sergio gaped, tone going hyper-squirrel with excitement. "Truly? But this is magnificent. MGM is casting for just such a character. If I could but meet this Danshov I might learn much."

Laney yanked her gaze from Rivera to Sergio.

There was a heartbeat of silence, then, "My apologies," he said, reading her mood with unmanly speed. Morab, it seemed, was not the idiot an equitable universe would require someone with his lusciousness to be. "There are issues here, real-life concerns to which I am not privy. Hence, I should leave you to your discussions." Yet he remained as he was, looking like he'd give his right kidney to be privy to those juicy tidbits.

"Perhaps that would be best," Laney agreed.

Rivera remained silent, but I believe his eyes said something like, *Fuckin' A.*

A moment later, Sergio had sauntered out the door, plastic sword and bulging pecs in tow.

Rivera scowled at my inoffensive front door, then settled his ire on me. "We need to talk," he said.

"Seriously?" My ovaries were not currently programmed for a mature conversation involving real words. They were, I was pretty sure, concerned about other details. "Maybe you should have thought of that instead of lying to me like a fu . . . " I gritted my teeth and glanced regretfully at baby Mac. Kids! I guess you're not supposed to swear around them. Go figure. "Instead of lying to me," I finished poorly. Turns out it's hardly worth speaking if you can't toss out the F bomb now and then.

"I didn't lie," Rivera said.

"Really? So your house actually *was* being attacked? So terrifying gang members were honestly about to burst into your kitchen, making me scurry for parts unknown like a hunted—"

"I was trying to keep you safe!"

"By sending me to Danshov . . . who, by the by, almost drowned me. Did he tell you that? That's the guy you thought would be a dandy choice to look after me during my time of need?"

A muscle bunched in his jaw. "What do you want me to do, McMullen? Challenge him to a duel? Pistols at dawn? Would that make you happy?"

"Pistols? No." I gritted a smile at him. "That would imply

10

you two were civilized human beings. I think I'd prefer a fistfight. Bare knuckles."

"Yeah?"

"No holds barred."

"Well"—he cocked his head at me—"if that's what it takes . . . " He pulled his cell from his back pocket. "I'll set it up right now. I assume you'll want to watch?"

I snorted. I was an enlightened woman . . . a feminist, in fact, but nothing would make me happier than seeing Danshov beat the crap out of Rivera . . . or, conversely, seeing Rivera beat the crap out of Danshov. It was, in my bloodthirsty opinion, a win-win. "Do I want to see you get your ass handed to you?" I scoffed. "Just let me know when and where so I can show up with a lawn chair and popcorn."

He stepped toward me. "If you think your little monk can touch me, you're even crazier than I thought."

I stepped toward him, hormones humming like honeybees. "You think you're such a hard-ass with your bulging . . . " I tossed a dismissive hand toward his chest and felt my breath hitch at the sight. "And your . . . " I motioned toward the smoldering rest of him. "But . . . " I inhaled heavily and took another step toward him. "You're—"

"All right! That's enough!" Laney snarled, maneuvering between us like a world-weary referee. "I don't want any fornicating around my baby."

"Fornicating!" I snapped, and yanked myself out of the lust-induced haze. There might have been some spittle involved. "I wouldn't fornicate him if he had the last dick on the—"

"Mac, please," she pleaded and held up a hand as if to ward off evil spirits. "Can't you two just discuss things like adults?"

"Well, I'm an adult," I said. "But clearly—"

"Adult? Are you shitting me?" Rivera whipped an arm toward the door through which one branded love slave had just escaped. "Is that what you call it when you jump the first oiled-up—"

"Enough!" Laney sliced a hand between us. "I was shooting too high. You don't have to be adults. How about human? Could you manage that much?"

Rivera ground his teeth. I looked away. Honest to God, I didn't want to be a moron. In fact, I wanted nothing more than to be lucid, sensible, maybe even—wait for it—classy, but he drove me bat-shit crazy. Okay, truth was, maybe I was a little bat-shit without him, but he brought all the excrement to the forefront.

"I'm sorry."

I zipped my gaze to Rivera, sure my ears were playing tricks on me. "What?"

"I've apologized before." His voice was no more than a simmering growl.

"In this lifetime?"

"Listen, McMullen . . . "

"Dammit!" Laney barked.

I gasped. Rivera gaped.

Laney, even pre-gestational, didn't swear. Now that baby Mac had boots on the ground, I was certain she would have expunged *all* four-letter words from her vernacular.

"I just . . . " Her expression shifted from anger to fear. "I love you, Mac." Tears swam in her otherworldly eyes. "I don't know what I'd do if . . . if something happened to you." And suddenly she was sobbing.

"Laney . . ." Stumbling forward, I wrapped her and the baby in my arms. "I'm sorry. I'm so sorry." I glanced over her head at Rivera.

His hands were fisted, his body tense, as if he were undergoing some terrible torture. But he managed to remain where he was, which was pretty amazing. I've seen men tear their hair out by the handfuls when Laney looked mildly dewy eyed.

"We won't fight anymore. Tell her we won't fight, Rivera."

"We won't," he said.

She hiccupped noisily, patted Mac's back. "You promise?" she asked and shifted her sorrowful gaze to Rivera.

He flexed his hands, probably battling a dozen fictional villains on her behalf. "We won't fight . . . today," he said.

She turned her gaze to me. "Mac? Do you . . ." She sobbed noisily, trying to control her emotions. "I'm sorry. I'm leaking hormones, but I just . . . I need to know you'll be all right. That you'll treat each other with the mutual respect you deserve. Promise me."

"I promise," I said.

"Really?"

"Cross my heart," I vowed and did.

"Okay," she said without a modicum of emotion, and turned casually away. "I'm going to head home, then. Traffic's going to be a bear and we're trying to get Mac on a decent schedule." I stared after her, remembering, rather belatedly, that (1) Brainy Laney Butterfield is an excellent actress, and (2) when she cries in earnest she does so in absolute silence. Histrionics are reserved for the camera. "But remember—" She stopped in my humble foyer. "There's a special place in hell for those who lie to new mothers."

"You're evil," I told her. "I don't know why I always forget that."

"It's because you love me," she said and left.

Three

"The fact that jellyfish have survived for millions of years without a brain must be the best news ever for you douche-nuggets."
—Chrissy McMullen to her brothers, following a particularly unappreciated episode involving superglue and hair

I shifted my gaze to Rivera, noticing for the first time that he looked kind of tired. Tired, grim, and heart-palpitatingly handsome.

"Can I get you something to drink?" My tone sounded a little bit saccharine, but perhaps that was better than pissy. Or its evil sister . . . horny.

"No." He exhaled, clearly trying to remain civil. It was a stretch for both of us. "Thank you."

"Hungry?"

"Not right now."

"Okay," I said and moved toward the kitchen. "But I think I'll have a little something if you don't mind."

I could feel him following me but ignored him. Trying to

lower my emotions to a boil, I glanced into the freezer. My recent exile from L.A. had changed everything: the way I thought, the way I exercised, the way I ate.

Except when it came to ice cream. Ice cream, clearly, was the one constant in a world gone mad, and the only thing likely to bring my mood back into the non-lethal range.

I took out the unopened tub of Häagen-Dazs, removed the lid, and dished a modest portion of brownies à la mode into a bowl. Plopping my leaner-than-it-used-to-be ass against the counter, I settled my gaze on my uninvited visitor.

"Why are you here?" I had meant the question to sound approachable, but the icy ambrosia had not yet numbed my rancor.

Rivera glared at me. "Do you still have that mermaid getup?"

"Tell me the truth, Lieutenant." I raised my brows at him. "Have you been sampling Narcotics' confiscated gains?"

The scar at the corner of his mouth twitched. Why, dear God, *why* did I find that sexy? "The getup you wore while you were playing Sherlock at Elaine's after-party, do you still have it?"

I took another nibble of icy bliss and considered pretending ignorance, but it was too much of a leap. "Laney was in danger," I said, remembering my incognito investigation on the oh so embarrassing night in question. Even Rivera's über-posh but philandering sire, the estimable Senator Rivera, had appreciated my disguise. "Some people, present company excluded, of course, try to help the individuals they care about instead of bursting in to call names, spew accusations, and periodically send them fleeing into more danger."

He ignored my rant, fished a spoon from my silverware drawer, and dug into the bucket. "So in that particular situation you thought dressing like a sea siren and pretending to be . . . Who were you impersonating again? A French prostitute?"

I considered a few choice swear words but I had bigger problems: my bowl was already empty. I gave that some judicious consideration, then began feeding directly from the tub. Our spoons sparred for an instant. "Why are you here, Rivera?"

His lips twitched again, probably at the reminder that he hadn't come solely to piss me off. "The mayor's charity ball is coming up."

I froze, utensil halfway to my mouth, and blinked at him. "Are you serious?"

He managed to look angry and confused at the same time. "Why would I make up something like that?"

"Are you asking me on a *date*?"

The confusion was gone now, replaced by increased anger and a smidgeon of defensiveness. "We've been on dates before."

"Can you remember any that didn't involve loaded weapons?"

He opened his mouth, probably to issue some ridiculous double entendre, but finally shook his head. "You want to go or not?"

I scowled, which was simply wrong. One should be ever joyous when brownies à la mode is involved. "When is it?"

"Couple weeks."

I quirked a cocky brow at him. "And you still haven't found some skank who'd agree to—"

"I thought you cared about her!"

I paused, baffled.

"Elaine. I thought your promise to *her*, at least, might mean something."

A thousand nasty rejoinders rushed to my lips, but I trapped them behind clenched teeth despite the fact that he only seemed to appear when there were other men interested . . . e.g., Morab the love slave. "Very well, I'll play nice if you will," I said, and smiling grittily, batted my stubby lashes. "The mayor's ball, you say?"

He eyed me. *Suspicious* didn't begin to describe his expression. "Yeah."

"How nice of you to ask." I fished out another morsel of ice cream, nibbled delicately. "Where might this auspicious event be held?"

"The Belasco."

Holy hell, the Belasco Theater! The mayor must have some big-ass balls. "I see," I said, tone cool. "And when exactly?"

A muscle danced a hot tango along his jaw, reminding me that we had, on more than one occasion, gone from frosty to fornication in a sizzling thirty seconds. "The twenty-eighth."

"Of this month."

"Yes." He might have ground his teeth.

"Well . . ." I smiled. "It's ever so flattering that you asked, Lieutenant, but I'll have to check my social schedule." I pattered to where my purse rested on a kitchen chair and pulled out my cell phone. Half the time I forget to punch in my future plans. The other half, those plans became mysteriously lost in the ether, but I was trying hard to join the twenty-first century. Unfortunately, the new millennium was fighting back; it generally took me half an hour just to *find* my digital calendar.

"Well?"

I glanced up at his growl. "Well, what?"

"Are you free?"

His impatience rang of jealousy, and as any woman with an ounce of honesty will tell you, jealousy from an ex is tantamount to winning the lottery. "Let's see . . . " I scowled at the tiny screen, nodded, and muttered softly, "Oh, yeah, Vincent. I'd almost forgotten."

"Vincent Angler?" he asked.

I was rather pleased that he remembered I was acquainted with the good-looking linebacker who played for the Lions. "Then there's Tavis . . . " I sighed as if put-upon.

"Who? Not that fucking Mayberry cop?"

"Oh . . . Vigo . . . " I crooned happily. My gaze remained on the screen, but I couldn't help noticing that Rivera had clenched his fists.

"What about him?"

"It's been ages," I said and raised my brows at his obvious displeasure. "We're just meeting for drinks. Nothing to get excited about."

"Where?" he asked, seeming not so much excited as well and truly pissed. "When?"

I smiled. "Looks like it'll just be a quick visit. I'm seeing Mr. Archer afterward."

"Are you shitting me?"

"Thennnnn . . . " I wobbled my head, having a jolly old time making crap up. "D, Micky . . . " I paused. "About which day were you inquiring again?"

His eyes were narrowed, his body language obscene. "The twenty-eighth."

I sighed, long and heavy. "I should probably be studying for my exam then."

"Exam?"

I raised my wondrously innocent gaze to his. "Didn't I tell you? I'm going back to school."

I wasn't entirely sure, but it looked as if he might have quit breathing. "What for?"

Sashaying back to the counter, I fished a luscious chunk of brownie from the ice cream tub. Savored it. "I'm studying to become a profiler."

For a second, I thought he might actually implode. Thought the throbbing veins in his neck might burst, ejecting his head right off his neck. "A profiler."

"Yes."

"For the police department."

I shrugged. "Or the FBI."

"Are you *trying* to get yourself killed? Is that it?"

"What's the matter, Rivera? Afraid I'll fall for some hot cop fresh out of the academy?"

His lips twitched, his hands flexed. Then he turned and stalked out the door like RoboCop on autopilot.

But that was okay. More brownies à la mode for me.

Four

"I'm beginning to believe you may never be old enough to know better."
          —Father Pat, who knew Chrissy fairly well

"Hey," I said, and stepping into my office at L.A. Counseling, closed the door behind me. Micky Goldenstone was standing with his back toward me as he stared out the window. His low-cut pants hugged his hips, his waffle-knit shirt was snug, his shoes leather. My view was considerably better than his.

"Doc," he said and turned. His smile, a twisted, kick-ass grin, looked both devilish and heartbreakingly vulnerable against his dark skin. But what was behind it? Worry, maybe, and the usual truckload of unrelenting guilt. "How you doing?"

"Good," I said, though I was still suffering from post-love-slave humiliation and after-Rivera gluttony. Sometimes it's hard for even *me* to believe I'm a reasonably well-paid and semi-respected psychologist.

"What are you doing here?" Micky hadn't made an

appointment—Shirley had called me during my dog-food-buying lunch break to inform me of his arrival. "How's Jamel?"

It was a good place to start. He'd learned the boy was his son fairly recently, was raising him as such, and was subsequently experiencing the joy/agony that any self-respecting child causes his parents.

"Good. We're planning a trip to King's Canyon. I'm letting him pick the camp sites." An almost imperceptible tremor quivered in his fingertips.

I sat, motioning toward the couch for him to do the same. He prowled the short length of my office instead.

"Just the two of you?"

"Yeah."

"That's nice. The sequoias are spectacular."

Silence pulsed between us for a beat.

"How's your grandmother?" I picked up a pen from my desk and fiddled with it as I silently analyzed.

"Terrifying," he admitted, and I smiled not so much because it was true but because my own horrific family remains a couple thousand miles to the east.

"Is work going—"

He turned toward me. The smile was gone, replaced by angst and ferocity. "What if something happens to him?"

I inhaled slowly, filling my lungs, calming my nerves. Sessions with Micky were never boring. "What's going on?" I asked.

"Nothing." He prowled again, brows low over his wildly expressive eyes. "Probably nothing."

"Probably . . ."

"He's safe. He's fine."

"Why wouldn't Jamel be fine?" I felt a niggle of worry low in my gut. There was something about Micky's son that had always stirred my soul. Maybe it was his stuck-out ears or the loss of his mother . . . or the fact that he was the product of rape; Micky had a hideous past. A past for which he'd spend the rest of his life making amends.

Micky huffed a laugh. "Because the world's fucked up, filled with fucked-up people."

"Any people in particular?"

He stopped prowling to look at me. "Me, maybe?"

"No," I said. "Not anymore." I liked to believe I had a little something to do with that. He had come to me years ago, burning with guilt, bursting with anger. Those elements still remained, but they were banked now, fueling his desire to make a better world for his son, for himself.

He snorted in disbelief, but his shoulders relaxed a quarter of an inch. "You planning to have kids, Doc?"

"Not today."

He sighed, rubbed his neck beneath his clean-cut hairline. "They'll drive you insane. Make you want to shove your head in the oven, or wrap them up in that . . . " He made a winding motion. "That plastic stuff."

"Bubble wrap."

"Yeah. Wrap them up in that shit so nothing can touch them. So nothing can hurt them. It's crazy. Scary as hell. Being responsible for someone else. Someone you'd die for. Someone you live for."

"You're a good dad, Micky."

"Yeah?"

"Yeah."

"What kind of *person* do you think I am?"

"On a scale of one to ten?"

He stared at me, then chuckled as I'd intended, relieving a little more of the tension. He sat finally, perched on the edge of the couch, expression troubled, palms, paler past the curve of his fingers, pressed together. "I don't know where to draw the line."

"Between . . . "

"Duty to my kid and duty to"—he shrugged as if lost—"society."

I raised a brow.

He tilted his head back and laughed at himself. "Jesus, I sound like an idiot. But I don't—" He rose to pace again. "How much are you supposed to give up?"

"Me?"

"Sure." He leaned against the edge of my desk and stared down at me. "You're a do-gooder."

"Me," I said again, and remembered, with a mix of horror and longing, a scene I'd played out just the day before in my living room. I was pretty sure do-gooders did not ride half-naked Brazilians like a proverbial untamed stallion.

"Saved *my* ass," he said.

I started to deny it, but I had kind of done just that. "Well . . . it was worth saving. Your life!" I corrected. "I mean your *life* was worth saving."

He cocked his head. "I'd be lying, Doc, if I said it doesn't do my heart . . . and stuff . . . "—that grin again, mischievous as hell—"good to know you're thinking about my ass."

I gave him a prudish scowl and he straightened, still grinning. "I bet your lieutenant doesn't appreciate you sticking out your pretty neck for an ex-Skull like me."

"What's this all about, Micky?"

For a second, I thought he might actually tell me. "You ever get tired of sleeping alone?"

I wondered if I had missed a segue somewhere but sometimes it was best just to let the conversation roll where it would. "I have a Great Dane. Takes up about ninety percent of the bed."

"Yeah? Maybe that's what I need."

"A dog?"

"Low expectations," he said, and leaning down, kissed me.

I would have objected, honest, but the kiss lasted only a moment before he drew back, then walked out the door.

I stared after him, mind whirring. That kiss had been a goodbye kiss, a condemned man's kiss—what was going on that Micky had been so reluctant to say? I had no time to get my bearings; Shirley was already buzzing me. It took me a moment to remember how to answer the intercom.

"Yes?"

"Rose Unger is here, Ms. McMullen." She was using her professional voice. I might have been imagining it, but I thought I could hear her *what the hell just happened in there?* voice being firmly squelched. Shirley is half receptionist, half mother bear, and all psychic.

"Oh, yes . . . " I glanced around, feeling lost. "Please, send her in."

A moment later, I was seated across the coffee table from my next client. She was as pale as Micky was dark, as prim as he was passionate.

"So, Rose," I said, lifting my gaze from my notes to her, "tell me a little about yourself."

"Well . . . " She pursed her lips. "There not much to tell, really."

According to my records, Rose was eighty-two years old. There had to be a little something to talk about.

"So you live in San Marino?"

"Yes, I have a little bungalow not far from the Mission."

"You live alone?"

"Ever since Orvill passed."

"And Orvill was your . . . " I paused, letting her fill in the blanks. According to her daughter, one Amelia May Langer, Rose had been acting erratically since her husband's death. But I would judge for myself.

"My husky," Rose said.

"It must be difficult . . . " I paused, staring at her. "Excuse me?"

"He was such a good boy. Most heavy-coated breeds don't care for the water. But he loved to swim."

I blinked, trying to navigate. "Orvill was your *dog*?"

She watched me in bland insouciance for several seconds, then grinned. "I'm sorry." Her expression might have contained a modicum of regret, but mostly she just looked impish. "I'm teasing. Orvill was my husband, of course. But I suspect you know that." She cocked her head a little, eying me. "Amy probably told you everything but my shoe size. Six and a half," she added. "If they run true to size."

I settled back a little. Rose Ungar, I thought, was a pistol. "Tell me why you're here."

"You want the truth?"

Generally speaking, the truth and I have a somewhat tenuous relationship. But maybe now wasn't the time to admit that. "Yes," I said. "The truth would be nice."

"Well . . . " She sighed heavily. "I used to blame the government."

I waited for some sort of explanation. When none was forthcoming, I nudged gently. "The government?"

"Lance, my son-in-law, worked for the State Department. Lance . . . " She shook her head, platinum curls bobbing. "Sounds like a knight or a cowboy or a firefighter or something, doesn't it?"

"He's not a knight, I take it."

"He's a dud is what he is. I mean, don't get me wrong, Amy wasn't ever going to be tearing up the roads with the Hell's Angels or anything, but once she married Lance . . . " She sighed again. "Do you mind if I smoke?" She drew a package of Camels from her handbag.

I tried to keep my eyebrows from popping into the stratosphere, but they seemed to have a mind of their own. "I'm sorry. It's actually against my landlord's policy."

"Is that right?"

"Yes."

"Wouldn't you know it, just when I'm ready to start a nice little bad habit." She tucked the box tidily back into her purse.

"So . . . you haven't smoked in the past?" I asked.

"Not for sixty years or so."

"And you still miss it?" If that was the case, it didn't look good for my own hopes of breaking the nicotine habit . . . for the four hundredth time.

"I don't know. Sometimes, I guess. It's just . . . " She shrugged, a birdlike bob of bony shoulders. "If not now . . . when?"

She kind of had a point, but I didn't say as much. "Do you think that's why your daughter wanted you to see me? Because of the smoking?"

"Could be, but I'm thinking it might be because of

Rodney."

"Your . . . " I took a stab in the dark. "Border collie?"

She chuckled. "Don't be silly," she said. "He's my gigolo."

"How important is sex?" I asked.

Shirley turned toward me like a bulky ballerina, face showing her surprise. "As a form of entertainment or as a means of perpetuating the species?"

Shirley was a high school graduate with seven kids, innumerable grandkids, and enough practical knowledge to fuel an East Coast think tank.

"Either."

"Well . . . " She settled into her chair behind the reception desk. Since she began working for me nearly two years ago, the place had come to resemble a well-tended jungle. One broad, variegated leaf threatened to tickle her left ear. "It's tough as hell to find a good movie these days. Plus, even the matinees will cost you ten bucks. Sex, on the other hand, is free."

"Usually," I agreed, remembering Rose.

"Unless you get a kid out of the deal—then it'd be cheaper to buy a nice little island someplace. Why? You thinking of giving it up?" Reaching under her desk, she pulled out a white bakery box and a bottle of milk.

I didn't bother to tell her that except on very rare but clearly remembered occasions, I had been celibate for years. I also didn't turn up my nose at the goodies contained in the box. I am, if nothing else, gracious.

I took my first bite of a maple-frosted long john and waxed philosophical. "Maybe it's not as important as our social mores would suggest."

"Sex?" she asked, as if thinking I might have wandered

onto another topic without informing her. Taking a bite from her own pastry, she gave me a dubious look out of the corner of her eye.

"Yeah."

"How long has it been since you've had any?"

I considered lying, but Shirley seemed to have inherited Laney's ability to read my mind. "A while."

"Could be you should get some soon to see how you feel about it."

"You think?"

"But only if you got yourself a really fail-proof contraceptive." Shirley was a huge proponent of birth control. I guess raising a litter of kids will do that.

"Hard to beat abstinence in that regard," I said.

"Yeah, but then you're neglecting your humming place."

I had heard her refer to such a locale before. "I'm not sure I've got one of those."

"Oh, you got one. You just been ignoring it is all."

Five

"I can refrain from swearing or I can refrain from poking you in the eye with a chopstick. You choose."

—Chrissy McMullen, with whom breaking up was not only hard to do but frequently dangerous

I considered Shirley's words on my drive home, ruminated on them over Chinese take-out, which I shared with Harlequin, my significant other of a different species.

Afterward, he licked my ear and promised never-ending adoration, while Shikoku, a malamute lookalike, watched with a mixture of disdain and indifference. Shikoku is a story unto herself. Suffice it to say she does not adore me, and yet we share an abode. An arrangement not entirely acceptable to either of us, but forced upon us by her master, Hiro Danshov, chef, self-defense expert, and purported assassin. Had I met him earlier in my life I would have said he was the most exasperating man in the world. But I've known Jack Rivera for some time.

By ten o'clock, we had watched enough *Walker, Texas Ranger* to convince me it was time for bed . . . or possible suicide. Gathering up our used crockery to prevent Harley from wearing it on his oversized snout, I marched it into the kitchen.

The phone rang as I was returning for the now empty Häagen-Dazs bucket.

The number on the screen was unidentified. I answered anyway. "Hello?"

"How you doing, white chick?"

It took a moment for my brain cells to clatter around enough to recognize her voice. "Lavonn?"

"Living and in the flesh."

Lavonn Blount and I have a short but colorful history. It involves abusive boyfriends, drugs, and badass dogs. Somewhere in that quixotic mix we had trauma-bonded.

"So how are classes going?"

I scrambled to catch up. "Classes?"

"I saw you in the library."

"What? How? I thought you were in Cleveland or something."

"Well, you know what they say. Be it ever so weird, there's no place like home."

"I'm not sure that's how it goes."

"I'm paraphrasing."

"So you came back to . . . " Honest to God, I was surprised at her return. Not long ago, Lavonn had fatally shot a dirty cop. That was followed by the shocking revelation that she'd been acting as sort of an unofficial undercover agent.

"Study for the bar exam," she said, completing my sentence.

"At UC? Why didn't you say hello if you saw me?"

"You were thinking really hard. Looked painful." She paused for a beat. "Charley says hi."

Charley was the above-mentioned badass dog. "How *is* he?"

"He misses you."

I snorted. Lavonn and I definitely had the kind of relationship that included snorting. Snarling and cursing were also acceptable forms of communication.

"Well, maybe he knows I saved his life." Charley had been seriously injured. Lavonn and I had dragged him to my vet, where I'd paid the ensuing bills.

"Yeah, either that or he's hungry for white meat."

"I had almost forgotten how awful you are," I said.

She laughed. "How's life?"

"About par."

"That bad?"

"I didn't say it was bad."

"Girl," she said, "par for you is one short step from the morgue."

"Huh . . ." I thought about that for a second. "I guess I'm ahead of the game, then."

"Nobody trying to kill you?"

"Not that I know of."

"Well, it's not even midnight yet."

"Did you call just to brighten my day?"

She laughed. "Actually, I wanted to talk to Mick."

"Who?"

"Mick. Micky. Michael."

"Micky Goldenstone?" I asked, remembering his agitation, his angst . . . and his kiss from earlier in the day.

"How many Micks you got there?"

"None," I said, but I glanced around, just to be sure. I had been pretty groggy during the last, say . . . sixty minutes of *Walker*. For me, evening television and Ambien are neck and neck in their ability to put me to sleep.

"Listen, I'm not his keeper. The two of you want to get your freak on, it's no skin off my ass."

"Get our freak . . . " I sighed and started fresh. "Why would you think he'd be here, Lavonn?"

"He is, isn't he?"

"Did he say he would be?"

"He didn't say he wouldn't."

Logic seemed to be in short supply. "Were there other places he neglected to mention?"

"Don't get smart," she said.

"I'm trying, but it's so hard. What's going on?" I asked and glanced into my fridge. A carton of low-fat yogurt from another century sat in the nearly empty upper shelf. Something blew past; I think it was a tumbleweed. But I spied the all-natural, no-good-tasting-stuff-included juice Laney had given me during my tempestuous rehearsal with Sergio. I pulled it out. Closing the door with my foot, I screwed off the top and took a whiff.

"You sure he's not there?"

"Wouldn't I have noticed?"

"I don't know. Maybe you've got so many brothers roaming around your house that one more would be superfluous."

"Superfluous?"

"I told you I'm back in school."

I laughed. Lavonn might have a hard-ass stance toward

authoritarian figures . . . and everything else . . . but I kind of liked her. Or maybe it was that stance that *caused* my foolish fondness. "What'd you want with Micky?" I had long known that she'd been crushing on her nephew's dad. "Besides the obvious," I added, and took a swig from the one hundred percent recycled bottle. The contents tasted like something that had seeped from a radioactive cactus.

"Jamel has school tomorrow."

I looked at the container, wondering if there had been some mistake in the labeling process. Perhaps the liquid was meant to light fires or something. "You've got Jamel?"

"Yeah. I've been taking care of him some now that I'm back in town."

"Is Micky usually this late?"

"We've yet to establish a pattern regarding his promptness," she said. The phrase was oddly legalistic.

"Well, was he late last time?"

"No. But I got the idea he'd called it quits with that Daphne chick a while back, so he was unattached."

"Who?"

"Daphne or . . . whatever. I think they work together."

I thought for a second. "Deirdra? The lunch lady?"

"Yeah."

At some point he *had* spoken of a friend in Branford Middle School's cafeteria. I had warned him about the pitfalls of dating a coworker, but he'd said it was nothing like that, just a few laughs . . . some high-protein recipe exchanges. If Micky's body wasn't a temple it was at least a nice little chapel.

"When did you expect him to return?"

"I don't know, but Jamel said his bedtime is at ten, so I figure it's probably really nine."

"Wow. You must have been a great kid."

She huffed. "Let me know if you hear from him, will you?"

"Didn't he say where he was going?"

"You think I would have called *you* if he had?"

"I *am* pretty charming."

"And yet I manage to resist."

"What was he wearing?" I asked.

There was a momentary pause, then, "How hard up are you?"

I remembered mounting Sergio like he was a grand prix jumper and thought it best not to answer. "Maybe we can extrapolate his plans from his ensemble."

"Oh, that's right, you're back in school, too."

I didn't bother to tell her that I'm so smart I used words like *extrapolate* in my sleep. "For example, if he was wearing grubby sweats I think we can rule out a tête-à-tête with Angelina Jolie. But if he's got those black biker jeans on . . . "

"Then what?"

"Then Jolie's back on the table."

"Shit. I don't think I can compete with a chick who's been doing the Brad."

"He was wearing the jeans?"

"And those fancy-ass shoes."

"The leather Oxfords?"

"Yeah."

I told myself I had no reason or right to be disappointed. But if I was going to be honest, I had kind of hoped he'd worn that sexy ensemble yesterday for me and me alone. An idea hit me suddenly. An idea, I'm not proud to say, that wasn't altogether happily received. "Maybe he dressed to impress *you*."

"He was in my house about seven seconds before he launched out of here."

I didn't know how to respond to that.

"Well," she said, sounding resigned, "at least we know he's safe from fifty percent of the population."

"How do you figure?"

"No woman in her right mind would hurt him when he's wearing his butt-loving biker pants."

She had a point. I told myself that after I hung up. Repeated it as I brushed my teeth. Made it my mantra as I brushed *Harley's* teeth. He curled his lip, giving me his I'm-too-sexy smile that made me laugh, then climbed up onto my bed like a giant mantis.

But ten minutes later, I was still sleepless. Yes, I realize some people habitually take several seconds to fall asleep, but sleep and I have a close, abiding bond. Usually. I got out of bed, paced through my abbreviated living room and into my pint-sized office.

The light was on in the Al Sadrs' house next door. It looked as if Ramla was still up. Probably still worrying about the sister she had brought to America, then subsequently lost to the vast wonders of that same country. To the right, beyond my fence, the Griffins' yard was dark and empty. Seventeen-year-old Bryn was not, for once, making out with her beau du jour behind the rosebushes, or perhaps she had simply become more adept at hiding her activities. At her age, I had resorted to entertaining "company" between Dad's workshop/sanctuary and the neighbor's broken-down RV. Romantic, it was not.

But none of that mattered. My neighbors weren't my concern. Of course, strictly speaking, neither was Micky

Goldenstone. He was a grown man. In fact, he had once been a prison guard, and you don't get much more grown up than keeping tabs on a few thousand guys who would just as soon eat your liver as look at you. More recently, Micky had become a middle school teacher, which might actually be scarier than the Folsom guard gig. In short, Micky was capable, smart, and experienced. I gave myself a mental nod as I made a beeline for my bed. Clearly, the man did not need to be worried over.

On the other hand, there's substantial evidence that we, as Homo sapiens, tend to worry about the wrong things. So, conversely, if I worried about Micky all would be well in his world.

Congratulating myself on such sound reasoning, I paced my bedroom. Harley watched me for the first lap, then sighed heavily and laid flat out, ribs rising gently, bony head dead center on my pillow. Shikoku, however, remained by the door, ever alert to the crazies she was fully aware could overtake my good judgment at any given moment.

I glanced at the time and felt my shoulders relax a smidgeon. It was still early, especially by a grown man's standards . . . a grown man with a grown man's appetites. He was simply out for the night. Safe. Probably had a few drinks, knowing Jamel's aunt would care for him as long as necessary. All was well, I assured myself.

Five seconds later, I was back on the phone. "How about his grandmother?"

"What is wrong with you?" Lavonn's tone resonated with that particular blend of frustration and wonder that seems to be reserved for me and me alone.

"I can't sleep."

"Well, I can. And I've got a nine o'clock class."

"Did you call her?"

"Grams?" She hissed the name as if afraid that if she spoke too loudly Micky's grandmother would be magically conjured up. Grams, it's true, is a singularly terrifying personality. That she had a woman of Lavonn's ilk buffaloed spoke eloquently of her superpowers. "Why would I do that?"

"Maybe he's with her?"

"You think he's wearing his ass-loving pants to spend the evening with a nonagenarian?"

Nonagenarian. Was that an old person or a terrifying person? I didn't ask. I didn't want the PhD police to take away my doctorate. "It's possible."

"You don't get out much, do you?"

"What about his shirt?"

She sighed. "The white waffle knit," she confessed, probably wishing like hell she hadn't called me in the first place. "With the short sleeves."

I nodded, remembering. There was something about white cotton against dark skin that made him look concurrently cuddly and sexy as hell.

"Kick ass arms," she said. "And a button-up fly."

We were quiet for a second, but finally the words slipped out.

"Easy access."

Surprisingly, we spoke the words together, then huffed in tandem. Lavonn and I, it seemed, had more in common than either of us was entirely comfortable with.

"He's fine," she said.

"Yeah," I agreed. Silence echoed between us for a moment. I spoke first. "You'll let me know when he shows up?"

"All right, but I've got to tell you, if the brother pops in at three in the morning looking happy as a clam, I'm not necessarily going to be in the best of spirits."

"I'd appreciate a call anyway."

I could hear the shrug in her voice. "If that's what you want."

The conversation had been weird as shit, but I still felt better after we hung up. Nudging Harley's head off my pillow, I claimed a sliver of mattress for myself and slipped blessedly into dreamland.

I'm not sure what woke me. One moment, I was wonderfully catatonic, and the next, I was fully awake. Awake and scared out of my mind.

Six

"If you were a real friend you'd quit cleaning your house before I come over. In fact, if you'd smear a little raspberry jelly on the carpet I think we could be BFFs."

—Chrissy, who doesn't like to get too obsessive about cleanliness

A tiny click of noise snapped my attention to the right. Shikoku was on her feet, silver eyes trained on mine. I shot my gaze at Harlequin. He was dead to the world. That meant nothing.

My limbs were heavy, saturated with dread, but my heart was thumping wildly in my chest.

"What's wrong?" My voice was gravelly.

Shikoku flicked one stiff ear toward the front door and back. Terror rippled to my fingertips, but this wasn't my first rodeo; far better to face the enemy head-on than cower in fear. Slipping my hand beneath the pillow once again confiscated by Harley, I pulled out my weapon. The hardwood floor felt cool

40

against the balls of my feet. I tightened my grip and held Shikoku's gaze. She studied me in rapt concentration for a blistering eternity. Then she lay down in the doorway and closed her eyes.

Relief sloshed through me. There were no strangers in my house—I was certain of that much. Shikoku never slept if others were present. Instead, she watched each newcomer with an intensity Harley reserved for ham bones.

Still, my joints felt creaky as I forced myself to the front door. The security light above my little stoop was dutifully standing guard between me and the darkness. It was still and quiet outside my living room window, evidencing the kind of spooky peace found only in the small hours of night. But a movement on the sidewalk startled me. A shadow leapt forward, then materialized into a frolicsome Doberman followed by his lagging handler.

"It's just a jogger," I breathed. Shikoku opened one eye as I entered the kitchen. "You've got to learn to chill." She lowered her piercing gaze to my weapon. "What? This?" I raised the bottle of wine death-gripped in my right hand. "Maybe I just wanted a little libation." Okay, I realize that a nice spumante makes a better after-dinner drink than a weapon, but the truth is guns scare me more than the bathroom scale after a late-night binge. And although Hiro Danshov had given me a rudimentary understanding of how to defend myself with a blade, the idea of threatening another human being with one still gives me the heebie-jeebies. On the other hand, I'm pretty comfortable with any vessel that contains large quantities of fructose.

I cleared my throat. "And the bottle just happened to be by my bed." Shikoku's silver eyes never blinked. "Well . . . *on* my bed." Why did they never blink? "Under the pillow, actually, and I thought . . . hey . . ." I took a deep breath, vaguely aware I was explaining my actions to a dog. "How about a treat? A little tuna maybe?" She watched me for a moment longer, then closed her eyes. A second later, Harlequin rambled in, looking sleepy but hopeful.

"You were probably worried, too, huh?" I said. "It's not just talk of food that woke you?" He whapped his tail, trusting and happy, making the world seem right. I fondled his ear with my empty hand as I opened the fridge. The bottle clanked against the handle. "Protecting the bed from any trespassers who might—Ack!" I stumbled backward. Cold air and refrigerated light sloshed over my winter-white legs.

The glass shelves were brimming with foodstuffs. Leafy greens sprouted from every corner. Knobby tubers bulged from a wooden bowl.

I creaked my head sideways as Shikoku sauntered into the room.

"How—" Something jangled. I jumped, bleating like a hapless lamb as the spumante, my number one line of defense, clattered to the floor when the phone rang again.

My hand was almost steady when I reached for it. My voice wasn't quite so optimistic. In fact, it might have sounded a bit like the croak of a dying cricket.

"What's wrong now?" Lavonn asked.

It took me a few seconds to recognize her voice, longer still to formulate an intelligent query. "Huh?" I turned on the kitchen light. No one jumped from the shadows to impale me on an asparagus spear. I tried to swallow my fear, but it seemed stuck on my epiglottis.

"You okay?"

"I'm not sure," I said and forced myself to goose-step to the living room. My fingers felt strangely disembodied, but when the LEDs illuminated the room, nothing untoward surprised me. Except, perhaps, the fact that I'm a bit of a slob.

"What's going on?" Lavonn asked.

"If the phone goes dead, send the cops."

She was silent for a second. "Are you playing me right now?"

"Maybe," I said and subsequently checked every room. Shikoku followed on silent paws, then gave me an I-told-you-so look when I came up empty.

"Is your life always this freaky?" Lavonn asked.

I exhaled finally. My house was small. Whoever had stocked my refrigerator was long gone. And of course, if I was going to be honest, I knew who that someone was. I glanced at Shikoku, who yawned as she settled back onto her rug. Her master, Hiro Danshov, had an odd fondness for highly nutritious food. His sense of humor was just as peculiar.

"So Micky finally arrived?" I asked, glancing at the clock on the microwave. It read 2:42. If I accounted for the expiration of daylight saving time that I had not yet acknowledged, then added seven minutes to adjust for the clock's lateness, the time was 3:49. Or 1:49. Or 3:37? Or . . . Giving up, I reached into my fridge for a snack. The most delectable tidbit was a carrot, frilly green top still intact. I sighed as I took a bite.

"No."

"What?" I stopped munching. "He's not there yet."

"No. And it's 2:42 in the morning."

"I'm sure you're wrong," I said and scowled at my microwave. The truth hit me like a cartoon anvil. The damned

43

intruder had not only defiled my fridge with nutritious snacks, he had reset my clock. I shook my head, refusing to let Danshov mess with my mind. "Have you called the police?"

"Jesus," she said, and I remembered her complicated history with law enforcement.

"Do you want *me* to?" I asked.

"I don't know," she said. "What do you think's going on?"

There were a lot of mysteries. I glanced at my refrigerator. It looked strangely smug about its own. "Maybe he just ran out of gas or something?"

"And forgot my phone number?"

She had a valid point; why wouldn't Micky call?

"You sure he's not with you?" she asked.

"Are you serious?" My tone sounded a little shrill to my tired ears.

Hers sounded razor sharp. "Yeah, I'm serious."

"You think I wouldn't have mentioned it by now?"

"I don't know. Maybe you're embarrassed about doing a client or something."

Or, more likely, if I were with someone as hot as Micky I'd be singing the "Hallelujah Chorus" from the rooftops. Instead, I was spending the evening with two dogs and a haughty refrigerator. I gave my favorite appliance a glare. "He's not here," I assured her.

"And he hasn't been all night?"

"No," I said and glanced apologetically at the fridge. I couldn't stay mad at it. "I don't think so."

"You don't *think*. . ."

"No," I repeated more emphatically. "So where is he?"

"How would I know?"

"Take an educated guess."

"You're his shrink!" She sounded peeved and sleep deprived.

Well, join the damned parade . . . or the parade of the damned. "I only see him occasionally." I didn't add that he had visited only hours before. The desperation in his questions sent a chill through me now. "We don't generally discuss his dating options."

"What *do* you talk about?"

"That's privileged information." And she was the last person on the planet I would tell. It was impossible to guess what she would do if she realized Micky had forced himself on her sister. Just as impossible to know why Kaneasha hadn't shared that truth with her family.

"So he *is* dating someone?"

"Listen, Lav . . . " My phone bleated. I pulled it from my ear and scowled at the screen before speaking again. "It's him."

"What?"

"Micky's calling," I said.

"Why would he call you instead of—" she began, but I cut her off.

"I'll get back to you." Then, "Micky," I said and held my breath. Generally, when I try to switch callers, I lose both parties and piss off everyone.

"Sycamore trees." The voice was eerily soft.

My heart thumped once, then stopped. "Hello?"

"And squirrels."

"Micky, is that you?"

"A park . . . " He paused, as if tired or disoriented. "Where we could play some catch."

"Micky! What's going on?"

45

He coughed.

"Micky!"

"I guess she was right."

"Who?" I pressed the phone tighter against my ear. "Who was right?"

"I was the one misbehaving." He chuckled. It sounded raspy and scary as hell.

"Where are you?"

He didn't answer. Silence stretched into the night. I tightened my grip until my fingers ached. "Micky, please tell—"

"Jamel!" he gasped. "Where are you?"

"He's with Lavonn, Micky! He's safe. He's fine. Where are *you*?"

There was a soft exhalation, then, "Tell him I tried."

"What are you talking about?"

"My boy. Tell him I wanted better for him."

I was outside now, though honest to God, I had no idea where to go from here. "Tell him yourself."

He didn't respond.

"Micky, you can tell him yourself!" My voice had risen toward hysteria. "But I need to know how to find you! Give me your address so I can—"

The phone went dead.

I pulled it from my ear and stared at the screen. I'd lost him. I hit redial, but my call went straight to voicemail. Jabbing spastically at buttons that suddenly seemed too small, I swore and prayed and swore.

"What'd he say?"

"Lavonn?"

"Where's Micky?"

"I don't know."

"What the hell are you talking about? What'd he say?"

"He was . . . I think he was out of his head."

"What? Like he was high or something?"

"Like he was . . . " I stopped before the word *dying* slipped past my lips.

"Like he was what?"

"He said I should tell Jamel he tried."

There was a silence punctuated with confusion, stamped with fear. "Call the cops," she said. It sounded ominous, but she was right. I hung up without saying goodbye.

After that, I called 911 and insisted that they find Micky Goldenstone. But the dispatcher didn't seem overly concerned. Granted, when I explained the situation it sounded a little less dire than it had when discussing it with Lavonn. The woman with the drier-than-dust voice to whom I spoke didn't seem to find it earth shattering that a man had remained away from home longer than expected. Neither did she gasp when I explained that he had sounded disoriented. But my gut was still churning when I disconnected.

I ran through the conversation in my mind, hitting the high points: Micky had expressed regrets about failing his son. Had assumed responsibility for misbehaving. But how had he misbehaved? The word sounded so sophomoric. Did it have something to do with his job as a teacher?

Lost, I hurried into my office, tapped my desktop to life, and googled Micky's school. I'd call the principal, see if he could shed any light on the situation. Yes, it was late and he'd probably be pissed, but I had to do something.

I scrolled frantically through the school's website, but no phone numbers were listed. Instead, there seemed to be endless columns of names. *Mr. G. Emerson. Mrs. H. Drake. Ms. B. Haven. Mr. . . .* I stopped abruptly. Ms. B. Haven? "Misbehaving?" I hissed, then checked the online white pages. Seventeen Havens were listed in the L.A. area, but only three had first names that started with B. One was Brandon. One was someone named Barbara, who, the site stated, was 65 or older. Probably not the individual for whom Micky had worn his biker pants. The final option was a woman named Brooke. I called her number and let it ring a dozen times. No one answered. But a quick glance at my computer screen gave me Ms. Haven's home address.

Seven

"Dumb luck—it maybe ain't the mother lode, but it's the best I got."
—Elmer Brady, Chrissy's most pragmatic grandparent

My cell phone rang. I turned down the volume of my weird-ass GPS without taking my eyes off the road that curved like a serpent toward the San Gabriel mountain range.

"Hello?" My voice was shaky. The caller's was pissy.

"Turn around."

"Rivera?" I'm not sure what it says about my state of mind that I was relieved to hear his voice, pissy or not.

"Go back home."

So he somehow knew about my call to the police. The call during which I had insisted that they find Micky. The call that might have included some mid-level swearing on my part.

"McMullen . . . " Rivera's tone had dropped from pissy to snarly. "Don't be stupid."

"So you think I'm being ridiculous, too?"

"What?"

"They treated me like a brainless twit."

"Maybe that's because you're *acting* like a . . . " He paused, then exhaled slowly, as if reminding himself to be civil or at least *human*. "Meet me at the station. We'll get this sorted out."

"Micky's in trouble."

"You don't know that."

"I *do* know that."

"You don't—" Another pause, then silence fraught with a toxic mix of anger and frustration. We'll call it franger. "What is he to you?"

"*What?*"

"Goldenstone! Shit, McMullen, he's a grown man, but every time he stubs his toe, you gallop to his rescue like a greyhound on a hare."

"'Gallop'?" I said, then, remembering past incidences, added, "'Stubs his toe'?"

The last time Micky had called me in the small hours of the morning, I had raced to Glendale in something of a functional trance. Once there, I had found him confused and suicidal, standing over a hopped-up drug dealer who was bleeding onto his rosewood flooring.

"That scenario doesn't exactly make your actions more sensible, McMullen." I wasn't sure if he was reading my mind or working off his own memories.

"What about his son?" I asked.

"What about him?"

"Maybe Jamel's had enough trouble, what with his mother dying of an overdose and all." I didn't mention the circumstances of Jamel's conception. No reason for Rivera to know. Sometimes people perform horrific atrocities. But sometimes . . . swear to God . . . sometimes those same people

50

will turn things around, will give their souls to make things right. That's how it was with Micky Goldenstone.

"It's not your problem. Tell me where you are and I'll—"

"Not my problem? Not my . . . " I was warming up to blast him, but a thought occurred before I could gather enough oxygen. "Can you track him?"

"What?"

"Triangulate his phone or something?"

"Triangulate his phone?" There might have been a tad bit of disbelief in his tone.

"They do it all the time on *CSI*."

"This isn't la-la land, McMullen. Here in real life we don't interfere with a perfectly capable man's life because he's stayed out past curfew." He sounded a little tired now and kind of preachy, which made me want to disparage his mother and hang up, but the truth was, I didn't really want to make this trip alone. I would rather be accompanied by a man who had disappointed me a dozen times and saved my ass a dozen more.

"If you track his phone I'll tell you where I am."

"Jesus H," he began, then stopped abruptly. I could imagine him gritting his teeth. "What's his number?"

"You'll do it?"

"What's his fucking number?"

His tone was so snotty, I almost refused to tell him. But sometimes it's best to restrict acting like an imbecile to nonlethal situations.

Pulling the cell from my ear for a second, I stared at the tiny screen, trying to remember how to look up a number while remaining online.

"Are you staring at your phone while driving?"

"I'm trying to find his—" But he cut me off.

"I'll get it. Just watch the damn road," he snarled and hung up.

I sniffed at his tone, then glanced up, squawked at the speed limit sign rushing at me, and veered left.

By the time he called back, I had my vehicle well under control.

"What'd you find out?"

"There was no heartbeat."

"What?"

"No ping. Either his phone's dead or he turned it off."

"Turned it off? Why would he—"

"Where are you?"

"Why would he turn it off? That doesn't even make sense. I was just talking to him a few minutes—"

"Where the hell are you?" he snapped.

I bristled but did my best not to pout. "Heading toward Azusa."

There was a moment of quietude broken by a feral growl. "Because?"

"He said he was misbehaving."

I swear I could hear him roll his eyes, but I stormed on.

"Ms. B. Haven is his coworker. She lives in Azusa."

"What the hell is that supposed to . . . Miss B. Haven." He put it together quickly. "Jesus. Is she married?"

"What?"

"He's probably sleeping with her . . . or someone else's wife. Hence the misbehaving and the foggy attitude. Believe me, McMullen, if you find him . . . and that's an astronomically big *if* . . . he's not going to thank you when you wake him from his after-sex bliss."

"He hasn't picked up his son yet."

"Good for him."

I tapped my brakes in an effort to avoid crashing to the bottom of the canyon that yawned beside the road. This wasn't my first rodeo. And I didn't want it to be my last. "He was talking out of his head."

"Maybe he got laid twice."

"He said to tell Jamel that he tried."

"So he got *drunk* and laid. We should all be so lucky."

"There's something wrong," I said.

"Spidey senses acting up again?"

"I mean it."

His sigh was deep and long-suffering. "Tell me what happened. Don't leave anything out."

"I was asleep."

"Alone?" His tone was grouchy but probing. I felt a warm wisp of pleasure in my gut. Jealousy was a healing balm to a woman of my flagrant insecurities. It was, in fact, so comforting that I chose to ignore his question.

"Lavonn called at about—"

"Lavonn Blount?"

"Yes."

"What time was that?"

"About ten. She asked if I'd seen Micky."

"Why would she think you had?" he growled.

"Holy crap, Rivera!" I said, simultaneously flattered and frustrated.

"Okay." There was almost an apology in his tone. "Go on."

"I said I hadn't."

He didn't ask if I was lying, but I felt his longing to. "What then?"

I paused. The rest of the scenario might make me sound a little desperate. "I asked if he was wearing his biker jeans."

"Do I want to know why?" His tone suggested fatigue.

I didn't bother to clear my throat. "He looks . . . umm . . . pretty good in those jeans."

"And?"

"And you call yourself a detective?"

"No."

"She said he *was*." I waited for him to connect the dots, but apparently that wasn't a game he wanted to play. "Ergo, he's probably with a woman," I deduced.

"Which brings me back to the sex idea."

Truth be told, *everything* brought Rivera back to the sex idea. But as much as I hated to admit it, he did kind of have a point. If I showed up at a cozy little triplex just in time to save Micky from post-coital cuddling, I was probably going to have to shoot myself in the brainpan. But it was too late to worry about that. I was arriving at Haven's house.

A pretty globed light illumined a tidy front yard and the numbers 14573 stamped into a tile beside the front door. "I'm here." I whispered the words. Don't ask me why.

"Stay in your vehicle until I arrive on scene."

"What if he's dying in there?"

"Do you see his car?"

I glanced around, heart beating overtime. "No."

"I don't care how horny he was, I doubt he hot-footed it twenty miles across town."

"Maybe she already ditched it."

"Ditched it? Jesus, McMullen, who are you channeling now?" he asked, but I ignored him.

A thousand deadly scenarios stormed through my mind. Micky Goldenstone was in every one of them. "Take care of Harley for me," I said and opened my door.

"Are you shitting me?" Rivera's voice had risen to ear-shattering levels. "Take care of Harley? That's all you have to say?"

I was already getting out of my Saturn, knees quaking like an L.A. high-rise. "And Shikoku," I added. "It's not her fault her owner's a douche."

"Get back in your vehicle and secure your locks, McMullen. Do you hear me? That's an order!"

"An order?" Even in my present state of bladder-quivering terror, an order was far more likely to convince me to proceed than to change my course of action.

"I'll be there in five. At least wait till—"

"An order?"

"Jesus Christ, I'm sorry, okay? Just get back in your car before you get yourself killed!"

I glanced disjointedly to my right. Nothing more fearsome than a trio of cacti caught my eye. No bullets whined. No mad dogs barked. Not so much as a purring engine disturbed the quietude.

"Why are you getting so freaked out?" I asked and tried to convince my urinary system that all was well; now was not the time to perform.

"It's the middle of the fucking night, McMullen!"

"In a neighborhood as innocuous as . . . " I stopped, heart thumping. "Something happened, didn't it? What do you know?"

"What do I know? I know you could stir up trouble in a convent."

"Well, yeah, in a convent." I tried to sound amused, but my voice shook a little. "You know how easy it is to tick off a nun? One little cherry bomb in a toilet and they're—"

"Get your ass back in your car."

I exhaled heavily and forced myself to move forward. "Luckily, I'm not applying for nunship," I said and stumbled toward Brooke Haven's house.

Eight

"If we can be anything we want, like Sister Celeste says, why'd you decide to be a dumbass?"

—Chrissy McMullen, to just one of several dumbasses with whom she was acquainted

"Chrissy . . . " Rivera snarled, but I spoke over him.

"Micky's in trouble," I said, and hanging up, rang the doorbell.

I could hear the tinny chime from inside the little bungalow, but no other sound reached my ears. I rang it again. And again.

Finally, somewhere in the interior, a light switched on. A soft thud reached my ears, then silence. I rang again, then added a knock.

"Who is it?"

I caught my breath and steadied myself. "Hello?" I tried to sound soothing, but the helium-high voice that reached my ears did nothing to bolster my courage. "Ms. Haven?"

57

"Yes?" It sounded more a question than an answer.

"I'm here about Micky."

There was a pause, then, "Who?"

"Please, Ms. Haven, I have to talk to you about Micky Goldenstone. May I come in?"

There was a long silence before she fumbled with the lock. The door opened. She was young, girl-next-door pretty, and honey blond. "What's this about?"

"Do you work with Micky Goldenstone?"

"Michael? Sure. Yes. Why? Has something happened to him?"

"I think—" I began, but a car was squealing around the corner. It raced toward my Saturn and slammed to a halt. A moment later, Rivera popped out of his Jeep and stormed toward us, looking angry and disheveled.

"What's going on?" Haven asked. She retreated a pace.

"Lieutenant Rivera," he said and snapped out his badge. "LAPD."

"I don't . . . " She sounded faint. "Is something wrong with Michael?"

"He—" I began, but Rivera interrupted.

"We're trying to determine if there's been some kind of mishap, ma'am. Could we step inside for a minute?"

"Yes. I guess." She backed into the foyer. It was as neat as a single-malt whiskey. Rivera closed the door behind us. She zipped her wide eyes to his. "Is Michael okay?"

"Have you spoken to Mr. Goldenstone recently?" Rivera asked.

"No. I mean, I left school early. I was planning a little get-together after work. Just a few friends."

"You had a party?" Rivera asked, eying the ungodly

neatness.

"Lou just left a couple hours ago. I thought Michael might drop by, but I didn't think too much about . . . " She clasped her hands, looking pious or scared. Or maybe they're the same thing. "Please, you have to tell me what this is about."

"Where could he be?" I asked.

"What?"

"Do you work with Mr. Goldenstone, Ms. Haven?" Rivera asked.

"Yes, but—"

"He was talking crazy," I said.

"What's going on?"

"I think he's in trouble. He called me. He sounded out of his head. Do you have any idea where he could be?"

"Out of his head? Like he was high or something?"

"Does he use illegal substances?" Rivera asked, honing in on her question.

I shook my head. "No!"

"What?" Ms. Haven seemed to be shrinking before our eyes.

Rivera softened his tone. Bad cop gone good. "How often does Mr. Goldenstone use recreational drugs?"

"He doesn't," she said and clasped her hands tighter . . . from pious to desperate. "I'm sure he doesn't."

"You're sure he doesn't? Or he actually doesn't?" Rivera asked.

She wrung her hands.

"We don't want to cause him any trouble," Rivera said. "We're here to help."

"He's an excellent educator," she said, voice pale.

"But?" Rivera questioned, gaze sharp on hers. She raised

her chin.

"And a wonderful father."

"He hasn't picked up his son," I said.

"Jamel?" She yanked her skittering gaze to mine. "Where is he?"

"With his aunt."

"And Michael hasn't returned for him?"

"Do you know his whereabouts, Ms. Haven?" Rivera probed.

She speared him with her blue-heaven eyes, then paced away. "I . . . " She roamed toward the kitchen but turned back before she'd reached the doorway. Not so much as a dust mote littered her hardwood floor. What kind of woman doesn't even own a dust mote? "No. Of course not. How would I?"

"We don't think he did anything wrong," I assured her, though the dark lieutenant's glare suggested otherwise.

She winced. "Have you talked to Marv?"

"Marv?"

"Full name?" Rivera asked and snapped open a small notebook probably retrieved from some hidden compartment known only to police officers and marsupials.

"Marvin," she said. "Marvin Lieberman, the gym coach."

"At Branford?" Micky and I didn't discuss his work much. The trauma of his childhood took most of his billable hours. But I heard the occasional story.

"Yes. Branford Middle School. I teach art . . . and . . . now with the cuts, I help out as a para. Michael and Marv and I . . . we're all educators. But Michael . . . "

"Michael what?" Rivera asked.

"I'm sure he didn't mean what he said."

"Which was?"

"Maybe I shouldn't—"

"You should," Rivera and I intoned together. He glared at me before turning back to her. "We're just trying to help him, Ms. Haven."

She twisted her narrow hands. "He said Marv wasn't a real teacher. He said he was . . . " She shook her head. Golden, shoulder-length hair brushed softly against her tidy T-shirt. "They've never gotten along very well."

"What did Mr. Goldenstone say exactly?"

"That Marv was a waste of oxygen. A blight on society." She winced before speaking again. "A fucking pervert."

"Why?"

"I don't know. I mean, Marv can be kind of . . . crude sometimes. But maybe he's just hiding his sensitive side. I think he had a rough childhood. He was—"

"Does he have sycamore trees?"

"What?" They turned on me in tandem, Haven surprised, Rivera pissed. He didn't like to be interrupted while in Spanish Inquisition mode.

"Lieberman, does he have sycamores in his yard?"

"I don't know . . . " She looked at Rivera as if she thought I might be one tree short of a forest.

"Do you know his address?" Rivera asked.

"Marv's? Yes. I mean . . . " She looked around vaguely, then shambled toward an antique secretary. "I think I have it here somewhere. He had a little get-together last summer. For faculty and friends and stuff. We grilled hotdogs and . . . " She pulled out a tattered little notebook and flipped through the pages. "Here it is. He's in Rosemead."

Rivera scribbled the address down. "Do you have his

number?"

"Number?"

"Phone number."

"Oh, of course, only I . . . I don't seem to have it here. But if you call the school . . ." She shook her head. "It's late. Or early. I'm sorry. I wish—"

"You've been very helpful. Thanks for your cooperation," Rivera said and, placing a hand on my back, nudged me toward the door. I went willingly, mind windmilling.

"What now?" I breathed finally and turned toward him with my rear end pressed against the door of my Saturn.

"Now I pay Mr. Lieberman a visit."

He looked hard and formidable. I felt small and frail. Lifting my right hand, I curled my fingers weakly into the front of his shirt. "I want to help."

"No," he said and, reaching around me, opened the driver's door.

"But. . ." I raised my imploring gaze to his. "What if Micky's hurt? What if he—"

"Go," he ordered. He grasped my wrist, pulled my fingers from his shirt, and pressed me into the Saturn's worn seat.

"Will do," I agreed, then, snatching the notebook from his hand, I slammed the door and hit the locks.

Nine

*"Cursing, both a form of communication and a viable alternative to
kicking handsy bastards in the gonads."*
    —Lily Schultz, Chrissy's longtime mentor and owner of the
Warthog Saloon

"Hey! Dammit!" Rivera yelled, but I had already started the
engine.

"McMullen!" He thumped a fist on my window. "Open
up."

I gritted my teeth, determined to leave him in the
proverbial dust, but I couldn't quite forget that when it came
to the saving-my-ass department, he was at the top of my list. I
powered down the window a couple cautious inches. "What?"

"Where the hell do you think you're going?"

I considered sarcasm, but I didn't have time to do it
properly. If a job's worth doing . . . "Rosemead."

"The fuck you are."

"The fuck I'm not."

He growled something inarticulate, then, "I'm coming with you."

He was already reaching through my window to pop the locks, sliding into the passenger seat before I could decide whether being saved was worth tolerating his domineering fucktardedness.

"Enter the address," I said. I wasn't crazy about my ass, but it was the only one I had; I nodded crisply toward the bulky GPS that brooded on my dashboard.

"McMullen—"

"Get the directions or get out."

He looked no happier than he had a second ago, but he lifted the antiquated black box and peered at the knobs. "What the hell is this thing?"

"It's . . . " I shook my head, not prepared to explain. "Just push the red button."

"What can I do to please you, my mistress?" The voice seemed to come from nowhere in particular.

Rivera growled something in return.

"Solberg's doing," I said, though it wasn't much of an explanation. Laney's husband, super nerd and all-around dweebster, liked to fiddle with other people's electronics when his wife was working on location.

Rivera was still staring at me.

"I was tired of getting lost, so he . . . " I shook my head, remembering to stay focused. "Just tell him the address."

"Him?"

"*It!* Give it the address."

"Does he have a name?"

He did, but I didn't really feel like sharing the fact that Solberg had bestowed the electronic navigator with the name

64

of one sexy-assed love slave to whom I would have gladly given my second virginity. "Do you want to get there or not?"

Rivera read the house number through gritted teeth, recited the city and state while glowering at me.

There was a moment of silence, then, "Who is this that intrudes on our time together, mistress?"

"What the hell?" Rivera snarled.

"Give me that!" I snapped and snatched the thing from his hand. I had found in the past that harsh words only upset this new giver of directions, so I cleared my throat and softened my voice. "Morab?"

"Oh, for fuck's sake!"

I shushed him. "Please provide the fastest route to the address given."

"Who is this strange man who invades our privacy, my beloved?"

My cheeks felt hot. I didn't dare glance at my passenger. "I'll explain later. Right now, a friend is in danger."

Morab sulked in silence.

"Please. It's life or death."

"Very well," he said. "If you vow that we will share time alone later."

"Sure. Yes." I glanced toward Rivera. "I promise."

"I look forward to those moments with bated breath. Every second apart from you is—"

"I'm going to throw that fucking thing out the window."

"Directions! Please," I begged.

"For you and you alone," he crooned and read off directions as if reciting naughty poetry.

I squealed onto Canyon Vista Drive. Rivera grabbed the oh-shit handle above his door and glared through the windshield as if trying to refrain from throttling me.

"Listen, McMullen . . ." he began, then slammed his foot against the floorboards, possibly in an effort to prevent us from careening into a mailbox that listed precariously close to the street. But there was no need. We missed it by a quarter of an inch at least. He rumbled something inarticulate under his breath and continued. "I appreciate your loyalty."

I glanced in his direction, wondering where he was going with this new and not altogether believable civility.

"Eyes on the road!" he snapped, then exhaled carefully and returned to his I'm-just-placating-the-crazies voice. "You're a good friend."

I snorted noisily as I screeched into a right-hand turn.

"But this is police business."

"The same police who didn't give a tinker's damn that Micky was missing?" I hot-wheeled it into another turn.

"Do you have any idea how many people call in about Uncle Fred going missing, only to find out that good ol' Freddy was getting shit-faced at the local bar?"

"Micky's nobody's uncle." I gunned it, racing along to Morab's sultry directives.

"Jesus, McMullen, will you just slow down for one damned minute?"

I wasn't sure if he meant literally or figuratively, but we were doing about eighty-seven miles per hour now. Turns out, four a.m. traffic is more fun than four p.m. traffic.

"Is this because of the Black Flames thing?"

"What?" I sent him a scalding glance, though the speedometer had just hit ninety and it may have been wise to take his advice about keeping my eyes on the road. The Saturn was beginning to shake like Harlequin during his after-bath ritual.

"I said I was sorry."

"That you lied?" I tightened my hands on the wheel and pushed the Saturn to ninety-two. "That you said my life was in danger from the most bloodthirsty gang in recent history? That you sent me off to be cannibalized by the Things, a pair of hillbilly twins the size of—"

"Your life *was* in danger."

I snorted.

"What? You think the Flames are some kind of joke? You think you can handle them now that Danshov has shown you a couple of slaps and a roundhouse kick? Is that it?"

Hiro Danshov, the chef/assassin I had met in dumbfuck nowhere, *had* taught me a few things, not least of which was that I could have the hots for someone who may or may not have intended to kill me.

"Or do you think Danshov will save you himself?"

"No one's going to save me but me," I said and sped onto Foothills Boulevard. "You've taught me that much at least."

Anger and frustration, melded into a quixotic mix, zipped across his face. But there was guilt, too. I felt a little bit of that same emotion sear me; the truth was, I would have been dead a dozen times over if it hadn't been for Rivera.

"I was just trying to keep you safe," he said.

"Turn right, my beauty, onto the vast thoroughfare you call the Two Ten," Morab breathed.

I tapped the brakes and skidded up the on-ramp.

Rivera grabbed the dash and swore under his breath, but we were already speeding west onto a nearly empty interstate. We were heading into a steady nose wind, making me think my little Saturn might lift off like a battered Cessna.

"Did you do him?" he asked.

"What?" I jerked my surprised attention to the right.

A muscle ticked in Rivera's lean jaw as if he were attempting to hold the question at bay, but it escaped, sending his snarl into the steamy ether between us. "Danshov! Did you sleep with him or not?"

My brows were still in my hairline, so my expressive arsenal was pretty much empty. "Define 'sleep,'" I said and blinked, going for innocence.

"Did you fucking fuck him or not?"

A laughed a little, feeling flighty, terrified, and strangely elated. "Fucking fuck—"

"Dammit!" he snarled and grabbed my arm.

I jumped like a startled bunny when our gazes clashed. Yes, Hiro Danshov had shown me a dozen ways to kill a killer. But Lieutenant Jack Rivera could still slay me with a glance.

"No!" I snapped. "I didn't sleep with him."

Silence dropped between us. He drew breath through his nostrils. They flared. It was sexy as sin, but I forced my attention to the road ahead.

"What about Goldenstone?"

I tightened my grip on the wheel. "If you're asking if I slept with Micky, I'm going to make you wish—"

"Did you?"

"He's a *client!*"

"And?"

"And do you have any idea what the board would do to me if they thought I had intercourse with a client?"

He huffed a laugh. "So that's why you haven't jumped him yet? 'Cause he pays the bills?"

"Geez, Rivera, if you could find *any* reason, any reason at all, not to do every lame-ass Skank Girl who slinks across your line of vision, I'd—"

"I didn't sleep with Skank Girl!"

"But you wanted to, didn't you?"

"Holy hell, McMullen! If I worried about every guy you *wanted* to jump I'd never sleep again."

"So you *did* want to."

"Eleven miles until you arrive at your destination. At your current speed that will take approximately two seconds, my courageous sweetling."

Rivera yanked his scowl to my speedometer. "How the fuck fast are you going?"

"I didn't ask for your help."

"Well, you're going to get it," he snarled.

"Why?"

"What?"

"Why are you going to help me?" I glanced at him. "Is it because you feel guilty?"

"Jesus! Watch that—" But I breezed past the sluggish Toyota in the right lane, then zipped onto the San Bernardino Freeway.

"Is it?" I asked.

"What would I have to feel guilty about?"

"You tell me."

"You're the one who fell elbow over ass into Professor What-the-fuck's bed."

"Marc was a gentleman and a scholar." I felt inordinately proud of my statement. I had spent months on end unable to remember his name in Rivera's presence, and that was while I was still involved with the good professor.

"Was that why you broke it off? Not yeti enough for you?"

"Go screw yourself, Rivera. Or are you waiting for Skank Girl to do that?"

His eyes bored into mine. "Maybe I'm waiting for you, McMullen," he said, voice dropping. "Maybe I've always been waiting for you."

"Wh . . . " I began, but Morab interrupted.

"Turn right, my dove. You shall find your destination on the left."

I careened to the curb, jolted to a halt. The houses here were separated by wide yards and giant palms. "What do you mean, you've always been waiting?"

Our gazes met, clashed.

"Are you saying you haven't had sex with anyone but me since . . . " I tightened my fingers on the steering wheel. "Since that first time in my kitchen? Is that what you're saying?"

His inscrutable eyes turned to scan the yard on the far side of the street. "You sure jerkoff there got us to the right address?"

"Is it?" I asked.

"Chrissy," he began, but something thumped in the darkness, yanking my attention toward the front of the house, barely visible in the uncertain light.

"What was that?"

"Stay in the car," he ordered, hot cop voice returning.

"What do you think it was?" I reached for my door handle.

He grabbed my arm. "Jesus, Chrissy, for once in your life—"

Something banged again. I twisted out of his grip and lurched outside. Another thump disrupted the night. I squinted at the house, creeping closer.

Rivera was beside me in a second. I could see now that the

screen door was opening and closing erratically. *The wind*, I thought. *It was just the wind.*

Then I noticed the dark shape lying on the stoop.

Rivera pushed me behind him and pulled out a gun.

I didn't argue, not with the position. Not with the weapon.

"LAPD," he said, raising the pistol in both hands. "State your name and situation."

The shape moaned. We inched closer. Overhead, an automatic light switched on.

Micky Goldenstone lay draped across the concrete, leather Oxford caught between the door and the house, white shirt blooming with blood.

Ten

"Just because a brother's hot, doesn't mean he ain't a douche."
—Lavonn Blount, who knows such things

"Micky!" Rivera tried to hold me back, but I ducked under his arm and raced forward. "Micky." I crouched beside him. His cheek felt cold. He didn't speak.

"Call nine-one-one," Rivera said.

I pulled out my phone with shaky hands, managed to punch in the numbers, to say the appropriate words. Rivera stood over me, legs spread, scanning every direction.

"Get back in the car," he ordered.

"I don't think he's breathing."

"Get in the fucking car!"

I slipped my hand to Micky's throat. My fingers bounced erratically, but I pressed them to his skin. He felt sticky and chilled but there was a flutter.

"He's still alive! I think he's alive."

Rivera crouched beside me, gun held steady. "Chrissy,

72

please—"

"Micky, it's me. It's me, Christina. Wake up, honey. Please wake up."

A noise sounded from inside the house. I gasped. Rivera rose, lithe as a panther, arms outstretched, his weapon an extension of himself. "LAPD," he said again, but his voice was drowned out by sirens.

Everything happened at once: The screen door thumping against Micky's buckled Oxford. Paramedics snapping questions, Rivera answering. Me sitting, holding Micky's icy hand until they tugged me away. I rose foggily to my feet and noticed that Rivera was gone. The front door of the house was open. Forgotten by everyone, I stepped inside. Rivera had his fingers pressed against the throat of a large, prone man. His jaw was square, his hair short, his gaze empty and staring.

"Is he . . . " I began.

"Dammit!" Rivera snarled and struck me with his no-hope eyes.

"Lavonn?" My voice sounded too loud and strangely bright, seeming to crackle against the just-played-out events.

"What the hell time is it?"

I tightened my grip on the receiver. There was blood on my free hand, dried but somehow still sticky. My stomach roiled. Dawn had arrived while I wasn't looking.

"Is Jamel all right?" I don't know if I was stalling or merely rambling.

"Course he's all right. He's sleeping. Just like I was. Why?" Her voice dropped an octave as premonition stole into her tone. "What's going on?"

I glanced toward the lobby of Alhambra Medical Center.

They had whisked Micky into one of the nearby rooms and were "doing everything" they could. "We found him," I said.

There was a pause, then, "'Bout damn time." Her bad-girl persona was firmly back in place. "You tell Mick I'm gonna kick his ass from here to Sunday if he doesn't pick up his boy double-quick."

I paused, wondering if I heard trepidation behind the bravado. "He's been shot, Lavonn."

She inhaled, long and slow, then, "Is he dead?" Her tone was flat, her lack of denial revealing legions about her past.

"No, he's . . ." I sucked in a breath. "His condition is guarded."

Silence.

"But they're doing all they can."

She huffed a laugh. "All they can?"

"I'm sorry."

"Where is he?" She was already pulling herself together. I could hear her gathering her keys, shuffling through her belongings.

"The hospital in Alhambra."

"On Raymond?"

"Yes."

"See you in half an hour."

"What? No." I shook my head. "I have to get home. Go to work." I glanced around, barely recognizing my surroundings. Everything seemed hazy, vaguely surreal. "I've got clients in—"

"So Mick don't mean much to you, huh?"

"Holy shit, Lavonn!" I rasped. "I was the one who found him, who searched—" I was clambering up on my high horse, but she had already hung up.

"What's going on?" Rivera's voice was little more than a rumble behind me.

Dismounting was neither graceful nor simple. Emotions clobbered me from all sides: worry, fear, hope, and strangely enough, guilt. Though I had already told myself a dozen times that I was not responsible for Micky's condition, some idiotic part of me wasn't buying it.

"Lavonn'll be here in half an hour," I said.

"Through morning traffic?" He looked tired and somewhat disbelieving. "She planning on flying?"

"I think she's got a broom."

He raised a brow at me. The guilt increased a hundredfold; the past few years of Lavonn's life had been hellacious. I had no reason to believe the first couple decades had been any better.

"I'm sorry. I didn't mean that." I exhaled, feeling as if I'd been holding my breath for hours. "That's what she said. That she'd be here soon. Not the part about the . . . not about the broom."

His eyes seared me, searching, but the corner of his mouth quirked a little. "You all right?"

Nothing that fifty hours of sleep and a lobotomy wouldn't cure. "Yeah. Sure." I rubbed my hand over my eyes. "Do you know anything?"

He glanced toward the doors behind which Micky had disappeared. "They probably haven't even filled out the forms yet."

"Forms! The man's dying and they're—"

"Easy," he said and, taking me by the elbow, led me toward a nearby bank of chairs. They were ugly. But at least they were uncomfortable, too. We sat in unison. "What's going on, McMullen?"

I reared back. "You think I'm responsible, too, don't you?"

He stared at me as if that lobotomy thing may have already taken place. "Should I?"

"No!"

"Okay."

I jerked to my feet, pacing fitfully. "I had nothing to do with this. Hell!" I flapped a hand at nothing in particular. "I didn't even know he was missing until Lavonn called."

"When was that again?"

"Ten or so. She said . . . Wait a minute." I shook my head, immediately and weirdly defensive. "She didn't do it either. She wouldn't, even if she knew. . . " I paused, mind free-falling before I could reel it in. "She wouldn't!"

"Even if she knew what?" Rivera asked.

I refrained from swallowing, from darting my eyes right to left, from wringing my hands. "Even if she was angry at him."

"Why was she angry?"

"I said *if*." I bumped a shrug and concentrated on looking casual, on slowing my heart rate, on not passing out. I hated secrets. But secrets told in psychiatric sessions were sacred.

"Okay. *Was* she mad?"

"I don't know. How would I? It's not like we're BFFs."

"Micky dropped Jamel off and hadn't come back for him. She probably has things to do this morning. It'd be understandable if she was pissed."

I forced a laugh. "She didn't shoot Micky because he was late picking up his kid."

He gave me a smile, but his eyes were narrowed in that I-know-things way that made me want to curl up under my bed . . . or punch him in the ear. "Why, then?"

76

"She didn't shoot him at all!"

"How do you know that?"

I didn't. Not really. But I felt a strange responsibility for Lavonn, had ever since we'd shared mutual danger and love for our dogs. "It was Lieberman!" I remembered the bloodied body with a jolt. Odd that I'd half forgotten those unseeing eyes until now.

"You know him?"

"No. But it was his house. It had to be him, right? He shot Micky."

"Before or after Micky shot *him?*"

I shook my head, remembering my true allegiance. "Micky wouldn't hurt anyone."

He looked as me as if I were hopelessly naïve. Or just hopeless. "Then who, Chrissy?"

"I don't know. How would I?"

"What aren't you telling me?"

"Nothing." Except that Micky had raped Lavonn's sister years before. Except that it was impossible to know how Lavonn would react if she learned the truth. Except that Micky had come to my office agitated and angry just hours before. "But Micky's not to blame."

"You don't sound so sure about Blount."

I huffed a laugh. "So you're back to the idea that she tried to kill him because he was late picking up Jamel? That's asinine. I mean, kids are a pain in the ass, but . . . " I managed a shrug, punctuating the falsehood that I had no desire for children, that I couldn't hear my biological clock ticking like a time bomb in my chest. "Lavonn wouldn't hurt anyone. She acts tough, sure, but she's really just a pussycat." What the hell was I talking about? That might be the stupidest thing I'd ever said in my life. Anyone who had met Lavonn for a minute and a half would know she might be a lion, a panther, or a flesh-eating cougar, but she was not a pussycat.

Rivera burned me with his eyes. "Why is it always like this with you?" Turning wearily away, he took a seat on one of the torturous chairs near the window.

"Like what?" I asked.

His gaze snagged mine. "Are you legally obliged to lie to me? Is that it?"

"I'm not lying," I said, but my voice had pitched up high. It was embarrassing. I was a better liar than that, had been for years.

He held my gaze for a second, then snorted and turned back to the window.

"I'm not."

"Do you distrust everyone?" he asked. Below us, a guy in baggy jeans and a hoody unzipped his pants. Without a backward glance, he urinated onto the driver's door of a red Honda. A muscle jumped in Rivera's jaw, but he remained where he was. This was concerning; the dark lieutenant usually teleports to the scene of the crime, no matter how trivial. "Or is it just me?"

My heart was drumming wildly in my chest, but I raised my chin and my voice in unified tandem. "Not everyone accuses me of murdering the man who intended to rape and dismember me."

In the doorway, a mother grabbed her daughter's arm and steered her back into the hallway. Touchy. Geez. I was, after all, just referring to the incident that had precipitated my first encounter with Rivera.

He chuckled and rubbed his eyes, as though exhausted.

"Dismember you?"

I gritted my teeth at him. "Maybe just rape, then. Maybe that's all Bomstad intended and that's no big deal, right?"

"So this is about rape, then?" he asked and rose abruptly. He seemed tall, suddenly, tall and angry and scary as hell.

"What? No!" I made a *fffssťing* sound, backing down immediately. "What are you talking about?"

He stepped toward me. "Did Goldenstone rape her? Is that it? Is this about revenge?"

"Of course not!"

"Tell me the truth." He grabbed my arms. "Did he rape Lavonn?"

"No!" The word rushed from my mouth like a sprinter on the starting blocks. "This doesn't have anything to do with Lavonn."

"Doesn't it?"

"Micky's the one who's injured. The one you should be concerned with."

"And I'm wondering why. Why was he shot? I'd ask Mr. Lieberman, but he doesn't seem to have a pulse. So I'm asking you."

"How would I know?"

He watched me. His eyes went flat and feral. "Did he touch *you*?"

"Who?" I actually stumbled back a pace. "Micky?" My voice had flown into the stratosphere. "Are you—"

"He was called Pit Bull, I believe, when he was inducted into the Skulls."

I should have realized Rivera would have checked into Micky's past. "That was a long time ago," I said. "People change."

"That hasn't necessarily been my experience."

I drew a deep breath, searching for my placid center. "Well," I said, "they can and they do." I was back on my high horse. I preferred the view from that vantage point.

"Is that your professional opinion, Ms. McMullen?"

"Professional and personal."

"And you think Michael Goldenstone is an upstanding member of the community now?"

"I know he is."

"One who just happened to be at Mr. Lieberman's house when he was shot to death?"

"Yes, I believe—"

"The gun's Goldenstone's."

"What! What gun?"

"The one that killed Lieberman."

I shook my head, confused and scared.

Rivera's expression was almost pitying now. The kind of expression one might give a concussed bunny that had wandered onto Highway 138, affectionately called Death Road by many fanciful Angelenos. "A nine-millimeter Hi-Point."

I shook my head again.

"Found it under a malnourished barberry near the front door. It's the Skulls' weapon of choice. Were you aware he owned a gun, Ms. McMullen?"

"You don't know he did."

"And you don't know him as well as you think you do."

"He didn't shoot anyone," I said. Rivera raised a brow, knowing better. Not too many months ago Micky had done just that. It had been justified and necessary, but still . . . "Recently."

"You sure of that?"

"Absolutely." But why had Micky been so upset earlier in the day?

Rivera snorted, half turned away, then swiveled back, teeth clenched. "I'm going to ask you again. What is he to you?"

"He's a client!" I snapped.

"A client you risk your life for at the drop of a hat?" He grabbed my arm.

I jerked away. "He's a friend, too. You've had a friend at some point in your life, haven't you, Rivera?"

He stepped closer, filling my senses like smoke. Dark, intoxicating, and strictly forbidden. "Why was he at Lieberman's?"

"How would I know?"

"Because you're buddies. Because . . . " He drew a deep breath as if trying to find balance, as if he was not entirely unmoved by my nearness. "They worked together, right?"

I eyed him, cautious. "I guess so."

"Were they adversaries? Conspirators? Lovers?"

"Lovers?" I tried a chuckle. It sounded disturbingly like the hack of a nicotine addict.

"Stranger things have happened," he said.

"Micky's not gay."

Another snort. "Like your gaydar's never been wrong before."

I raised my chin. My high horse seemed to have hightailed it, and I missed him. It was true that I had, on more than one occasion, dated guys who had turned out to be somewhat less heterosexual than I had hoped, but I was not the cause of their predilection. I was sure of that . . . really, I was.

"He's not gay," I repeated.

"So he and Lieberman were adversaries then," Rivera

deduced.

"What? No! What's wrong with you? People don't have to be one or the other."

"But they usually are."

"No, they're—"

"Where is he?"

We snapped our attention to the doorway as Lavonn rushed in.

"Mick!" She looked at me like I was half crazy. Which may actually have been giving me the benefit of the doubt. "Where is he?"

"In the ER," I said.

"Where's that?" She turned with such pugilistic fervor that I was forced to grab her arm.

"You can't go in there."

Her jaw was set, her eyes deadly. "Who says?"

"Everyone." Hadn't she seen a single episode of *Grey's Anatomy*? "They're doing all they can."

She huffed a laugh.

"You must be Lavonn," Rivera said.

She turned to share her glower, but yanked up her brows at the sight of him. "Who are you?"

"Jack." Their hands met in an elongated greeting. I examined his face for any sign of feral aggression. Nada. Hers seemed to be equally lacking in ferocity. Weird. "Jack Rivera."

What? Where was the growling lieutenant? Hell, where were the thumbscrews? Or did he save those particular instruments of torture for women who didn't have smooth-as-chocolate features and despicably narrow waists?

"You know Mick?" she asked. She, too, had lost a good deal of her usual abrasiveness.

"Pit's worked so hard to turn his life around."

Her expression softened a little more. "How is he? Really?"

"They don't tell us anything."

She blew out her breath.

"What happened?" he asked. "I thought he and Lieberman were friends."

Her brows had taken a downward bend again. "The gym teacher?"

"Am I wrong?" His tone was confusingly affable, but I was beginning to catch on.

"Is that who shot him?" she asked.

"He was found at Lieberman's house. Was there tension between them?"

"What does Lieberman say?"

"He's dead."

She winced. "And you think Mick did it?"

"Maybe I would have a few years ago, but not now. He's different now."

She tilted her head a little. "You from the old neighborhood?"

"We go back a ways, Pit and me. I just don't know—"

I had heard enough half-baked lies to last an eternity. It was time Lavonn understood the dark lieutenant's devious ways before she offered to bear his children. "I have to use the facilities," I interrupted. "Lavonn, come with me."

"Since when are you scared to use the biff alone?"

"I'm feeling a little faint." As half-baked lies went, it wasn't my best.

"I'll get you a nurse," Rivera said.

"I just need a little cold water on my face," I said, but he was already gripping my arm.

"Excuse me," he said, calling on a smocked passerby. "Can you help me, please? My friend here isn't feeling well."

The nurse in question was young and cute and conscientious. Just my fucking luck. But worst of all, her ring finger was horrifically devoid of any symbol of ownership. It took her a moment to wrench her attention from Rivera to me. But one glance seemed to convince her of my impending death. "I'll get a wheelchair."

"I don't need—"

"Come sit down," she crooned, tugging me toward the ugly chairs while speaking to Rivera. "What are her symptoms?"

"She's pale, erratic . . . irrational." He shook his head. "I thought she'd quit using."

"Go screw yourself," I suggested.

He gave me an early-carnivore glance. "I think she might just be coming down from a high."

The nurse nodded, oozing empathy. "I don't like her color," she said and placed a touchy-feely hand on my brow.

I turned my head away and didn't bother to tell her that I'm *supposed to be* the hue of curdled milk. Instead, I tugged at my arm while simultaneously glaring at Rivera. He had already turned back toward Lavonn, disgustingly handsome face etched in an expression of concern.

"How's Jamel holding up?"

"I didn't tell him anything yet," she said. Guilt and worry creased her face. "He and my boys were still sleeping. I didn't want to leave them, but . . . " She shook her head. "I just left a note."

Touchy-Feely was trying to nudge me into a chair.

84

"He's lucky to have you," Rivera said.

Lavonn raised her gaze to his, gratitude laced with interest. "I don't know. I'm kind of..." She paused, looking uncharacteristically uncertain. "Short with the kids sometimes."

"You're too young to be Mother Teresa. And far too pretty. How about we—" he began, but I broke away from my captor with a sharp "Hah" of victory.

"He's a cop!" I snapped, and watched Lavonn's brows lower toward impending retribution.

Eleven

"You are beauty personified. I worship at the altar of your loveliness."
    —Morab . . . the GPS, not the love slave (unfortunately)

"What?" Lavonn asked.

Rivera shifted his dark-hell gaze from me to her.

"What'd you say?" she asked again.

I cleared my throat, feeling strangely traitorous. "He's a police officer," I said, and snapped my arm out of Touchy-Feely's grip when she tried to snag me again.

Lavonn straightened her back as she faced him. "That right?"

"Lieutenant Jack Rivera," he said. "LAPD."

She inhaled heavily, studying him. "You know Albertson?"

"The dirty cop who was pushing drugs to schoolkids?"

"I shot him in the head." Her tone was kick-ass belligerent.

His was steady, honest, matter-of-fact. "Been meaning to thank you for that."

"Yeah?"

"Yeah." His eyes were narrowed, his body language unspeakable. "Fucker should have died twice."

She smiled a little. It looked disturbingly good on her face, transforming it from attractive to beautiful.

"There's the doctor," I said, then snarled when Touchy tried to grab me again. "Will you quit that!"

"Don't make me call security," she warned.

"Rivera . . . " I growled his name. It took a moment for him to shift his attention from Lavonn's milk-chocolate face to my milquetoast complexion. A little longer for his eyes to clear, as if he might have temporarily forgotten my presence. Finally, he nodded.

"I'll take care of her." He said the words as if I were just one of a dozen troublesome hounds begging for leftovers.

"Are you certain?" Touchy asked. "She seems kind of fractious."

"No more than usual."

"Well . . . " She looked doubtful. "Call me if you need anything," she said.

"I'll be sure to do that."

"Do you need my number?"

"Are you fucking kidding—" I began, but Lavonn interrupted my rant.

"You the doctor?"

I turned.

"Surgeon." The woman who corrected her was short, abrupt, and homely. I liked her immediately. "Doctor Mi. Are you related to"—she scowled, clearly having no idea who she'd been working on—"the patient?"

"He's got a name," Lavonn snapped. "It's Mick. Mick Goldenstone."

The doctor redirected her scowl. "Who are you?"

"His sister." Lavonn had never been overly fond of absolute honesty. Neither was she particularly PC. Some might call her refreshingly blunt. I'd probably have to go with *rude as hell* under ordinary circumstances. *Intolerable* when under duress.

"You should take better care of your brother," Mi advised.

"What's that?" Lavonn asked, drawing herself up.

The two of them faced off. "I'm tired of putting your gangsters back together."

"Gangsters?"

"Took me an hour to stop the hemorrhage. An *hour!*" she repeated, as if personally outraged by the loss of blood. "Not to mention the transfusions. He'll need a couple more units before we're done. And for what? Just to see him back in here again next week?"

"Who the hell—" Lavonn began, but Rivera stepped forward.

"LAPD," he said and flipped open his badge. I would have rolled my eyes if I hadn't been preparing to duck and cover. "When can I talk to him?"

Dr. Mi pulled herself up to her full garden-gnome stature and eyed him as if he had just slithered out from beneath something slimy. "So you're a cop." She drew out the final word with even more disdain than she had used for *gangster*. "Are you the one who shot him?"

"I'm the one who saved him."

"What were you doing when he was getting another bullet put in him? Eating donuts?"

I'll say this for Rivera: somewhere along the line he had learned how to ignore an insult. I don't mean to brag, but I'm pretty sure I can take credit for the lion's share of that acquired ability. "*Another* bullet?"

She stared at him a moment, then shifted her gaze to me. I resisted shriveling. "You get shot, too?"

"No."

"Why are you so pale?"

"I'm not sick," I insisted, but Rivera spoke again.

"He's been wounded before?"

Dr. Mi scorched him with her eyes. "You'll have to give him a few days to recuperate before you can accuse him of causing his own injuries."

"So he's going to be okay?" Lavonn asked.

"Do I look like a fortune teller?" she snapped, then, turning on her comfort-first shoes, she marched away, already giving orders to some poor schmuck who happened to cross her path.

"When was he shot before?" Rivera asked.

Lavonn shook her head, admitting nothing. Probably wisely.

"How about you?" he asked, but I was still busy being worried and befuddled and intimidated all at once. "McMullen, what do you know about Goldenstone's prior injuries?"

I exhaled, coming back to myself. "I know there was an incident on the subway."

"An incident?"

"The Crips were harassing a girl." I glanced toward the door through which Dr. Mi had disappeared. She reminded me disturbingly of Sister Celeste of Holy Name fame. Or Hitler.

"What girl?"

I shifted my attention back to him. "A stranger."

"And?"

89

I drew a deep breath and tried to focus. "He saved her life and was shot twice for his trouble."

"Where'd you hear that?"

"His grandmother told me." It was the cross-my-heart truth; those were some of the few dozen words I'd ever exchanged with Micky's Grams.

"What's her name?" Rivera demanded.

"Why?" I felt strangely protective suddenly, though God knew Esse Goldenstone could defend herself. Hell, she could probably take on Dr. Mi.

"I'll need to question her about Goldenstone's relationship to Lieberman."

"You going to lie to her, too?" Lavonn asked. "Like you did me? Pretend you're Mick's friend when all the time you're just trying to get the dirt on him."

So Rivera's an asshole. That's a given, but he's an asshole who doesn't back down. "I'm a cop, Ms. Blount."

"And an asshole." Told ya.

"An asshole who'd like to get some justice for Mr. Goldenstone," he said.

A little of the air left her sails. Mine were still wafting. "Did he do it?" she asked. "Did Mick shoot him?"

"It doesn't look good."

She swallowed, glanced away.

"Is there anything you can tell me that will help me believe otherwise?"

"He's a good guy." She said the words softly, earnestly.

"I don't think that's going to hold up in a court of law," Rivera said, but his voice had softened, too, almost as if he cared, as if he was human. "What time did he drop off his son?"

She exhaled, thinking. "Seven? Maybe a little after."

"What was his mood?"

"I don't know. I mean, I got my own kids. Plus Jamel. Things were pretty hectic."

"What was your first impression?"

"That he looked good," she said and shifted her gaze to mine. "He was wearing his biker pants."

A muscle ticked in Rivera's jaw. Welcome back, Lieutenant. "And that was significant?"

"I got the idea maybe he had a date."

"Because of his attire."

"Plus he smelled good."

A tic danced in his opposite cheek. "Did you ask him about his plans?"

"Sort of." She shuffled her feet. She was shod practically in powder-blue water shoes that complemented her figure-flattering skinny pants to a disturbing degree. "I asked him who was the lucky girl. He said it was me 'cause I got to spend time with his kid." Her voice broke. "He's a good papa. Jamel's . . . " She cleared her throat, then speared Rivera with her killer eyes. "He didn't do it. He didn't shoot that teacher."

"What makes you believe that?"

"'Cause he'd walk on water to be with his boy. If he was put away . . . " Her voice quavered again, but she continued. "He wouldn't see his kid no more."

Twelve

"Once upon a time, there was a beautiful princess who believed in fairy tales. She met a handsome prince. They got married and had four kids. Now she believes in highballs at 6:00."

—Connie McMullen, not your conventional storyteller

We were silent as I drove Rivera back to B. Haven's to pick up his Jeep. Thoughts stormed through my brain like sewage.

"What do you know about Lieberman?" he asked finally.

I glanced to my right. His face was just visible in the light of the console. That fantastical, heart-crushing face. "Just what Micky told me in his sessions."

"Which is?"

Heart-crushing or not, I was a professional. "Privileged information."

He chuckled. "And a little thing like murder doesn't make you think maybe you should share that intel?"

"Micky didn't kill anyone," I said. And I was sure it was true, even though Micky was a wildcard. A sweet, caring, considerate wildcard with sharp edges and a sometimes volatile temper.

"That's right. You just know these things." His tone was taut with derision, ripe with frustration. "Jesus, we should sign you up with the precinct. We wouldn't have to bother with all that pesky investigation nonsense. Just ask you to divine a suspect's innocence or guilt. You could wave your magic wand and inform us of the results." I knew sarcasm when I heard it. Hell, if I hadn't been the inventor I was at least its major contributor, but I kept myself out of the tar pit of his cynicism.

"It is a wand, isn't it, McMullen? Or do you prefer tarot cards?"

"Scrying." I could feel his gaze on me as I turned back to the road with a serene little smile plastered over my gritted teeth. "That's what we call it when we use a crystal ball."

He swore again, but without his usual conviction.

"I scry with my little eye." I made it kind of singsong. Maybe to drive him crazy.

"Scry with anything you want," he said. "Just as long as you stay in your house with your doors locked and your damned security system activated."

"Are you worried about me, Rivera?"

He snorted. "You? Not after that kick-ass training you got in Hillbilly Heaven."

"I wouldn't have been in Hillbilly Heaven, as you so poetically call it, if you hadn't lied," I said.

"I didn't lie."

"How would you like to refer to it, Rivera? Reclining? 'Cause it sure wasn't stand-up honesty."

"You want honesty?" he asked.

I shrugged. "Or we could happily regale each other with

fairy tales about my life being in imminent danger from the Black Flames."

"Okay, here's one for you: Once upon a time, there was a little girl who always wanted to be a cop."

I snorted.

"But instead, she settled on becoming a psychologist."

"Smart little girl," I said.

"She was never quite satisfied, though, so she kept sticking her little busybody nose into police business."

"Was it because the cops kept screwing up?"

Anger bunched in his jaw. "It was because she was a meddlesome . . . " He stopped himself. "She kept prying into things that were out of her league and putting herself in constant danger, forcing the good officers of the law to save her ass on a thousand fucking occasions."

"This little girl sounds very brave. I'd like to meet her someday."

"Well, you can't," he snarled. "Because she's going to get herself killed if she doesn't stay home and keep her damned doors locked!"

I scowled at the sweep of road illuminated by the Saturn's headlights. "I'm no expert on the subject, but I think you just broke about forty-seven cardinal rules of storytelling. Tense, for instance. I think you're supposed to—"

"Stay out of it!" he snarled.

I tightened my grip on the steering wheel. "He didn't do it!"

"The Hi-Point's his."

I didn't know if that was true. "So what if it is? We don't even know if it's the murder weapon. You haven't had time to get a ballistics report or—"

"Ballistics report? What do you think you are now? The damned Mentalist?"

"Simon Baker." I sighed heavily. "He is a cutie, but—"

"You're not a cop!" he snapped. "You're just a snoopy civilian who's going to wind up dead if she doesn't mind her own business."

I smiled and gave him a quick just-you-wait flick of my eyebrows.

He ground his teeth. "You're not really planning to follow through with your idiotic forensics degree."

"What if I am?" The question might have sounded childish, but if it did, it wasn't my fault. Jack Rivera could bring out the na-na na-na boo-boo in the Dalai Lama.

"You'll get yourself killed, that's what."

"What are you talking about? Forensics specialists just work behind the scenes where—"

His cackle interrupted my lovely soliloquy. I refrained from killing him. Despite my kick-ass training from Hiro Danshov, I was still going to need at least one free limb to knock Rivera unconscious . . . more to dispose of his rotting carcass. And three quarters of my limbs were currently involved in driving.

"Jesus, McMullen, that's rich."

I smiled, playing along with the jest. "I'm glad you think so."

Twisting slightly, he rested his right shoulder against the passenger door. I vaguely considered popping the locks and hitting a hard left turn. Would the doors hold or, perchance, would the irritating lieutenant be tossed into the darkness like so much dirty laundry? The Saturn still had some hidden tricks up its metaphorical sleeves.

"As if you're not capable of getting in trouble at home on your own couch."

"Well, if I'm going to do it anyway, I might as well find somewhere more interesting to . . . do it." I gave him a crafty smile for the double entendre. "And with someone more . . . " I eyed him up and down. "Appealing."

He stared at me a second, then chuckled and shook his head. "So it's come back to sex already."

"I didn't say sex."

"Here I am trying to keep you safe, and all you can think about is banging me."

"*You?* Huh! The only way I'd bang you is on the head with a . . . " I motioned wildly. I was at a loss. Thinking about sex with Rivera has a tendency to scramble my brain cells like fresh-cracked duck eggs. "A big, giant . . . whatchamacallit."

"A hammer?"

"No! A . . . "

"Joiner's mallet?"

"Mallet! That's it. I'd bang you any day of the week with a mallet," I promised, but the threat had lost a little punch.

"Sorry," he said and grinned. "I think I left my mallet with my planer."

"Your . . . "

"But I promise to give you some time with my Lenker rod if you'll let the police handle the Goldenstone situation."

It took all my concentration to resist staring at his crotch, but finally his words sunk into my blood-deprived brain. I cocked my head at him. "Are you trying to bribe me?"

"Let's call it a suggestion . . . with maybe a little bit of an offer."

I blinked, amazed, appalled. And a little . . . squirmy.

"You're actually trying to bribe me with sex?"

"It's been a long time, McMullen." His words were low and quiet, tugging at an über-sensitive thread deep inside me. I pulled up behind his Jeep, shifted into Park.

"Apparently for you," I said.

His eyes sparked. "Not for you, I take it?" He folded his arms across his chest. "Who's the lucky guy?"

A number of possible comments flew through my mind. But I didn't know which one to choose. *Who isn't?* might sound a little skanky. Naming names seemed like a bad idea . . . since I wasn't bright enough to conjure up a group of really great fictional lovers that quickly. "I don't kiss and tell," I said.

He huffed a laugh, maybe knowing better than to believe such a crock of bull doo-doo. The first time I jumped Rivera, I told everyone but the mail carrier.

"Was it that boy you were with at the Blvd a few months back? What was his name?"

I squinted at him. He knew Tony's name. Hell, he'd probably learned everything but the man's circumcision date. But maybe Rivera didn't realize embarrassing circumstances had convinced me to avoid Tony Amato and his coffee shop ever since our one and only date. "What about you?" I asked. "Any new skanks in your remuda?"

"Remuda?"

I raised a brow.

"Where do you—"

"Are there?" My voice, velvety smooth just moments ago, had taken a sharp turn toward murderous.

"Are there what, Chrissy?" he asked.

I tried to think of a mundane question, but the idea of him

with someone else seemed to be causing my canine teeth to elongate. "Are there other women?"

"Besides you? About three billion, I believe."

For one wild second, I actually considered biting him. Don't ask me where that came from. I mean, I hardly ever bite anyone anymore. Kicking, I have found, is so much more practical. If I could just wrench my leg over the emergency brake, I was pretty sure I could give him a good solid heel strike to the eye. Although I'd been told that, considering the hardness of my cranium, head butting might be my best bet. "Shall I assume you've slept with all of them or just a couple thousand?"

His lips quirked, causing the scar at the right side of his mouth to dance. "It's nice to know you have such faith in my sexual prowess."

"I have a great deal of faith in your ability to act like a—" A light flickered inside Brooke Haven's house. I jerked toward it.

"No," Rivera said.

I shifted my attention back to him more slowly. "No what?"

"Don't even think about harassing her."

"I'm not going to harass her."

"You're not going to talk to her at all. Not about Lieberman *or* your boyfriend or anything else."

"Micky's not my boyfriend."

"Not for lack of effort, I'm sure."

"Screw you, Rivera."

He shook his head. "Not until you promise to leave things alone. But . . . " He opened his door and stepped out. "You can dream about me all you want on your way home."

"I'll dream about kicking you in the eye!" I barked and leaned down to deliver that edict through the passenger door.

He laughed, giddy as a schoolgirl. "Go home," he said, sobering wearily. "'Cause swear to God, if I hear you've been poking into police business I'll throw your sexy ass in lockup."

Thirteen

"If it looks like a dick and acts like a dick it's probably my ex-boyfriend, who . . . in case you're not catching the subtleties here . . . is kind of a dick."

—Pretty much every living, breathing woman at one time or another

I drove home in a daze. Not because Rivera thought I had a sexy ass. *Pffft.* Thanks to Danshov's training/torture, I *knew* I had a sexy ass. On the other hand, Rivera *was* an ass.

I tapped my thumb on the steering wheel. Threaten me, would he? I had no intention of poking at anything, much less police business. Micky hadn't killed Lieberman. That would be proven forthwith. I was semi-sure of it. Besides, I thought as I parked the Saturn outside my little Tudor, I had clients to see in less than four hours. Clients who had bigger psychological problems than Rivera's even. Maybe.

"So do I do it?" Angela Grapier wore a little stud in her

left nostril. Her hair was pixie short, as green as a shamrock, and so cute it made me wish I had my own leprechaun. She now lay upside down on my couch, legs in the air, heels against my wall. And no, she was not one of the clients who had more problems than Rivera. She was, in fact, fun, funny, and funky. I was taking the credit for all of the above since she had begun coming to me with some pretty major issues almost three years ago.

"Are you asking me if you should have sex with Granger?"

"Yup," she said and twisted her neck so as to study me from her back-assward position.

"And you expect me to say yes or no." Angela had been intentionally celibate since her ill-advised relationship with a kid I had secretly dubbed Kelly the Animal. Kelly the Animal had introduced her to Ecstasy and unprotected sex. Kelly, I had therefore decided, should be shot with a long-range dart gun, ear-tagged as dangerous, and locked away for the rest of his unnatural life.

She swung her legs down and curled them under her bottom. "Actually, I think you'll say something like . . . " She narrowed her eyes and lowered her voice into some kind of nonsensical baritone. "While some think of intercourse as a purely physical act, there are often psychological repercussions that must be taken into consideration before entering into such a life-altering activity."

I curtailed my smile. "I don't sound like that."

She cocked her head at me. "You sound exactly like that."

"Do not."

"Ask Shirley."

I smirked. "Okay, maybe I sound a little bit like that, but it's still a valid point."

"I didn't say it wasn't. I just said you sound like you have a stick up your butt when you say it."

"Actually, you *didn't* say that and I could have gone the rest of my life without hearing it."

She laughed, young and cute and happy, light years from the angsty teenager brought to me by her father years before. And again, not to belabor the point, but that happiness, that carefree joy is because of my guidance as her—

"She was pregnant."

I slammed the door on my self-congratulatory party. "What?"

She glanced out my window toward Sunrise Coffee. And there it was, that hollow sadness, that ragged loneliness.

It came to me finally. "Ally," I said.

"Yeah." Ally was her sister. She'd died of a drug overdose a little more than a year ago. During the following months, I had been afraid we might lose Angie, too. But she'd fought her way back. Angie was a scrapper.

"Where did you hear that?" I asked.

"Creole told me."

I shook my head.

"Conrad Wilson. They call him Creole. He was her . . . one of her boyfriends. He's a meth head."

Oh Jesus. "Do you believe him?"

"He had an ultrasound image."

I considered that, then grasped for a straw. "You're sure it was hers?"

"They stamp the date and name on them."

I stifled a wince. As a psychologist, I had an obligation to be perfectly honest with my client, but mostly I just wanted to see a smile back on Angie's pixie face. "Maybe Mr. Wilson altered it somehow. Perhaps he isn't being entirely—"

"She wrote on the back." She swallowed, picked at a wrinkle in her leggings. "Misty Blue Grapier. Drew a big pink heart around it." Silence echoed in the room. "She used to dot her I's like that. With a lopsided little heart." Her lips twitched. "She was my age when she died."

I wanted to hug her, to pull her into my arms and save her from the horrors of the world, but I remained professionally upright . . . or perhaps more correctly, I remained as if I had a stick up my butt. "Does your father know?" William Grapier had made some mistakes, but he had cared enough to bring Angie to me and was, as far as I could tell, a pretty decent egg.

"Yeah, Creole told us together." Anger warred with worry in her eyes, but she tucked them both away. Sometimes I try to be staid like that, but to be honest I'm more comfortable with blatant emotion than with silence. I welcome passion. Hell, I welcome *curses*. I believe they're cathartic. Maybe that's because I'm a therapist. But more likely it's because I'm Irish. And mean.

"How'd your dad take it?" I asked.

She shrugged, as if with that simple motion she could set it all aside. "He quit drinking. Did I tell you that?"

"No, you didn't."

"Yeah, no more booze. At least that's what he says, but you couldn't prove it by me."

"What do you mean?"

"He's not around much."

"Where is he?"

"I don't know. Work?" Another monumentally casual shrug. "Doesn't matter. I've got things to do myself. Anyway . . . " She bounced a little and gave me a crooked grin.

"We're getting off track."

"Are we?" I asked.

"Yeah. I mean, there's nothing I can do about any of that, right? I just wanna know what I should do about myself. And Granger. I mean, what would *you* do?"

"About having sex."

"Yeah."

"With your boyfriend?"

She laughed. Some of the hollow agony had left her eyes, or maybe it was just buried deeper. "Theoretically, he'd be *your* boyfriend."

"Ahh, well, is he pressuring you to perform?"

"You."

"What?"

"He's yours now, remember?"

"Okay, is he pressuring *me* to perform?"

She sighed, looking put-upon as only an almost-twenty-year-old can. "That's your lead question? Seriously?"

"I think it's a bad idea to have sexual intercourse just because someone else wants you to."

"You!" she reminded me. "Geez, Doc, for a woman with a PhD you kind of suck at this. Aren't you gonna ask about his butt?"

"I wasn't planning to," I said, and refrained from doing so.

"Well, Tiffany says it's primo. And Tiffany knows her butts."

"Tiffany?"

"Tiffany Court, from my physics class. She says she'd do 'im."

"Because he has a primo butt?"

She bobbed a shrug. "There are worse reasons. Aren't

104

there?"

"I suppose there . . . " I began, and paused. "I'm not sure. That actually could be the bottom of the barrel."

She laughed, then sobered. "What's the right reason?"

Damned if I knew, but maybe it was time I gave that question some sagacious consideration. "If I had to nail it down to a singular objective I'd say it's to create life."

Her eyebrows winged toward her lucky-charm bangs. "Are you seriously saying you shouldn't have sex unless you're making babies?"

It had kind of sounded like that. "Perhaps that's a bit literal."

She studied me for a moment, a smart girl with a lot of history. "You mean sex should *improve* life."

Ummm . . . sure. "Just so. Would sex with Granger improve circumstances?"

"His or mine?"

"Both, I suppose."

"Well, his for sure. According to him, he'll die if we don't do it soon."

"What's his life expectancy without it?"

She laughed. "I'm not sure, but he has Saturday all planned out. Like a date thing. There's a club downtown that he's been wanting to take me to, then dinner at his place and euphoria till dawn."

I managed not to give her the *are you fucking kidding me?* look. "That sounds like he might be pressuring you."

"He's a guy."

Yeah, but were guys required to be dumbasses? I rephrased the question in my mind, popped in a few euphemisms, polished it, and added some PC. "Perhaps granting him leniency because of his gender does no one any good."

"Is that like saying dudes shouldn't be assholes?"

I didn't say "Bingo," but maybe my expression implied that she should be awarded a kewpie doll. "How about yours?" I asked.

For a second, she was lost in her own thoughts, but she got her bearings. "Will it make my life better?"

"Yes."

She inhaled slowly, then released her spent air just as gradually. "For a couple minutes probably."

"A couple minutes?"

She grinned. "Should I hold out for half an hour?"

"I was thinking a little more long-term. Such as, will the remainder of your life be improved because of your time with him?"

"You know I'm only nineteen, right?"

"Which means you could have a lot of years to regret it."

"It kinda sounds like you're telling me not to do the dirty."

"It's not my place to make your decisions for you. Besides, you have a good brain, a deep soul, and a father who cares about you."

"Please." She made a huffing sound and glanced outside again. "I can't compete with Security Mutual."

William Grapier was an investment banker for a lucrative local firm. "Are you resentful that he doesn't take more interest in your life?"

"No," she said, which was interesting. She rarely lied to me.

"Are you sure?"

"Yeah. I mean, I make my own rules. It's cool. I just

think . . . " That popping shrug again. "Maybe we could have a breakfast bagel together every once in a while." Her simultaneous need for freedom and security might seem like a paradox, but if so it was a paradox shared by the vast majority of us; we want freedom, but we also want someone to rein us in sometimes. It was a truth that transcended age, gender, and intellect.

"Do you think you might be contemplating sexual intercourse because you're lonely?" I asked.

"I'm not lonely."

The defiance I'd first seen in her was back. Defiance, anger, and a touch of hopeless desire.

"You lost your only sister." It felt unspeakably cruel to dredge up the past, but it wasn't as if she'd forgotten. "Your father's seeming indifference must—"

"She was his favorite."

I paused, scrambling to catch up.

"Dad and Ally. They were tight." She nodded at her own words. "She could make him laugh at the dumbest things. I can't even get him to . . . " She pursed her lips. "He didn't give a crap when Creole told him."

"About her pregnancy."

"Yeah. He just said . . . said it would have been a pretty baby. Then he went back to work."

I felt my heart twist. "It's difficult, Angie. I'm sure he's trying to figure out how to cope."

She thought about that for a second, then shook her head.

"Nope. He didn't care. And if he doesn't care about Ally, he sure as hell doesn't give a shit about me."

"Angela," I said, leaning forward in my chair. "This is a difficult time for you. I know that. But it's hard for him, too.

Try to—"

"I'm gonna do it," she said and bounced to her feet.

I straightened. "What?"

"I'm gonna do Granger."

"Are you—"

"Listen, I've gotta scram." She was already heaving her backpack over one shoulder, a tiny girl with a burden as big as tomorrow. "See you later."

"Angie?"

She turned toward me. I felt torn and strangely desperate.

"It's not my place to tell you what to do," I said, maybe reminding myself more than her.

"But?"

"Everyone deserves to be happy."

"So?"

"But it's not your job to make sure your boyfriend is."

Fourteen

"I'm not racist. Believe me, I hate everyone."
　　　　　　　—Lavonn Blount, who really does

I had two more clients after Angie, but I struggled to keep my mind on business. I know therapists are supposed to treat each and every patient with impartial consideration, but the pair of them were as boring as walnuts, making it difficult to concentrate when a dozen problems and a million questions were storming through my mind.

I called Alhambra Medical, but they didn't have much to tell me. Micky was still unconscious. I dialed Lavonn's cell next.

"What?" her tone was breathless.

"Lavonn?"

"He's dead, isn't he?"

"No. Micky's . . . " I wanted to say "fine," but he wasn't fine. "His condition remains guarded."

She didn't respond.

"He's still unconscious, but—"

"Damn white supremacists."

"What?"

"Lieberman. The fucker's a Bambi killer."

"What are you talking about?"

"And a murderer."

"Who'd he kill?"

"Mick. He killed Mick."

"Micky's not dead, Lavonn. He's going to be—"

"He's gone and you know it. They just haven't put him in the ground yet."

"Lavonn, people recover from this sort of injury all the time."

"Maybe in your world."

For a moment, I had forgotten that although only a few miles separated us, our expectations were worlds apart.

"He's going to be all right," I said, and hoped I sounded more confident than I felt.

She exhaled a sharp breath of disbelief and disdain. "Well, thanks for that, Miss Sunshine. Now I've got to go tell Jamel that his daddy isn't coming to get him."

"Lavonn!"

There was a pause during which I realized she was crying. "What?" she said.

"Don't do that. Please. Not yet at least."

I could tell she was holding her breath, but finally she huffed it out on an expletive. "I gotta go."

I nodded, thinking we had probably had enough of each other, but those damned questions . . . "What did you mean when you said Lieberman was a Bambi killer?"

"The man had an arsenal in his house."

My heart hiccupped in my chest. "How do you know that?"

"What?"

"How do you know that, Lavonn?"

"We were BFFs, didn't I tell you?"

"You and Lieberman were—"

"Holy crap! How do you think? I checked his Facebook profile. He's holding a gun as long as my leg and grinning over the top of a dead deer's head. Creepiest thing I ever saw."

"What about Micky?"

"What about him?"

"Does he have a gun?"

"How would I know?"

"Maybe he mentioned it in passing or—"

"You think that because we're black we spend our time discussing weapons?"

"You knew about Lieberman's."

"Maybe you think we's talkin' 'bout whose ass to put the next cap in."

"Listen—"

"Or how to jack a car. It's all we's good at, after all. Don't have no—"

"Shut up!" I snapped.

There was a moment of silence. I took full advantage of it. "Just answer the question." For a second, I thought she would continue her harangue, but when she spoke next her voice was cool.

"It makes no difference whether or not he had a weapon," she said. "He didn't do it."

"You're right." I found my balance with some difficulty. "I'm not going to worry about it. Micky's innocent. The police will figure that out soon enough."

She laughed. The sound was coarse, but her voice was still smooth as a centerfold's ass. "Certainly they will. Now I must go shoot rainbows out my butt and ride my unicorn to the moon."

"They will," I said and prepared to hang up.

The silence was stretched tight now. "So you're bailing on him, too."

I tried to end the conversation, but my hand wouldn't pull the phone from my ear. "No, I'm not bailing on—"

"Doesn't matter. It's fine. I can figure it out on my own."

"Figure what out?"

"I've gotta go. The forty-eight-hour window is closing."

"What forty-eight . . . What are you talking about?"

"Just tell me one thing: How did you know where to find him?"

"Who? Micky?"

"No. The king of England. Of course, Micky. How'd you know?"

I debated whether or not to tell her before I spoke. "I talked to one of his coworkers."

"And?"

"And she said Micky had disputes with Marvin Lieberman."

"Disputes. Does that mean Mick didn't want to be pen pals anymore or that he threatened to shoot him in the face with an Uzi?"

"He called Lieberman a pervert."

"Why?"

"I don't know."

"That's all she said?"

112

"Actually, it was a *fucking* pervert."

"Well, that makes all the difference," she said, and hung up.

I shook my head as I did the same.

"Problems?" Shirley asked, stepping into my office.

I glanced up, brows pulled together like mating caterpillars. "Am I racist?"

My receptionist's own caterpillars popped into her hairline. "Is this some sort of trick question that could get me fired?"

"What? No. Crap. You think I'm racist, don't you?"

"Well . . . " She sighed as she examined the leaf of an unidentified plant near the window. Her ivory blouse was perfectly pressed. Her gabardine trousers were cuffed, and her fingernails matched her lipstick. Cranberry rose. "No more than the average person."

"The average person *is* racist!"

She shrugged.

"You think I'm racist," I repeated and waited for her to deny it. She didn't.

"If it makes you feel any better, I'm racist, too."

I eyed her askance. "Really?"

"It's human nature. We've got to be a part of this world, live the reality, absorb the pain, and learn what we can from it."

"That sounds really intelligent. I wish I had some inkling what it meant."

She chuckled. "It means we only get slapped so many times before we learn to duck."

"And you've been slapped by the white population?"

She raised her chin a little. "I've taken a few blows from black folks, too, but I do what I do. It's none of their business.

I like working here."

I was officially confused. "That's . . . good. Does someone think you shouldn't?"

"It doesn't matter if they think I'm working for the man."

"I'm *not* the man."

"But it sounds better than 'working for whitie,'" she said.

A little bit of outrage was beginning to seep through my confusion. "What's wrong with working for me?"

"Some folks think I'm selling out."

"Who? Who thinks that?"

"But it doesn't matter. So what if I could make more dropping fries at Wendy's? I'm happy here."

"Wendy's employees make fifteen dollars an hour?"

She flapped her hand at me. "And you're helping people. *My* people, if we're going to divvy things up by color."

I winced, remembering Micky and trying to put the rest of this mess behind me. "Do you think he did it?"

"Mr. Goldenstone?" Her face creased into a frown.

"Yeah."

She eased her bulk onto my client couch. "He's got his demons, sure enough."

"I know, but I thought I was . . . " I paused and reprimanded myself. This was *not* about me.

"You *were* helping him," Shirley said, reading my mind with no visible effort. "Don't you ever think different."

"It's not about me," I said and snuck a peek at her face, because who was I kidding? Of course it was about me. *My* failure. *My fault.* "Lavonn thinks I'm bailing on him."

Shirley nodded, thoughtful. Her thoughtful expression looks a lot like her hungry expression. "Love'll make folks say crazy things."

"I don't think she *loves* me."

She gave me a don't-be-stupid glance.

"Oh. You meant Micky."

"Yeah."

"You think she loves him?"

She didn't seem to believe that question merited more than a single but emphatic nod.

"How do you know?"

"We all have our gifts."

I winced. I wouldn't say I was feeling insecure. But that doesn't make it any less true. "Do we?"

My front door dinged. Shirley rose to her feet, light as a feather. "Yours is to help folks find their way . . . white, black, or lime green with polka dots." She stopped with her hand on the doorknob. "And not to do something stupid about this Micky thing."

In a second, she was in the lobby.

"Mr. Albright. It's nice to see you again."

He murmured something in response. Mr. Albright didn't like to talk . . . not to people anyway. But I was back to considering whether I was really making a difference in anyone's life. I had considered Angela Grapier to be one of my successes. But even she was struggling. And Micky, usually so solid, was alone and unresponsive in Alhambra Medical.

But Shirley was right. I straightened my spine. I *was* good at my job. Mr. Albright, for instance, had only been coming to me for a matter of months and he was already showing signs of choosing a more . . . normal path. A path that would lead toward better communication with his fellow human beings. A path that would—

"What's that? You want me to talk to your stuffed panda

so he can translate for you?" Shirley asked.

My forehead fell with a clunk to my desktop.

Fifteen

"Sleep . . . like being dead but without that long-term commitment shit."
—Jimmy Magna, one of Chrissy's most cerebral ex-beaus . . .
and what does that tell us, really?

Despite fatigue heavy enough to drop me face first onto my hardwood floor, I spent that evening on my computer.

Lavonn was right; the picture of Lieberman with the dead deer was creepy as hell. But it was the image of him with Micky and two women that intrigued me the most. There was no caption, no explanation, but they had their arms wrapped around each other's backs. My internet skills being what they are, it took me most of an hour to learn that the woman on the far right was an English teacher named Sharon Cross. She was what medical professions would probably call morbidly obese. But was she looking at Micky with more than casual interest? I leaned closer to my computer screen and thought perhaps there was a sparkle in her eye as she gazed at him. But what did that tell me?

117

I did a Facebook search and found Ms. Cross's page after only a few minutes. It told me nothing. Nada. Zilch. Not a single entry. Not a solitary picture. As if she'd set up the account, then been swept into an abyss. Weird. What kind of person doesn't want the entire universe knowing every mundane detail of her life?

I returned to Lieberman's site and peered at the woman sandwiched between the two men. She was attractive, early thirties maybe, with a curvy figure that was pressed close against Micky's right hip and a dark mass of hair that swept past her shoulders in come-hither waves. Her dress was blood red and tight as an onionskin. She was smiling coquettishly at Lieberman, who gazed back at her with an expression I couldn't decipher.

I learned her name fairly quickly. Deirdra Mills. When Micky had spoken of the food services lady, I had envisioned a hairnet-wearing spinster with age spots and maybe some dental issues. Wrong again. Deirdra's social media sites boasted a couple thousand photos. Half of them were of her with men of every possible race, age, and physical description. The other half seemed to involve food. I studied the pictures. But they told me nothing, except maybe that Deirdra liked men. And that I was kind of hungry.

I fixed myself a peanut butter-and-honey sandwich and obsessed about everything that had happened in the past twenty-four hours. By the time I crawled into bed my mind was muzzy with fatigue. I was never going to be able to sleep. I was overtired and restless and . . .

That was my final thought before I dropped like a rock into unconsciousness.

My phone rang, bursting into my troubled sleep. I jumped,

heart thumping. Clawing Harlequin's paw off my face, I sat up groggily and checked my phone. By dint of being magically controlled by a satellite, it was the only reliable timepiece in the house and read 1:07. Laney's picture filled the screen beneath it. It was not an image of her as the heroic Amazon Queen or even as the glamorous actress others knew her as. It was, instead, a photo from a bygone era. One that featured her in orthodontic headgear and lopsided pigtails. See, that's the trouble with old friends: they can be mean. But I wasn't feeling so inclined at the moment. Deep-seated terror was my number-one emotion; the past twenty-four hours had been extremely traumatic, setting my nerves on edge, and she'd been abducted in the past.

I pressed the appropriate button with manic speed. "What's wrong?"

"Mac?"

"Where are you? Who's got you? If he's male, grunt. If he's female . . . Who am I kidding? He's not female. Is it someone who's proposed marriage or just fantasized about—"

"Is Shirley painting your office again?"

"What?" I asked, desperately trying to decipher her code.

"Have you been sniffing the fumes?"

"Are you still in the city or—"

"I'm fine, Mac." She said the words with enough weary humor to make me almost believe her.

I took a careful breath. "You sure?"

"Yeah. I'm a little worried about you, though."

"Why?" I quit breathing again. "Have *I* been abducted? Was it a male or—"

"Mac, seriously, take it easy. Nothing's wrong."

"Really?"

"Yes."

I slumped back against my pillows, relaxing a little. "Then why are you calling me in the middle of the night?"

"Check your clock."

I did . . . and winced.

"You mistook the ten for a one again, didn't you?"

"No. Maybe."

"Rivera called me."

"What'd he say?" I tensed again as memories of the previous night stormed in.

"He's worried about you."

I remembered him threatening to throw me in jail and huffed a snort.

"He is," she said. "He's afraid you're going to do something stupid."

"When have I ever done anything—"

"Mac . . ."

"Yeah?"

"Please don't do anything stupid."

"I don't know what you're talking about."

"Leave this for the police."

"I'm going to. I am."

"I know Micky's more than a client to you."

I exhaled, letting my shoulders slump. "He's a good guy, Laney."

"I know, honey, but he's got a bad past. Maybe it's caught up to him, somehow."

"Or maybe . . ."

"No. Please, Mac. No maybes. No what-ifs. Just let the police handle it." Her voice sounded strained.

"Are *you* okay?"

She sighed. "Just tired, I guess. Tell me the truth, do you think this baby will ever be happy sleeping without me?"

"I don't know why he should be different than any other male on the planet."

"Let's start with the fact that he's still an infant."

"You might have a point."

"I do," she said. In the background, baby Mac cooed. Or it might have been her husband. Sixteen months ago, the geekiest geek on the planet, J.D. Solberg, had somehow convinced Laney to marry him. When I found the witch doctor who'd conjured up that nonsense, we were going to have words. "Still, I don't think he's too young for a pony."

"What?"

"Are you busy tomorrow?"

"Well, I do have this little thing called a career."

"Let's buy a farm."

I was silent for a moment. "Good idea. Then later we can purchase a nice little galaxy far far away."

"What would we do with a galaxy?"

"What would we do with a *farm*?"

"Milk cows, ride horses, card wool, grow vegetables, make—"

"Laney . . ."

"Yes?"

"I don't know how to break this to you, but you're an actress. A star, actually."

"So?"

"Stars don't ride cows and milk horses."

"Be ready at one o'clock, okay?"

"I have clients who are badly in need of—"

"Your afternoon's entirely open."

"You're wrong. I'm seeing a new client who's having delusional episodes."

"Mr. Wellberg cancelled his two o'clock."

"What? No." Clinical psychology is an odd occupation. I mean, being the benevolent individuals we are, we want the best for our clients. But in order to remain financially solvent, we kind of need those same clients to remain neurotic, phobic, and borderline irrational. Luckily, in L.A., mental disorders sprout like fungi in a rain forest. "He was quite concerned about his delusions and wanted the first possible—"

"Turns out there really was a naked woman in his gum tree. Now he's feeling fortunate rather than irrational."

"I'm starting to think Shirley might not be great at this client-confidentiality thing."

"Come with me, Mac. Please," she begged. I was prepared to refuse, but Laney never begged.

"Will you buy *me* a pony, too?"

"You're not ready for a pony. But I could probably get you a pig."

Sure enough, due to the presence of a real, live naked girl in Mr. Wellberg's favorite tree, he had, in fact, canceled his afternoon appointment. Mia Taublib, however, showed up late and harried for her ten o'clock.

Mia's about my age. She's small, softly contoured, and funny. Her eyes are caramel colored, her face round and pretty.

"How was your weekend?" I asked.

"Good." The hint of southern twang in her voice strengthened a little. "Well . . . " She rethought her statement. "Tade Jr. came down with the flu, so I'm kinda tired. If *kinda tired* means I'd sell my left boob for an hour's nap."

I laughed but didn't inquire why only her left one was on the auction block. "You don't have anybody who could watch him for a while?"

She shook her head. "All my kin are in Tennessee. Down in the dirty south, as they say."

I had never heard the phrase before. "Who calls it that?"

"Tade," she said, then hurried to add, "but he's just joking."

"So your husband's not home yet?" Tade Sr. was stationed in Honolulu, where air pollution is virtually nonexistent and the water is as blue as a love slave's eyes. For just a second I considered joining the military.

"Not for another week or so."

"I suppose he'll be able to take some of the load off when he's finally stateside."

"Yes. Sure. He's great with the baby. They're best buds. I'm so lucky. But I don't know if I'll be able to get in for an appointment after he arrives. Things are going to be pretty hectic for a while."

"How so?"

"Tade Sr.'s great! Really great. But he doesn't like . . . " She paused, shrugged. "There's just a lot going on."

I watched her, wondering about the great Tade Sr., but I let her ramble. Because it's important to allow clients to choose the course of our discussions . . . and because my mind kept wandering down a thousand paths involving Micky Goldenstone.

By the time her fifty minutes were up, we'd discussed her chunky childhood, the haunting allure of bread pudding with rum sauce, and the unlikely possibility of obtaining fat breasts while keeping everything else skinny.

At 12:55, we were standing in the lobby, chatting about nothing in particular, when Laney pulled up outside in a ruby red Tesla. At least, I thought it was Laney. She was wearing a bonnet the size of Pluto and glasses dark enough to eclipse the sun.

But Mia still gave her a quizzical eye. "Is that—" she began, then shook her head as if she was most certainly wrong about whatever was going on in her head. "Your next client?"

Since Laney's weird-ass rise to fame, it was becoming increasingly difficult for her to live any kind of normal life. "No," I said. "Just a friend."

"She looks familiar."

"She has that kind of face."

"The kind that's made Jessica Alba richer than God himself?"

I laughed. "I hope to see you next week."

"Me, too," she said and left, but not without a long glance through Laney's windshield.

A minute later, I was sitting in the passenger seat beside the Amazon Queen.

"How's Micky?"

"The same, I guess." I'd called the hospital just a couple hours before.

"I'm sorry."

"Yeah," I said and tried to put Micky on the back burner for a while. "Where are we going?"

"Santa Clarita."

The drive was the best part of my day. I know I should shoot higher, but having an uninterrupted conversation with Laney is as good as it gets for me. We only stopped once, and then just long enough for her to nurse baby Mac, strap him back into his car seat like a precious antiquity bound for shipment, and move on.

By the time we pulled up beside the realtor's vehicle, we were almost talked out. Perhaps we hadn't solved all the world's problems, but I felt as if a weight had been lifted from my shoulders. Such are the restorative powers of friendship.

"So who are you today?" I asked and glanced at the person standing beside an SUV big enough to undo all the Tesla's hard work. Short, stocky, and topped by an oversized Stetson, he was facing away to admire the vista. And I had to admit, it was pretty admirable. Miles of white fences bisected the hills. Outbuildings big enough to contain spaceships dotted the property. But it was the house, a manse the size of Mount Olympus, that really drew the eye.

"What?" Laney asked.

"Are you Elaine? Patricia?" I shrugged, awed by the five garages, the manicured lawns, and finding in some strange way that I missed the old days, when Laney lived in an apartment the size of a shoebox and only caused minor disturbances when she walked down the street. "Daisy Duck?"

"I've always wanted poultry," she mused.

"Yeah? Well, maybe you can keep them in your . . . " I shook my head and bent, trying to see the top of the house through her windshield. "What would you call that? A citadel?"

"Citadels are so last millennium," she said, also gazing at the thing. "I think it might be a turret."

"For . . . "

"I'm not sure. Fighting the British?"

"Uh huh. What if the realtor passes out when he sees

125

you?"

"It's a woman."

I squinted at the figure. "Are you sure?"

"Gladys Singer, mother of five."

"Huh," I said when she turned her squat little body toward us. Sure enough, there was a fair chance she was female. "You're actually going to deprive some poor guy of the thrill of seeing the Amazon Queen in the flesh?"

"It seemed best."

"Might be too much excitement for the average man's heart?"

"Jeen said she's got a knack for finding the perfect home for every client."

"Was she responsible for his purchase of the Ice Palace?"

"It's not that bad." The fact that an earth mother like Laney lived in Solberg's sterile environs made me think (not without the occasional shudder) that she might actually like the little dweeb. Don't get me wrong. Solberg has his positive attributes: He could build a personalized global positioning system or hack an electronic account with the worst of them. But when it came to the marriage department, I'd rather exchange vows with an arthropod.

I put that thought aside, glanced at the fortress in front of me, and felt a ping in my heart. What had happened to the ugly little girl with the orthopedic headgear who cared more about panda bears than prestige? "So you're planning to live in Buckingham Palace and . . . Ohh," I said, reality dawning. "Solberg chose her. The realtor."

"Don't blow this out of proportion, Mac."

I grinned, thinking of the irritating little nerdling who used to spew come-ons like chewing tobacco. "Did he cry when you told him you were meeting someone?" I asked.

"You're such a bully."

"And beg you never to talk to another man as long as you live?"

She sighed. "Why do you think I had you running lines with Sergio instead of doing it myself?"

I stifled the wave of embarrassment that flushed me at the reminder. "I assumed it was because of my stellar acting abilities."

She gave me a dry glance. "Besides that."

"Poor Solberg," I said, realizing what it must be like to have your spouse clutched in a love slave's manly embrace. "If he just hadn't called me *babekins* quite so many times, I might actually feel sorry for him."

"No, you wouldn't."

"No, I wouldn't."

"You've got to admit, Sergio would be hard on any man's self-esteem."

"So how much worse for those as-of-yet-unidentified species, right?"

"Mac . . . " she reprimanded, but the realtor was heading our way.

"Quick," I said, "tell me how I'm referring to you or I'm going with Foghorn Leghorn."

"She knows who I am."

"Or should I call you Wily . . . Wait . . . you actually gave her your real name?"

"I guess she sold a house to Beyoncé. This place belongs to Clark Gable's grandson. So unless I'm carrying a scepter and wearing the crown jewels, she's unimpressed."

"Huh," I said. "Remind me though. Why am I here?"

127

She caught me in her evergreen gaze. "I need you to be around, Mac. To help with the baby. To keep me sane. To make sure I don't make any ridiculous decisions."

"You never make ridiculous decisions," I said, but suddenly remembered her husband, the GPS-programming nerdster. "Except that one time." I laughed, trying to lighten the mood, but she grabbed my arm in eagle-strong fingers.

"Tell me you won't do anything stupid about this Micky thing."

"Define . . . "

"Please." A single earnest tear slipped down the perfection of her cheek. "Please."

"I won't," I promised. "I won't do anything stupid."

Sixteen

"It's time you learned the truth, Pork Chop. Life sucks and then you get run over by a gravel truck."
—Glen McMullen, who actually had been run over by a gravel
truck

I was about to do something stupid. Guilt rolled through me as I remembered Laney's tearful request. But Micky was in trouble. And I wasn't racist. Nor was I, generally, stupid. Lavonn was planning something. She'd mentioned the forty-eight-hour window and I'd watched enough hard-core police procedurals to realize she was talking about those all-important first hours after a crime. Oh yeah, she had something up her sleeve. And although she could be as abrasive as sandpaper on my butt, I felt the need to make sure she didn't get thrown in the slammer for her trouble.

Which made my current ensemble perfectly logical. I was parked two blocks down and one block over from Lieberman's house and dressed incognito as one Fani

Kolarova. My French-actress disguise had served me well in the past. Even Rivera's philandering ex-senator father hadn't recognized me. Not that anyone was going to see me this time. But in case some passing civilian happened to glance my way, they would see a buxom blonde dressed in a black exercise suit snug enough to double as plastic wrap.

I had to learn the truth, and this was where it began. But I hadn't yet screwed up enough courage to exit my vehicle. Maybe, I thought, there was another way to figure things out. And maybe, if I was really lucky, that way involved sitting in my kitchen with a tub of Häagen-Dazs and a . . .

Something struck my window. I squawked and twisted left.

A giant stood beside my car. A dark, hulking . . . No, wait a minute . . . it was . . . Holy crap! It couldn't be! It couldn't possibly be Lavonn Blount. But it looked suspiciously like her.

She made a casual circular motion with her hand, then stuck it into the pocket of her hoody and stared at me.

I stared back, blond wig undulating to my well-padded boobs. She couldn't have recognized me. I was incognito. She probably just had car trouble or something, happened upon me, and was about to ask for help. Or maybe she'd been out for a jog and had lost her—

"What the hell are you waiting for?" she asked.

I turned the key to the accessory position and powered my window down a scant few inches. *"Quelle?"* It was one of the dozen foreign words I remembered. The majority of the others referred to private body parts; I'd learned the bulk of my French long before reaching the level of maturity I now possess.

"What the fuck are you doing in that thing?" she asked, nodding toward my sumptuous wig.

I reared back. *"Excusez-moi?"*

"What's wrong with you?"

I felt the blush start at my ears. *"Excusez—"* I began again, but she stopped me with a snort.

"Come on," she said, jerking her head in the direction of Lieberman's house.

"What? Why?"

Her scowl deepened. "You saying you dressed like an East Side hooker and parked three blocks from his house just for giggles?"

"Oui?"

She shook her head, looking tired.

"Every Monday and Friday." I said the words in English but added a smidgen of accent just to make sure she knew I wasn't really Christina McMullen.

"It's Thursday," she said.

"Are you sure?" Things had been confusing, but I was almost certain . . .

"You coming or what?"

I reared back. "Coming where? Why?"

"To learn the truth," she said and turned away.

"No." Panic was bubbling up like agitated Coca-Cola. "What truth?"

"Why did Mick call the dead dude a pervert?"

"I don't know."

"Me neither, but I'm going to find out," she said and marched away.

It took me half a minute and a good deal of cursing to force myself out of the Saturn. Longer to catch up to her long-legged strides. "Lavonn!" I was already panting, but I managed to grab her arm. "You shouldn't be here."

"Because a brother with an ugly past isn't worth your trouble?" she asked and yanked out of my grip.

I gazed longingly down the street toward my waiting car. It looked so lonely there in the dark. Maybe I should return to its loving embrace and hustle back to Sunland, where people tried to kill me with less regularity than they did in other environs. And . . . perhaps I was being unfair to Lavonn. I mean, did my presence here suggest that she was incapable of taking care of the situation? I didn't want to belittle her abilities. Or seem racist. In fact, if it took my absence to prove my even-minded fairness, I would just have to return home and . . .

"So what if Jamel won't see his daddy except through bars?"

I clenched my fists, swore, and stormed after her.

By the time I reached her side, it felt like my lungs were being squeezed in a cider press. "Holy crap, you're easy," she said but didn't bother to glance at me as we turned onto Lieberman's block.

"Am not."

"Are . . . What was that?" She froze, fingers gripping my arm like talons. The *yip-yip* sounded again. All I could see in the darkness were the whites of her eyes as I tried to pry loose from her grasp.

"I don't know. Coyotes, maybe."

"Coyotes!"

I controlled my grin and ignored the fact that my arm was going numb. I had seen Lavonn scared before, but only when being threatened by hopped-up drug dealers with bad attitudes. A few wild dogs howling in the distance seemed as innocuous as cotton balls by comparison.

"I think so," I said.

"Like"—her fingers tightened on my arm—"wolves?"

"Kind of. But they're harmless. Until dark," I said and stepped forward.

She dragged along behind. "It *is* after dark," she hissed.

"I know it's—" I began, then froze. She bumped into me, striking me with enough force to make me stumble.

"What—"

"Shh," I warned, and quick-stepped behind a nearby tree.

"What's wrong?"

"It's a stakeout." I could barely hear my own voice. But when I peeked around the palm's sturdy trunk, I saw, again, the dark SUV parked a few hundred feet away.

"What?"

"Shh."

A man stepped out of the vehicle, stretched, and rotated his neck.

"Cops," I breathed.

"Watching his house?"

"Yeah."

"How do you know?"

My heart was pounding like a gong in my chest. "Haven't you seen *Stakeout*?"

"Who?"

"Richard Dreyfuss and Emilio Estevez?"

"Are you playing me right now?"

"It's a classic."

She shook her head. "Why would they watch his house?"

"I don't know. Maybe they think someone's going to try to break in."

"Who would do that?"

"We've gotta go," I said and tried to tug her back toward

safety, but she remained unmoved.

"You're going to have to distract him," she said.

"*What?*"

"You distract the cop. I'll sneak through the back door."

"Are you out of your mind? I can't distract him."

"You kidding me?" Reaching out, she unzipped my boob-hugging sweatshirt. "You could wake a corpse with those things."

I glanced down. Plumped, padded, and prodded upward, they *were* fairly impressive.

But I swatted her hand away. "What are you doing?"

"Improving our odds."

"Forget it!" True, I was incognito. But now that it came down to it, I wasn't all that confident in my ability to fool a cop. Hell, Lavonn had recognized me through the Saturn's smudged windows, in the dark. "I'm going home," I said.

"Fine." She turned away. "If you don't care about Mick and his kid, you go on home and take a nap. Maybe cuddle up in your La-Z-Boy with some popcorn."

Popcorn did sound good. And the thought of my Boy reclining all alone almost brought tears to my eyes, but I snagged her sleeve again. For a moment, I thought she was going to deck me. Instead, she just gritted her teeth and lowered her brows.

I steadied my resolve. "*You* distract him. I'll sneak in."

"You crazy?" She reared back a little. "They see a long loaf of whole wheat like me struttin' down White Bread Avenue, they'll slather me with butter and eat me alive."

"What the hell are—"

"What would you do in there anyway?"

"Whatever you're planning."

"Yeah? You bring one of these?" She pulled a tiny something from the pocket of her jeans. I squinted at it. "Zip drive," she said. "To collect evidence."

"That's your plan?"

"He's a teacher."

"So?"

"You think he left a note on his fridge that says, 'Here's why I'm a pervert . . . and oh yeah, I shot Mick Goldenstone'?"

I wasn't sure if I should shake my head or run for the hills.

"It'll be on his PC," she said.

"But—"

"Now go show some cleavage," she ordered and tugged the sweatshirt from my shoulders.

I yanked it back up. "Why can't I have the zip drive?"

"Because it's *mine*. So quit your whining, unless you don't think Mick's worth the trouble."

I tried to think of a good excuse, but I was fresh out. "How long are you going to need?"

"I don't know. A couple hours?"

"A couple of *hours!*"

She snorted. "Give me like . . . fifteen minutes."

It might as well have been two weeks. "How the hell am I going to distract him for fifteen minutes?"

"I don't know how you white chicks do it. Faint or something."

"Faint? I've never . . . " But truth be, I'd fainted just a few short weeks ago. In my defense, I'd just been abducted and saved and . . . Another long story. "Listen, if you're not out in ten minutes I'm going to have to . . . faint. Or something."

She grinned at me, white teeth gleaming. "Go get 'em, girl."

I felt a little wobbly as she disappeared from sight. Kind of lightheaded as I removed my sweatshirt. Heading toward the nearest alley, I turned left, leaving Lieberman's house behind as I tied my sleeves around my waist. The tank top I'd pulled over my push-up bra was pink and topped with lace. Still hidden from view, I took a few deep breaths, fluffed up the girls, and turned the corner at a jog, heading straight toward the cop I wanted to avoid more than cellulite.

Seventeen

"The primary function of breasts may be the feeding of our young, but their ability to make blithering idiots out of relatively intelligent males should never be underestimated."
　　　　　—Lily Schultz, bar owner, philosopher, and realist

Even when chased by mad dogs, I'm not a fast runner. (This has actually been proven.) But this time I jogged particularly slowly, giving the officer, who had returned to his vehicle, plenty of time to see me coming. And, of course, to notice that the girls were bouncing like water balloons in a truck bed.

I stared through his windshield, trying to make sure he'd seen me, but it looked, from my limited point of view, as if his gaze was still focused on Lieberman's house. Gritting my teeth, I hopped up on the curb, ran two strides, hopped down, did another two, then repeated the process. Extra cardio, extra bounce, extra opportunity to fake the injury I was planning so I could capture Officer Stakeout's attention and—

"Shit!" I swore as I fell. My ankle twisted a microsecond

before my hip struck the asphalt with jackhammer gusto. My right elbow hit next. I rolled onto my side, clutching my arm to my chest and wondering if my foot had snapped clean off my leg.

"Are you all right, miss?"

"No! I'm not—" I stopped myself and blinked at the light shining in my direction. It took me a moment to realize my plan had worked better, and more painfully, than I had hoped. "*Oui*, yes." Tears bleared my vision. At least I thought they were tears. In actuality, my wig had slipped slightly. I held my breath and tugged it back into place with a shaky left hand, sure Officer Stakeout would have noticed. But... huh... turns out my injured arm was still pressed snug against my boobage, funneling every iota of his attention in that direction. "I am well."

"You sure?" He shifted the beam of light to my elbow. It looked like mashed strawberries. My stomach churned at the sight. I pulled my gaze away, settling in on him. He was short, earnest, and looked to be about as old as the lettuce in my crisper drawer. On the upside, he was considerably cuter. "That might be broken. I'd better call an ambulance."

"No!" I gasped, then soothed my voice into something possibly resembling a cool Frenchwoman's. "Please, *monsieur*, I cannot afford to miss the work." And I sure as hell couldn't give anyone my real name. Half of California's police force knew me as Rivera's main squeeze. Or possibly as his main ex-squeeze. Which is like, what... lemonade that's gone rancid?

"I wouldn't worry about that," he said. "I'm sure your employer will understand. Besides, they'll probably be able to get you fixed up before your shift."

"But you do not understand." I looked up through my

lashes. Luckily, they were still enhanced with the buttload of mascara and the trowel of eyeliner I had applied earlier in the day. "I must be ready at the four a.m."

"Four o'clock?" He squatted. "That's almost as bad as my hours. What do you do?"

"I am worked for by the Paramount Pictures."

"You're an actress?" He settled comfortably on his well-defined haunches, looking increasingly interested. But why wouldn't he be? Half the populace of L.A. hoped to see themselves on the big screen. If they were young, fit, and cute as bunnies, you could increase that to about 150 percent.

"*Oui.* And this is my . . . how is it you say . . . my big . . . " I hugged my arm more tightly to my chest, making my boobs swell like rising dough above the pink lace. To my right, Lieberman's house remained as dark as the center of my questionable soul. Did that mean Lavonn had failed to gain entrance or that she was exceptional at the task and was already inside? "My big break," I said and gave him a shy grin.

He grinned back. Yikes. Turns out he might even be cuter than bunnies, but I kept my head.

"Please . . . " I looked up imploringly. "If you could but help me to my feet."

"I don't think that's a good idea."

"*Si*, it . . . " Dammit! I can barely speak the King's English. Trying to be bilingual while under duress is laughable. And while slipping from bastardized French into mangled Spanish might have been comical in any other circumstance, doing so while trying to keep the cops off a pseudo friend was not quite so humorous.

I flexed my biceps, urging my right boob higher. Young and earnest is all well and good, but it's no match for healthy and horny. Stakeout's gaze dropped dreamily toward my cleavage. "Please"—I made my tone breathy, like an overtaxed porn star's—"I must not be late for my bedroom scene," I said and tried to rise to my feet. Pain ripped through me, but I refrained from cursing. Neither did I manage to rise, however. My ankle gave out, tumbling me back toward the street, but he caught me, hands steady and strong on my arm. Unfortunately, it was my injured arm. "Son of a . . . " I hissed but halted before any of my favorite Americanisms slipped out. He eased me back onto the asphalt.

"Sorry, miss. I'm sorry." He winced as he released his hold.

"That is okay, Mr. . . . " I shook my head and gave him an adoring gaze. "Here you have come to the rescue of me like a knight in shining armoire and I do not even know your name."

"It's Rick," he said. "Rick Lawson. *Officer* Lawson," he corrected.

I managed a confused mien, though honest to God, it was hard to resist collapsing into moans and rocking over my ankle like a palsy victim. I was pretty sure the damned thing was about to burst into flames and burn to ashes "Officer? Are you the soldier?"

"The . . . oh . . . no. I'm a cop. A copper. A . . . " He searched wildly for the correct term to suit my questionable place of birth. *"Guarda?"*

"A *policier*? Truly?" I reared back a little. "How exciting that is."

He glanced at Lieberman's house, and I thought I saw a smidgeon of disillusionment in his expression. He had, after all, been sitting alone in the dark watching an empty house. Well . . . a supposedly empty house.

My mind skittered to Lavonn, wondering if she was inside. If she had found anything. If—

"What's your name?" he asked.

I jerked my mind back to the matter at hand. A first-class lie was in order, but even a maestro has to stretch a little before the opening aria; I drew in my right leg and exaggerated a wince.

"I should call an ambulance before—"

"No!" I grabbed his sleeve, imploring. *"Non. S'il vous plait."*

He drew back, suspicion creeping around the corners of his lips. I eased up on his shirt.

"I am sorry. You are so kind, and I am, how you say? Queering you out."

"Ummm . . . weirding me out?"

"Oh, *oui.*" I chuckled softly, kind of wishing I had never been born. "I am not so good at this your language."

"But you still got a job with Paramount?" He had probably read for them with all the verve of Olivier and hadn't gotten so much as a call back. Not wanting to cause any bad feelings, I backpedaled madly.

"Oh, I . . . " I shook my head. "I do not have the part that speaks."

"No speaking part? Just a walk-on then?"

"Well . . . perhaps, you could say . . . just a *lie* on."

Quizzical might have described his expression. *What the fuck* would have summed it up more succinctly.

"I am to be in the bed with . . . " I paused, searching frantically for a believable male actor. I should have warmed up my lying muscles more carefully. "Mr. Cruise."

"Tom Cruise! You have a love scene with Tom Cruise? What's your name?" he asked again.

In for a penny, in for the whole damned money market. "Fani. Fani Kolarova. Mayhap you have heard of me?" I tried to sound really pathetic. It wasn't even difficult.

"I don't think so."

I shook my head sadly. "And never you will," I said, "if I do not get to the work on time."

It looked like he was weakening. I leaned in, figuratively and physically.

"I have come to this great country of yours on the temporary visa. I do not have so much of the time left. I must be gainful employed."

He exhaled, then scowled at Lieberman's blank slate of a house, thinking. "Let's have a look at that ankle."

I bit my lower lip and leaned back on my one, unsmashed elbow. He slipped off my shoe, then tugged at my sock. The pain was ripe enough to coax a hiss from my lips, but I locked the curses behind my clenched teeth. Miraculously, my legs were freshly shaven (both of them) and the muscles of my calves pretty firm.

Color was beginning to bloom like azaleas across my lily-white instep. I could see that much even in his weak-ass light.

He sighed in sympathy. "Are you sure you don't want an ambulance?"

"I do not have the funds to cover such an expense," I said. "And I must get home."

"Where do you live?"

Tricky. This was tricky. If I had him return me to my little domicile in Sunland, he would, of course, be able to determine my true identity.

"Paris."

"I meant here, in the States."

"Ahh, but of course. I live . . . Oh!" I gasped and leaned over my ankle again.

"Are you okay?"

"*Oui.* Yes. But perhaps . . . if it is not too much of the trouble, you might fetch ice for the swelling and something for the . . . " Another masterful wince. "Pain?"

"I wish I could, but I have to stay here," he said and started to glance over his shoulder.

Inside Lieberman's house, a shadow crossed the window. I leaned abruptly forward. The movement drove a mad stake of pain through every fiber of my being, but it did good things for my boobs. Officer Lawson came to attention like Harley spotting a lamb chop.

"It is a must that I be fit for my scene," I said.

"Well . . . " He cocked his cutie-pie head a little. "*Mission: Accomplished*, I'd say."

I laughed at his cleverness. "Tell me true, you are the actor, too, *oui?*"

"Me?" He jerked his gaze from my chest and set a careful hand on my foot. His fingers felt cool and soothing against my skin. I was probably going to burn in hell for the lies I was telling, so it seemed wise to enjoy his comforting touch while I could. "No. Not that I haven't considered it. Mom always said I'd be . . . " He shook his head, possibly remembering he was a duly appointed officer of the law and not some moon-eyed starving artist. "Being a cop's good, too. I get a chance to help people." He probed my ankle gently. "I'm afraid the swelling is spreading."

"This is unfortunate," I said but kept my gaze on his eyes. His lashes were very long.

"I'm sorry."

"*Non*," I said and pushed my borrowed hair behind one self-owned ear. "I meant, it is unfortunate that you are not the actor. Your face, it would look good on the silent screen."

"What?"

"The silent screen. The . . . " I paused in faux frustration.

"Silver screen," he corrected. "You think so?" He grinned a little, making me realize that I wasn't so far from the truth. He had Patrick Dempsey hair and a Will Smith smile . . . full-on and no holds barred.

"*Oui.*" It wasn't difficult making my voice sound breathless.

"Well, maybe you can get me a spot as an extra."

"I fear I do not have much clot as of yet, but perhaps one day I will be the big star, *oui?*"

"I wouldn't doubt it at all."

"Then it will be me who says the shots."

"What?"

I considered trying a seductive pout. But I'd known since I slipped my first diaper that while other girls looked adorable in full sulk, I just appeared constipated. "You know, I will be the person whom others must obey."

"Oh. You'll call the shots."

"*Oui.*"

"Well, when you do, I want to be a gladiator."

"*Quelle?*"

He amped up his grin and curled an arm, making his biceps pop. I felt something stir deep in my gut. Good morning, hormones. "Or maybe a boxer. Something . . . "

"Sexy?" I purred and put a hand on his bulging arm.

He blushed. Even in the questionable light I could see color infuse his cheeks. Holy hell, he was adorable. If I were

144

brain-dead enough to consider dating another cop . . . one ten years younger . . . and you know, not lying my ass off, I'd be on him like superglue.

"Well . . . " He cleared his throat and glanced behind him. "I'll bring up my car."

I zipped my gaze to Lieberman's house, wildly scanning the windows. They looked as black as my soul, but I couldn't afford to be careless.

My ensuing moan would have put Linda Lovelace to shame.

My poor little starter cop actually jumped. "Are you okay?"

"Of course. *Oui*. I will bear the pain."

"You'll feel better when you lie down for a while," he said and rose to his feet.

I tried to draw him back, but something flashed in the window behind him.

"What the hell?" he rasped and yanked out a gun.

I gasped, but he was already calling for backup, already racing up Lieberman's walkway.

"Don't leave me!" I wailed. He ignored me completely. Finding the front door locked, he raced around to the back.

I struggled to my feet just as I spotted a dark shape zipping across the neighboring yard. Lawson picked up speed. As for me, I hoped like hell Lavonn had kept up her cardio. Turning, I made a gimpy gallop for parts unknown.

Eighteen

"You look like I need a drink."
—Glen McMullen, upon seeing his daughter with yet another
note from her teachers

"You okay?" Shirley hadn't even stepped into the office before voicing the question.

I raised a brow at her from behind the reception desk, going for haughty. It was 8:52 in the morning, but I was bathed, groomed, and dressed to stun in a white silk blouse and black pencil skirt. Amazing, really, since it had taken me a full thirty minutes to find my car on the previous night. After turning the corner at a dead limp, I had spotted an elderly gentleman walking his cockadoodle in the predawn stillness. Knowing the propensity of the geriatric for reporting strange goings-on, I had hidden in a bougainvillea for half an eternity. I was still picking petals out of my hair when I reached home. After that, I had tried to contact Lavonn but she hadn't picked up. Smoking had taken up the remainder of the night.

Don't get me wrong, I kicked the nicotine habit years ago. But when I'm sure the cops are about to haul my pretty-good ass off to the slammer, I allow myself a couple of cigs . . . 'cause, you know, they're hard to come by in the big house. But despite my chain-smoking vigilance, nary an officer showed up at my door. By six a.m., I was certain Rivera knew about my nocturnal activities but was delaying the arrest just to torment me.

"Yes, I'm fine," I said.

She lowered her brows a little.

"Why do you ask?"

She shoved her key into a handbag the size of Luxembourg and stepped inside. "You're early," she said.

"Yes." I quit fussing with the tape dispenser before I hurt myself. Believe me, office equipment can be capricious. At least that's what I'd told Mom when my brother Michael appeared with a stapler-shaped hematoma in the exact center of his forehead. Recalling that fond memory, I carefully aligned the client cards Shirley had placed on her desk the night before. "Well, I thought I'd get caught up on some paperwork."

"Now?" Stepping around the corner of the desk, she watched me as if she had stumbled into an alternate universe. One with new and startling species.

I forced a laugh. "You act as if you've never seen my face before noon."

"Mr. Otterson isn't due until nine. You're eight minutes early." She didn't mention the fact that I usually come fishtailing into L.A. Counseling's parking lot about thirty seconds before my first client steps through the door, but that was just kindness on her part. "What's going on?" she asked.

"What do you mean? Nothing . . . " I began, then remembered she could smell a lie like a mother.

"I hurt my ankle," I said.

She canted her head, waiting me out.

"At the gym. On the Stairmaster. Then I . . . I got to feeling sorry for myself . . . and couldn't sleep. So I . . . " I let a little honest guilt seep in. "I had a cigarette."

She watched me, sifting through the guilt, stealthily ferreting out the real source.

"Or two," I corrected and winced. Once, while on a masochistic binge, I had read a plethora of articles on the effects of nicotine. I was pretty sure I could feel the density of my bones drop while that of my arteries increased exponentially. "Or . . . twelve."

She shook her head and bent to stow her purse in the bottom drawer of the desk. "Those things'll kill you."

I should be so lucky, I thought, to be offed by something as innocuous as cigarettes. The smart money was on my being snuffed out by some gun-wielding neighborhood patrolman . . . or Rivera.

"I know, but I was in a lot of pain."

She straightened, a big woman with the poise of a runway model. "Your knee feeling better now?"

"Yes, it's . . . " I began, but I sensed the trap a second before it was sprung. "It's my ankle," I corrected.

"Uh huh," she said and removed a dead leaf from a hovering philodendron. "What'd you learn?"

"What?"

"About Mr. Goldenstone. What'd you find out?"

"I spent the night at home," I said. "I mean . . . after spraining my ankle at the—"

She propped a capable fist on a cocky hip and glanced over her shoulder at me.

"The police are handling the investigation," I reminded her.

"Ms. McMullen . . . " She sounded tired as she dropped her fist and settled her weight onto the edge of the desk. "You've got to quit doing this."

"Doing what?" I tried to look like a dumb blonde. I'm pretty sure I was fifty percent successful, despite the fact that I had left my borrowed wig hidden in the back of my underwear drawer.

"Sticking your nose into police business, else one of these days someone's going to snip it off."

Shirley was right, of course, I shouldn't stick my nose into places it didn't belong, and I *didn't* want it snipped off. But I had three hours before my next appointment and I couldn't forget the photograph of the foursome on Lieberman's Facebook page.

Perhaps he and Micky had never been BFFs, but apparently they had not always been enemies. So what had happened? Maybe the woman in the skintight dress could shed some light on the situation.

Phone calls to Branford Middle School had assured me that Deirdra Mills had not shown up for work in the cafeteria. Thus my journey up the dreaded 5 to Van Nuys.

Ms. Mills lived in an apartment building that had all the appeal of an appendectomy. It was a long, white building that boasted a flat roof and the ability to make any other place in the world seem homey by comparison.

I stepped into the narrow lobby and after a moment's search pressed number 112. Finding her address had not been difficult. Deirdra was not what I would call reclusive.

"Yes?" Her voice was softer than I had imagined.

I made mine the same, so as not to scare her off. "Deirdra?"

"Who's there?"

For a moment, I considered telling her I was delivering flowers or pizzas, or a large check from California Lottery. But I've done that sort of thing before. It usually ends with me learning nothing . . . besides the fact that I'm kind of an idiot.

"My name's Christina McMullen. I'm a friend of Micky's."

She said nothing.

"Do you have a minute?"

"Not really." She paused as if searching for an escape route. "I'm pretty busy."

"It'll just take a minute."

Another pause. "You alone?"

I glanced behind me, immediately paranoid. "Yes?"

"Okay, but I don't have much time," she said and buzzed me in.

She opened the door while I was still shuffling painfully down the hallway, shut it immediately upon my stepping inside, then backed away. Her eyes were red, her hair bunched up in a messy knot at the top of her head. Gone was the sexy social butterfly I'd seen in a hundred photos.

"I'm sorry about what happened," I said and watched her, trying to read body language, expression, nuances.

"Me, too," she said and wrung her hands.

"You were friends with Marvin Lieberman?"

"Well, I don't know." She darted her gaze to me, then paced into the kitchen. It was a tiny thing stuffed with hanging copper pans and littered with what looked to be dozens of colorful photographs. "I wouldn't say friends. I mean . . . we worked together." She winced. "Sort of."

"You're a cook?"

"Yeah." The first light of enthusiasm shone in her eyes. "I was sous chef at the Bistro until . . . well . . . it's way over in Anaheim and the Five is murder during . . ." She winced, apparently remembering there really *had* been a murder. "You're a friend of Micky's?"

"Do you have any idea what happened?"

"No! No." She turned away again. "How would I? I mean . . ." She shook her head, shuffled pictures around on the aging Formica. "No."

I stepped closer, trying not to crowd her. The word *skittish* wouldn't come close to describing her paranoia. "So . . ." I glanced at the photographs. They were pictures of food. Bright, evocative images of beautifully presented menu items: entrees, salads, desserts. "You took these?"

"Yes. I'm creating a cookbook. *Deirdra's Dream Dishes.*"

I shuffled a picture of lasagna a little closer to me. It had been baked to perfection. The cheese was still melty, just bubbling to gold. The sauce was as bright as the fresh cut tomatoes that had surely been used to make it. "They're beautiful."

"Apartments in Los Angeles . . . even this one . . ." She glanced around and stifled a shudder. "I need another income if I'm gonna stay."

"You're not from here?"

She shook her head. "Des Moines."

"What brought you to L.A.?"

"The fact that it wasn't Des Moines. Listen, I really do have to get going."

I nodded. "I was just hoping maybe you could shed some light on the situation."

She swallowed, looked like she might cry. "How's Micky doing? Do you know?"

"He's still unconscious." She made no comment. "Were you close?" I asked.

She shook her head immediately. "No. Not really. I mean, he was . . . *is* . . . he's a great guy. I just . . . I'm sorry . . . " She drew a fortifying breath. "I have to go . . . do laundry."

As excuses went, it was pretty lame. "I could help you if you like."

"No! No. It's just down the street."

"You don't have facilities in your building?"

"Washing machine's broke. Has been since I moved in."

"Oh, well . . . you're sure you don't know what could have happened between Micky and Mr. Lieberman?"

"I have no idea."

"You never heard them argue or—"

"No. Never. They was friends. I don't know what could have gone wrong," she said and, pacing to the door, ushered me out.

I got in my Saturn, drove around the block, then pulled in behind a Chevy Malibu that was parked a hundred yards down the street, and waited.

Fifteen minutes later, Deirdra appeared, lugging a canvas bag big enough to carry a body. I sat up abruptly, then slouched back down, heart racing.

Tailing her wasn't difficult. Still, I employed my very best stealthy detective techniques: always keep a few cars between you, drive past when she parks, and . . . that about covered it.

A half hour later, I left her at the Suds 'N' Go. I felt gritty, tired, and kind of silly. Turns out the contents of her oversized laundry bag were nothing more damning than actual laundry.

My two o'clock appointment was late. Lavonn Blount showed up instead. She stalked into the reception area like a pugilist prepared for battle. "We need to talk!"

"What?"

"What's going on?" Shirley asked and rose, spreading her legs in a stance that would make many a lineman green with envy.

Lavonn shot her gaze to my receptionist but spoke to me. "Call off your gargoyle."

"What have you gotten Ms. McMullen into?"

Lavonn raised a brow, tacitly threatening to tattle about our antics of the previous night.

I cleared my throat and stood gracelessly, elbow bitching, ankle throbbing.

"We'll just be a minute, Shirley," I said. "Please hold my calls."

"Hold your calls?" she repeated. True, I could count the number of calls I got a day on one toe, but I kept walking, concentrating on each step until I reached my office and closed the door behind me.

I turned with gracious poise. "I'm glad to see you got home safely after—"

"How much do you know about Mick?" she asked, drilling me with her eyes.

I retreated a stumbling step. "What?"

For a moment, I thought she was going to take me down like a panther on a piglet, but finally she paced to the far wall, where she turned to face me. "Why were you in such a hurry to get to Lieberman's?"

"What are you talking about? You were there first."

"Was I?"

"Yeah, you . . . " I stopped short, breath corked in my throat. "What did you learn?"

Maybe I expected her to deny knowing anything, but instead she stood mute and inscrutable.

"Lavonn . . . " I took a limping step toward her. "What's going on?"

She looked away, jaw bunching. "Why does he come here?"

I shook my head, uncomprehending.

"Here." She threw out a hand like a slap. "What does he need? What does he talk about?"

The tension between us, already tighter than Superman's undies, cranked up another notch. "That's privileged information."

Rage flamed in her eyes. "Not if he's a fucking pedophile!" she snarled.

Nineteen

*"I hate surprises, unless they involve hot naked guys and very large cakes.
Even then, they'd better be topped by some pretty great frosting."*
—A hopeful Chrissy, upon learning of her impending birthday
party

"What?" I felt as if the floor had just dropped from beneath
my feet, leaving my body suspended before the inevitable
plunge.

Lavonn watched me in silence. "Is he?"

"Is he what?"

She slammed her palm on my desk, making my knees
bounce and my heart leap to my throat. "A pervert. Is he a
fucking pervert? Tell me the truth." She straightened slowly,
intimidating as hell in her quiet rage.

"What did you find in Lieberman's house?"

"What do you know?"

I knew that her sister had been raped . . . had been
impregnated . . . by the man they'd both admired. I also knew

155

that man was doing everything in his power to make things right. But I could share neither of those facts.

"Have a seat, Lavonn," I said, motioning toward my client couch like Vanna showcasing a Hawaiian vacation. "I can see—"

"I don't want no fucking seat!" she snarled and grabbed me by the front of my silk blouse. "I want to hear you admit it."

I've been threatened by the best of them: cuckolded husbands bent on revenge, wrinkled octogenarians hoping to increase their fortunes, and, of course, your run-of-the-mill assassins. So you'd think a skinny mother of two busting her hump to pass the bar wouldn't be anything to write home about, but her eyes were bat-shit crazy.

Still, Micky was a client. I swallowed my bile, steadied my hands, and tried not to pee in my proverbial pants. "I can't give you confidential information." My voice was little more than a croak.

She ground her teeth in my face, then dropped her hand and stepped back.

"No reason to pretend anymore." She shook her head and slumped onto my couch. "I know."

I took a wobbly step toward her, not quite trusting my legs. "What . . . uhh . . . what do you know?"

"The truth," she said.

Relieved terror sluiced through me. This was for the best—she had a right to know—but the aftermath of this little clusterfuck was going to get ugly. Cataclysmic ugly. End-of-days ugly. I drew a careful breath. "I'm sorry, Lavonn."

"Yeah." She chuckled. "Funny thing is, I was hoping he had the hots for *me*."

"You . . . " I paused, mind spinning. "What?"

"Wouldn't you know I'd be beat out by Snow White with a PhD."

"Snow . . . " I tilted my head at her. "Are you talking about *me?*"

"You can't be as dense as you seem."

"You'd be surprised," I said and glanced out the window, making sure we hadn't been teleported to that alternate universe Shirley had probably suspected earlier. But no, Sunrise Coffee was still as it should be. A blond lady in chinos and a leather jacket was just exiting. She carried a steaming to-go cup and a white paper bag.

"Mick's got it bad for you."

"For me." I tilted my head, thinking, perhaps, that a different perspective might clear things up. "That's what he told you?"

"He didn't have to *say* it."

I remained silent for a moment. "So what would make you believe it?"

"You really so pitiful that you have to fish for compliments?"

Duh! "No. I'm just curious how you arrived at this conclusion."

"He said you were razor."

"Ahh . . . "

"Sharp! Mick always had a thing for the classy chicks. Even back in the day."

I resisted preening. "He thinks I'm—"

"Kaneasha was like that."

"Your sister." I remembered suddenly that we were discussing real life here. Real issues. Real tragedies.

"She had eyes big as Bambi. And she was smart. Could have been anything. Could have had anyone. But she had a thing for Mick. Told me she was gonna marry him." She grinned. The expression was lopsided. "Told me that when she was twelve. But I . . . I said . . . " Tears swelled like dark oceans. "He wouldn't be interested in no skinny-assed schoolgirl like her," she warbled, and began to cry.

My heart, generally made of stone, cracked. "Lavonn . . . " I dropped to my knees and reached for her hand. She took it in a grip of steel.

"I was shit to her! I was shit. 'Specially after I found out she was pregnant. Called her a slut. Said she was going to burn in hell." Her face contorted. "She was my sister." She shuddered breath through her open mouth, turned her swimming eyes back toward me. "Only one I had."

I tightened my hand around hers. "We're often worst to the people we care about most."

She huffed a laugh. "Well, that's just fucked up, ain't it?"

"I believe we're biologically programmed to . . . "

Her brows rose.

"Yeah," I agreed. "It's fucked up."

"You know the worst part?"

Good God Almighty, we hadn't gotten to the worst part yet?

"I still wanted him for myself. Even after the baby was born. But this . . . " She shook her head and gritted her teeth. "If he's laid a finger on one of my kids, I'll neuter him like a fucking poodle."

I felt my stomach lurch. Felt the floor shift beneath me. "What are you talking about, Lavonn?"

She drilled me with her stare as if she could read my mind.

"You don't know? Honest to God?"

"Don't know what?"

"About the pictures. Swear to Jesus?"

"Ms. McMullen . . . " Shirley's voice sounded like a bomb over the intercom system. I ignored it.

"What pictures?"

"Mr. Fullman has arrived," Shirley announced.

Lavonn inhaled again, deep and long, as if fortifying herself. "I got into Lieberman's house."

I nodded, slowly, scared to receive more information.

"Easiest thing in the world to hack into his computer. Found a file right off. Had three pictures in it."

"And?"

"They were of children. Pretty kids no older than my Keifon."

"What are you saying?"

"They were naked."

I shook my head, relieved, terrified. "That doesn't mean . . . "

"Mick was in one of them."

I released her hand and rose slowly to my feet. "No."

She stood, too, expression stony. Without shifting her gaze she pulled a trio of papers from her back pocket and tossed them onto my coffee table.

I bent slowly, picked them up with fingers that had gone cold.

The top image was of a girl, twelve, maybe thirteen years old. She lay on her back, slim legs bent to the right. Her eyes were closed, lips curved into the hint of a winsome smile. Her hair, a variegated blend of blonds and browns, was artfully arranged behind her. She wore no shirt, no pants. Instead, a long sweep of bronze satin flowed between her pale breasts before floating away to meld with her hair. As if both were caught in unseen eddies.

The next picture was similar. But it was the third that made my breath catch in my throat. That made my stomach twist. It was of a girl with black hair and a pale complexion. She lay on a river of red satin that covered her most private areas. Beside her, with one hand gently placed on her trim hip, lay a man whose skin was as black as hers was white.

Micky.

I swallowed my bile and shook my head. "This can't be."

"Well, it is!" she snarled and snatched the images from my hand. "It is! And I want to know if he told you about it. If he told you he was a perverted fuck."

I shook my head. Protocol be damned. "He's not." I was sure of that. Yes, I'd misjudged before. But not this time. Please, God, not this time. "He's got demons, but he would never do . . . " I felt a little sick, a little dizzy. "This isn't right."

"No shit!"

My mind snapped to the artful photographs I'd seen scattered across Deirdra Mills' counter. "Someone tampered with the pictures."

She chuckled harshly. "You always this naïve?"

"There's some mistake. Has to be."

"Why?" Her tone was tortured, her expression twisted. "Why does there have to be?"

"What?" I shifted my gaze to hers, half forgetting where I was.

"Tell me why he can't be a perv," she breathed.

I shook my head, trying to think, to pick my way through the landmine. "He loves kids. Would do—"

She laughed, interrupting my ridiculous inanities. "Love? That's all you got? Hell, the shelters are filled with kids who're *loved* by the folks who put them there."

She had a point. Of course she had a point, but I shook my head.

"What about the subway?"

She raised her chin, watching me. "Just 'cause he was willing to take a couple hits for some chick on the train don't mean nothing." She chuckled. "Maybe she was white and had her a PhD."

I ignored her sarcasm. "Why would a man who'd die for a woman he didn't know willfully hurt children?"

She was silent for several seconds before she spoke again. "You got a thing for him, too. I know you do."

I considered denying it, but we seemed past that juncture. "I was attracted to David Hawkins, too."

"You making some kind of sense that ain't immediately apparent?"

"He was a psychiatrist. Smart, wealthy, handsome. He tried to kill me with a fillet knife."

Her brows had risen considerably.

"You know the good thing about murder attempts perpetrated by respected mentors?"

"Not off the top of my head."

"It teaches you not to take physical attraction too seriously."

Twenty

"If opposites attract I should be looking for a guy with a normal family and a whopping big bank account."

—Chrissy McMullen, age fifteen, already fairly cognizant of her familial and financial situation

"Hey, sis."

"Pete?" I scowled at my office phone. I hadn't talked to any of my brothers in months. Hadn't *wanted* to since I was old enough to understand the meaning of the word *troglodyte*. In fact, I was surprised Peter knew my work number. And not happily surprised. The last time he had visited L.A. there had been a lot of shots fired . . . most of them in my general direction.

"How you doing?"

"I'm fine," I said. It was an out-and-out lie. I was shitty. My ankle throbbed and my mind was still whirling from the bombshell Lavonn had dropped on me not six hours before.

"You still banging your lieutenant?"

"I'm not *banging* anyone."

"Hit a dry streak, huh?"

"I haven't . . . " I could feel my right molar starting to pulse in concert with my ankle. Some people feel familial connections in their heartstrings. I feel like I'm in need of a root canal. "Did you call for a reason?"

"Dad's sick."

"*What?*"

"Dad, you remember him. Stocky guy, flattop haircut. Doesn't talk much."

"Of course I remember him," I said and felt an odd meld of guilt and panic zip through me like Mexican tequila. Don't get me wrong; Glen McMullen and I have never been close. In fact, half the time I'm entirely unsure if he's aware of my existence. "What do you mean, sick?"

"You want everyday terms or will only the Webster definition do now that you're all hoity-toity?"

"What's wrong with Dad?" I snarled.

"Might be cancer."

"What?" The word escaped like gas from an air hose. "No. That can't be . . . " I was sputtering, speechless, floundering. Dad couldn't have cancer. Dad was indestructible. Like shoe leather or Ho Hos. "You're kidding," I said.

He breathed an expletive. "You must think I've got one hell of a sense of humor, sis."

"Well, it certainly wasn't delivered by the deities."

There was a moment of confused silence, then, "Anyway, I thought I should call."

It occurred to me all at once that I hadn't spoken to our mother in weeks either. In fact, I tended to avoid all contact with her if humanly possible. Guilt morphed seamlessly with grinding fear. "Why didn't *Mom* call me?"

"Guess they're busy with tests and stuff."

"What kind of tests?"

"This is all pretty fresh yet, Chris. I don't have much info. Maybe you could get ahold of *them* if you ain't too important."

"Don't be an ass. I never said I was too—"

"Listen, I gotta fly. I've got a load-and-go at the convention center. Talk at you later."

"A what? Wait! Where's Dad? What kind of—" But, story of my life, he had already hung up. I drew the receiver from my ear and blinked stupidly before settling it carefully into its cradle.

My door opened. Shirley stepped inside and set a container on my desk. "Peach cobbler," she said.

I blinked at her, fighting my way through the fog. "What?"

"Peach cobbler," she repeated and waved vaguely at the compostable container she'd just left in front of me. *Sunrise Coffee* was written in a flowery font across the top. "Mr. Amato brought it by. Asked me to give it to you when I thought you needed a lift."

"Oh. Thanks."

"I thought that time might be now," she said and shut the door behind her.

"Okay."

"Was I right?"

"What?" My voice sounded kind of dopey.

Her face scrunched into that expression between worried bunny and angry bear. "You doing okay, honey?"

"Yeah. Yes. I'm fine," I said, but it wasn't one of my better lies.

"Was that your brother on the phone?"

"Pete." I nodded and exhaled, searching hopelessly for

normalcy. "Peter John."

"He don't call here much. You sure everything—"

"He said it was a good thing I was smart."

"Peter—"

"Dad." I rose jerkily to my feet. My ankle bitched, but not loud enough to drown out the screaming memories. "Said it was lucky I was smart 'cause fat girls were out of style."

She absorbed my words for a moment. "I take it you wasn't skinny."

"The refrigerator and I could barely fit in the same room together. Which was problematic, because I spent most of my time in the kitchen."

"There's nothing wrong with having a little meat on your bones."

"How about being *called* meat?"

She patted the back of my couch. "Sit down, honey. You gotta get off that ankle."

"My ankle's fine," I lied mildly. But I sat.

She lifted the little box from my desk and pressed it into my hands. "Here you go," she said.

"I don't want any cobbler."

She handed me a spoon. "It's fresh made."

I opened the box and tried a test sample. For a moment, I was distracted by the sheer peachiness, but finally I raised my eyes to Shirley's. "I bet you never called any of your children Pork Chop." That nomenclature had ground at my self-esteem like a millstone for a couple of decades.

She sighed. "I love them kids," she said. "But I gotta tell you, when they're going through the dog-ate-my-brain years, which can last most of forever, they'll make a body do all sorts of things that maybe wasn't never approved by Dr. Spock."

I scowled at the cobbler, which was patently unfair. It was primo. "If I ever have children . . . " I shook my head. Since Brainy Laney had squeezed baby Mac out of her bottom, I'd been weird, intermediately disgusted, and . . . not jealous, exactly. I mean, not jealous at all! Since accepting the fact that I actually *was* blood kin to the apes that called me sister, I had suspected the McMullens were not meant to procreate. But it wasn't until Pete's failed streaking attempt that the idea firmly cemented in my brain. Supposedly, the senior class had offered him ten bucks and a keg if he would entertain at graduation by running naked between the stage and the seated guests. But somehow his feet had gotten tangled in his discarded boxers and he had fallen flat on his face, causing considerable facial lacerations, a broken tibia, and a visit from a tired-looking police officer.

No, the McMullens should use every kind of prophylactic known to mankind. Still, I always felt an odd little niggle of something when babies were mentioned.

"If you ever have children what?" she asked.

"You should taste this," I said and lifted the box toward her. She scowled, looking increasingly concerned. Maybe because in her nearly two years of employment at L.A. Counseling, I'd rarely offered to share so much as a piece of Juicy Fruit.

"Just because he called you Pork Chop don't mean he didn't love you," she said.

I caught her gaze, then breathed a soft snort and continued consuming the cobbler. My eyes stung despite the yumminess. I lowered them.

"My momma used to call me Wally," she said. "Said I looked just like the sea lions we used to visit at La Jolla."

"What's wrong with parents?" I asked.

She was silent a second, then, "I'd give every dollar I got in the bank to see her one more time."

Swallowing was suddenly difficult, but I managed it. "How long has she been gone?"

"Nine years now. She used to say, 'Wally, you ain't never going to be the prettiest sea lion on the shore. But you remember this . . . '" She paused. I looked up. "'You're the most loved.'"

My lips twitched. "I wasn't," I said.

"What?"

"I wasn't the most loved."

"I'm sure you're . . . "

"No." I cleared my throat and set the remainder of the cobbler aside. Shirley managed not to faint. "I'm not feeling sorry for myself." And the glaciers weren't melting. "It's just a fact." I glanced out the window and smiled a little at the memories. Sometimes they were mean little bastards, but sometimes we got on all right. Today's self-pity orgy would have to be chalked up to the former. "I wanted to be a cheerleader."

"Who don't?"

"But it was an elected position."

I scooped up a little whipped cream. Tony used all organic dairy products; the cows had worked so hard . . . it didn't seem right to eschew their produce just because I was feeling a little off.

"And you wasn't elected?"

I didn't bother to answer. The mean little bastards were piling on now. "Glen McMullen was a practical man. Said the marching band needed a tuba player and luckily I was 'stout' enough to carry the load."

"Did they get to wear them fluffy plumes on top of their heads?"

I smirked at her, but honest to God, I had kind of loved that plume. "Well . . . " I rose to my feet. "Thank you, Shirley, but I'm—"

"What's he got?" she asked.

"What?"

"Your daddy . . . what's wrong with him?"

I considered denying everything. Instead, I smoothed my skirt and tried for hauteur. "They think it might be cancer."

She opened her mouth to respond, but the phone rang before she spoke.

"Will you get that, please?"

She thrust out her chin. "Call him."

I laughed. "We don't have that kind of relationship."

"That's why you gotta be the one to reach out."

I made a go-hither motion with my hand and she finally exited, jaw set.

I sat alone for a moment, fiddled with my stapler, considered updating records, then pressed the phone button for line two and dialed.

"Hello?"

"Mr. Grapier?"

"Yes."

"This is Christina McMullen. From L.A. Counseling."

There was a moment of silence as he caught up. "There's no trouble with Angie, I hope."

I held my breath for an instant. Calling Angela Grapier's father might not have been absolutely acceptable from the board of psychology's point of view. There was, after all, a little thing called client confidentiality. But his daughter was hurting.

"I was just wondering if you've been able to spend much time with her lately."

"What?"

I fisted my free hand on the desktop. "These last few months have been extremely difficult for her. As they have been for you, I'm certain. I was just hoping the two of you have been able to find some time."

There was momentary silence, then, "It's a busy time of year."

"Yes, but—"

"One of the top-tier guys took a job with Fidelity; we're scrambling to cover his clients."

"I'm sure it's difficult."

"If I play my cards right I can maybe make partner by Christmas."

"That's great," I said. "I'm sure you're more than qualified, but perhaps your daughter's mental state is more—"

"What? Oh, yes. I'll be right there," he said, speaking to someone else before returning to me. "Listen, I'd love to chat, but I have to go. My boss—"

"You're going to lose her!"

There was a silence, long and labored.

"What?"

"Maybe not physically. She might survive your neglect," I said, and quashed every dire warning issued by the tiny member of the board of psychology who slavered on my left shoulder. The angel on my right was notably absent. "But if you don't take the time to put her first, she'll find someone who will."

The silence continued. Good sense suggested I should leave well enough alone, but good sense and I were barely within shouting distance.

"Probably someone young and male who doesn't much care if she gets knocked up before her twentieth birthday," I said and thought of the daughter he had already lost, the one who had been pregnant and hurting and addicted to meth.

His chair squeaked abruptly. "Are you saying Ally's . . . situation . . . was my fault?"

"No," I said. "I'm not. I'm just wondering how you'll feel if the same thing happens to Angie."

"And I'm wondering what the psychiatric board will think of your conduct."

I almost chuckled. If they found out about this phone call they'd chew my ass up one side and down the other. Then they'd probably take my license. In fact, tarring and feathering might come back into vogue. "I believe the board would agree that I'm acting in the best of my client," I lied.

There was a tense pause, then, "I've got to go." He hung up before I made any more attempts to ruin my own career.

Out front, the doorbell rang. Relief struck me in tandem with the arrival of my next client. Far simpler to deal with someone else's problems than my own, and Ted Carson had a buttload of—

"What the hell do you think you're doing?"

I jerked to my feet with a gasp, half wondering how the board had heard the news so quickly.

But no overeducated psychoanalyst had arrived to snatch away my PhD. Instead, an overexcited psychotic stood in the doorway.

And he looked pissed. But that was nothing new for the

dark lieutenant.

Twenty-one

"Please! I'm not in love with him. In fact, half the time I hate him more than cauliflower. The other half, though, I do kinda wanna nail him like a two-by-four."

—Chrissy McMullen, following an overdose of NyQuil

Our gazes struck like sabers. Blazing lightsabers. Blazing lightsabers on steroids.

"Lieutenant!" Shirley said, bursting in behind him. "How nice to see you."

He turned his lethal lightsaber eyes toward her. "Did she tell you?"

She raised one holier-than-thou brow. "Did she tell me what, Lieutenant?"

His voice was low and steady, humming with an anger so starchy it made the hairs on the nape of my neck stand at attention. "Did she tell you she broke into Lieberman's house?"

Shirley shifted her gaze to mine for the briefest of seconds.

Guilt rushed through me, but I kept my expression firmly set on bland. "I'm sure you're wrong," she said. "Ms. McMullen is a good-hearted citizen who—"

"She tampered with evidence."

Shirley pursed her cranberry-rose lips. "False accusations are an evil thing, Mr. Rivera. But false accusations about a fine, upstanding citizen like Ms. McMullen—"

"Ms. McMullen will be lucky if she doesn't get her ass thrown in Lompoc for—"

"Could get you in a good deal of trouble," she rasped and leaned forward.

That's when I stepped into the fray. It was also then that my ankle gave out. I tottered, fell, and was scooped up, none too gently, by a fuming Rivera.

"What the hell's wrong with you?" He growled the question from very close quarters. I could feel the heat of his chest against my left boob, the hard muscles of his arms beneath my bent legs.

"Nothing," I said, but I didn't quite manage to meet his eyes.

He snorted. "I wouldn't believe that even if we *weren't* talking about your mental state. What happened to her?" he snapped and turned toward Shirley.

She looked worried and a little shaken. "She injured her ankle."

"How?"

Shirley's brows had lowered, perhaps remembering her own suspicions of just a few hours before, but she is nothing if not loyal. "Working out. At the gym."

I contained a wince and knew beyond a shadow of a doubt that I should have chosen a better alibi. One that couldn't be proven or disproven by the logs those damned gyms keep. The dog park, maybe. Or the morgue.

"The gym." He shifted his Hades-dark gaze to mine.

I refrained from peeing in my pants and gave him a nod, prim as a Puritan.

"Where?" His tone was so macho, his attitude so righteous, that I was tempted almost beyond control to spit in his eye. But Shirley had just called me good-hearted.

"What's your plan, Rivera?" I asked. "You hoping to interrogate the Stairmaster responsible?"

"Where?" he asked again.

I tried to remain civil. Hell, I tried to remain good-hearted. But there was something about his I'm-the-shit attitude that brought out all the crazy monkeys at once.

"In Nevermind," I said and wriggled gracelessly out of his arms. "At the corner of None of Your Damned Business and Go Fuck Yourself!"

A muscle jumped in his jaw. Fire flared in his eyes. But before we tore out each other's throats, the doorbell rang again.

"That'll be Mr. Carson," Shirley said. There was relief in her tone. There was also a good deal of *holy shit what is wrong with these two*. But she stood her ground. Perhaps with the arrival of my next client, she expected Rivera to trot out of my office like a well-behaved schnoodle. But if the dark lieutenant were a dog . . . which . . . you know . . . he kind of *was*, he'd be something a little less cuddly. Like a werewolf. Or maybe one of those hellhounds that guard the underworld. "Come to discuss his troubles. Ms. McMullen is a godsend to this community. Without her . . . "

"See to the client," Rivera ordered, still nailing me with his eyes.

Shirley watched him for a second, then stuck out her bosom. I mean, her bosom always sticks out, but when she puts her back into the effort, it's truly impressive. "I respect the police," she said. "They've got a tough job, and for the most part they do it well, but you won't be coming in here harassing good honest folks like Ms. McMullen."

Rivera turned his carnivorous gaze on her, but God bless her, she didn't back down. Instead, she narrowed her eyes, spread her well-shod feet, and propped capable fists on solid hips. "Not unless you want an ass whippin'."

A half dozen uncensored emotions flashed in his eyes. Surprise was the first, followed swiftly by anger. After that, several whizzed by too quickly to catalog, but I'm pretty sure I saw some WTF and a spark of admiration in the mix.

"Shirley . . . " My tone was a little breathless. "Thank you." I gave her a look that I hoped conveyed the fact that she was Erin Brockovich, Norma Rae, and the dude who saved all the soldiers in that Mel Gibson flick, all rolled into one. "But I'm sure the good lieutenant has no intention of harassing anyone. Please, take care of Mr. Carson. I'll only be a short while."

Her scowl darkened, and for a moment I thought *I* was the one about to get the ass whipping, but she finally turned her glower back to Rivera. Their gazes met, held, then she gave him one stern nod and left the room.

"Tell me the truth," he breathed when the door closed behind her heft. "How the hell do you do it?"

"Do what?"

"Get half of L.A. ready to do battle for you while the other half is trying to kill you."

"Who's trying to kill me?"

"Have you ever even considered the danger you put your friends in?"

"Someone's trying to kill me?"

"Or do you just go bobbling around like a princess in a—" he began, but I grabbed him by the front of the shirt and dragged myself to his nose.

"Who the fuck is trying to kill me?"

"You tell me." His voice was as bland as one of those weird little gourds people buy in the fall but never know what to do with. "You're the one who broke into Lieberman's house."

I eased up on the fabric a little. "You're wrong," I said.

"We lifted your prints."

Panic zipped through my system like a firestorm, igniting all the high points. It took me a moment to remember I hadn't gone into that house. He was bluffing. And not for the first time. I smiled a little. "I don't even know what you're talking about."

"I'm talking about the year you'll spend behind bars for breaking and entering."

I shook my head, snorted a laugh and released him. "You're full of crap."

"I'm talking about sharing a cell with a woman named Squash who'll shave her name into your—" He stopped, narrowing his eyes and thinking harder than I ever wanted to see him think. "No," he said, gaze locked on mine.

Seconds ticked away until I found, to my chagrin, that I was holding my breath and that my knees wanted, rather badly, to drop me face first onto my aging Berber carpet. "No what?" I was trying to sound bored. I might have managed coherent.

"Lawson said there was a blonde."

"What's a Lawson?" I asked, remembering Mr. Stakeout's adorable smile and impressive biceps.

He ignored me. "A blonde with a French accent and a really nice . . . " He dropped his gaze to my chest. "Swear to God, woman, I'm going to handcuff you to your headboard."

I managed to raise my chin in defiance. "You wish."

"What the hell were you thinking?"

I almost admitted the truth: I was thinking that Micky was a friend who needed help. That Lavonn was as worried as I was. And that Lieberman's house would surely shed some light on the situation. But I hadn't completely lost my mind . . . yet. "I was thinking that cops are a clutch of barely restrained junkyard dogs, and a smart girl will go to the gym just to be fit enough to hold her own against the barbarous likes of—"

"Who was inside?" he asked, grabbing my arm.

I gasped, partly because I was jumpy, but mostly because I was pissed to be interrupted during a pretty fine tirade. "Let go of me," I insisted, but he leaned in, teeth gritted.

"Who the hell was inside Lieberman's—"

"Lieberman's dead!" I reminded him. "Micky's comatose. Why are you hassling me instead of finding the culprit?"

"For all I know you *are* the culprit."

"Me! Me?"

"Got any better ideas?"

"Yeah! How about . . . " I searched frantically before coming up with a name. "Haven. What about her?"

"Brooke Haven?" he scoffed.

"Micky mentioned her name. When he called me. Remember?"

"No, I don't remember. Because what he said was that he was the one misbehaving not, 'Hey, Ms. B. Haven capped

177

Lieberman, then shot me just for kicks and—'"

"So you're not even going to question her?"

He didn't answer.

"Tell me the truth. Is it because Micky's black or because she's white? Or it is the fact that she's cute as a bug's butt? Is that why you're bothering me instead of—"

"Amber Daun was there past one on the night in question."

"Amber Daun—"

"Lou Ellen Chambridge stayed half an hour longer."

"Who's—"

"They had drinks with leftover Halloween candy and watched horror flicks on Ms. Haven's flat screen. She never left the house. But she did spend time on the phone with her eighty-nine-year-old mother."

"She made a phone call? Did she leave the room?" I gasped. "I bet what they heard was actually a prerecorded message. I bet—"

"What's wrong with you?"

"What's wrong with me? What's wrong with *you*? Just because she's adorable and blond and absent a single dust mote doesn't mean she couldn't have faked a conversation, snuck out of her house while her friends were watching the tube, then shot Lieberman and Micky before they knew—"

"She didn't leave them," he said. "Not all night. Not once. Both agree on that. We have no reason to believe they're lying."

"Oh. Well . . . " Fuck. "Okay. Maybe . . . " I shook my head, floundering.

"Who broke into Lieberman's house, Chrissy?"

"I don't know what you're talking about."

"Was it one of the fucking morons who's been sniffing after you?"

"What? I don't—"

"Was it Solberg?"

I leaned away, surprised, pissed, and more than a little insulted. "Laney's husband?" I crossed myself distractedly, hoping to ward off any evil spirits incited by speaking his name. "Have you lost what little sense you—"

"One of your clients, then, or . . . " His brows lowered even farther. "Manderos!" He said the name like a curse, grip loosening.

I shook my head, too surprised to realize that that might have been a dandy time to make a break for it. "*Julio?*" I hadn't seen Rivera senior's hired body double (long story) in months.

"Angler? Archer? That fucking cop from"—he waved wildly—"nowhere?"

I did the head shaking thing again, fascinated, like a titmouse about to be devoured by a cobra.

"Jesus!" He stopped short, body all but reverberating with ire. "It wasn't Danshov, was it?"

"Who?"

He tightened his grip. "Hiro Danshov. Was he there?"

"Why would he—"

"Because you've twisted him around your finger like taffy."

"What kind of taffy do you twist around—" But he moved in close, body pressing against mine.

"Don't get involved with him, McMullen."

I was finding it a little hard to breathe. Impossible to move away. Sadly, I managed to speak. "If you didn't want us involved, Lieutenant Ravings, you shouldn't have sent me scampering out in to the netherworld like a—"

"He was there, wasn't he?" Rivera seared me with his eyes. "Wasn't he?"

"Where?"

A tic danced in his jaw. I could see that without breaking eye contact. "God damn it, McMullen! Do you do this intentionally? Do you drive me mad out of spite?"

"Spite? No," I purred and leaned closer, letting my boobs graze his chest. "I just do it 'cause it's so easy."

"What does he mean to you?" he asked, clamping an arm around my waist.

"Who?" I rasped.

"Danshov!" Irritation mixed with something sharper, headier.

"Oh." I remembered the antihero with a sharp pang of something I had never quite figured out. Danshov was scary and incomprehensible and hotter than hell.

"He's dangerous," Rivera said and grabbed my rear end.

"You're an ass," I snarled and curled my fingers into his hair.

He thrust his crotch against mine, hard as kryptonite, knocking me against the edge of my desk. Something clattered to the floor. "That's not all I am."

I gasped like a starving starlet, breathing hard, breasts heaving. He lowered his gaze to my uplifted boobs. His lips followed. They burned on contact and suddenly I was grappling with his belt, struggling with his fly. He popped out, eager as a boy scout, big as an eggplant. He was already rucking up my skirt. I took him in both hands. Our arms tangled for a moment, but we synched finally.

"Ms. McMullen?" Shirley said from the doorway.

Rivera growled something. It might have been obscene. Or

poetic. Or sexy as sin.

"Shirley!" My voice was squawky and raspy at the same time. I leaned sideways to peek around Rivera.

Her brows had sprung toward her hairline like Mexican jumping beans. "You okay?"

"Yes. Of course. I'm fine." I shot my gaze to the hot lieutenant's. His teeth were bared, as were other parts. He did nothing to hide either. "We were just discussing . . . " Holy fucking hell, I was panting like a greyhound. "Current events."

"Uh huh."

I stiffened my back at her tone, though honest to God it couldn't hold a candle to Rivera's stiff stuff. "You really should use the intercom if you wish to converse with me."

"I did," she intoned. "Twice."

"Oh." I shot my gaze guiltily toward the phone "It must not be—"

"I could hear it from my desk."

My face felt warm. I cleared my throat. "Was there something you wished to discuss, Shirley?"

"Me? No," she said. "But there's an Officer Lawson out front who'd like to have a word with you."

Twenty-two

"You're the most beautiful woman in the whole wide room."
—J.D. Solberg, light-years before he met Brainy Laney and
quite a while before he morphed into an almost tolerable
human being

My heart stopped dead in my chest, but I managed to speak without assistance from my cardiovascular system. "An . . ." Dear God. Dear God, dear God! "Officer . . ."

"Lawson," she repeated calmly, but her eyes showed a good deal of white around the iris. "Shall I tell him you're busy?"

"No!" Surprisingly, Rivera and I spoke in unison. I darted my gaze to him and away.

"No," I repeated, voice marginally more dulcet. "I'll ummm . . . I'll be there momentarily. Please . . ." I stepped away from Rivera, simultaneously smoothing my skirt. "Please impart that information to the good officer for me."

"Okay." Her brows had lowered a little. "I'll impart. But

you should probably . . ." She motioned toward her impressive chest before exiting. I glanced at my considerably more modest one, only to find that I was not modest at all. My hands shook as I buttoned up.

"Don't do anything stupid," Rivera said and zipped his fly.

Now you tell me, I thought, but I raised my chin like a martyr eyeing a burning pyre. "I don't intend to."

"Breaking tradition. Good idea," he said. "Maybe he won't recognize you."

I winced and tried to hold my tongue, but the question slipped out. "Twelve months for breaking and entering? Really?"

He closed the distance between us in two strides.

"What happened?" His voice was soft, his hands the same as he touched my arms. I wanted desperately to unburden, to admit, to fall against his chest and confess everything. But I wasn't entirely crazy.

That muscle in his jaw jumped again. "Were you in Lieberman's house?"

"No." At least that much was true.

He held my gaze, seemed to find truth, and nodded. "How are you going to play this?"

I drew a breath through my nose. "Dumb?"

He nodded. "Smart to use your strengths," he said but lifted his hand to my cheek. His palm felt warm and firm against my skin.

I raised my gaze to his, terrified.

"You're Christina McMullen," he said. His voice was earnest, almost reverent. "PhD."

I watched him, unblinking.

"Not some cheap wannabe starlet from Paris."

"I don't know what you're talking about," I whispered.

"Thatta girl," he said and, releasing my arms, remained behind as I stepped into the hallway and reminded myself, on threat of twelve months in the pokey, not to limp.

By the time I reached the reception area, I had almost quit hyperventilating.

"Ms. McMullen, this is Officer Lawson," Shirley said before turning toward my client. "Mr. Carson, you can accompany me. Ms. McMullen will be free momentarily."

I barely noticed them leaving. I stepped forward. My handshake was firm, if a little damp. "What can I do for you, Officer?"

He didn't look quite as cuddly this morning. Could be his superiors weren't too thrilled to hear that he'd been distracted by a Parisian jogger with a lot of visible cleavage and a poor accent while he was on stakeout. "Have we met before, Ms. McMullen?"

Oh sweet Jesus! "You and I? Not that I recall. Am I forgetting something?" I raised a haughty brow.

He scowled, then glanced down at the notebook in his square-tipped fingers. "Can you tell me where you were at approximately ten o'clock on the night of November fifth?"

My mind skittered in surprise. He didn't want to know my whereabouts on the previous night. He wanted to know what I was doing . . . when Lieberman was killed. Holy fuck! He wasn't going to accuse me of B&E. He was going to accuse me of murder. I tried to think, but I could barely remain upright. Thinking was out of the question. "Why do you wish to know?" I kept my tone professional, my back ramrod straight.

"Answer the question, please."

"At ten o'clock."

184

"Yes."

"The night of Marvin Lieberman's death." It would be stupid to pretend I didn't recognize the date. Wouldn't it?

"That's correct.

"I was . . . " I wanted to say . . . was *desperate* to say "in bed." With . . . someone . . . anyone who could collaborate my story. But wait a minute. I hadn't done anything wrong *that* night.

"I was home," I said, and reminded myself sternly not to expound. No expounding.

"Alone?"

I gave the haughty brow an extra lift. "I rather doubt that's any of your concern, Officer."

"I'm sorry, ma'am," he said and blushed. Actually blushed. I wasn't sure if I should be thrilled by my ability to embarrass an officer of the law, or pissed that I'd just been *ma'am*ed. He'd called Fani *miss*. He continued on. "My department is determined to find justice for Mr. Lieberman."

I nodded. "And Micky Goldenstone."

"What?"

"You're investigating the shooting of Mr. Goldenstone, too, I assume."

"Yes, ma'am," he said. I resisted slapping him, both for his terminology and his apparent disregard for Micky. "I believe you were first on the scene."

"Myself and Lieutenant Jack Rivera," I said.

"I read his report."

"Then I would think anything I had to say would be superfluous."

"I . . . " he began, then tilted his head ever so slightly. "Are you sure we haven't met?"

"Quite."

He nodded, almost seeming convinced. "What can you tell me about the evening of the fifth?"

I ran through the details one by one. He wasn't the interviewer Rivera was. And by that, I mean I didn't feel flayed within an inch of my life. In fact, he was refreshingly polite. "Thanks for your time, Ms. McMullen."

"You'll keep me informed?"

He didn't answer. "What are your thoughts on the matter?"

I raised my brows, surprised that an officer of the law might think my opinion worth considering.

"You're a psychologist," he continued. "With an . . . interesting past concerning crimes. Mr. Goldenstone was your client. Why would he shoot Mr. Lieberman?"

"You're assuming he's guilty." I wasn't ready to tell anybody about the damning pictures Lavonn had discovered. But maybe I was doing Micky an injustice. Maybe if a good investigator had those photos, the truth would be learned that much quicker.

"His prints were the only ones found on the murder weapon."

"So you believe he killed Lieberman, then tried to take his own life."

"It's not uncommon for someone in his situation to feel regret, fear . . . turn the gun on himself."

"Is it common for a person to try to commit suicide by shooting himself in the side?"

"It's not . . . unheard of."

"Really?"

"Do you have a more likely scenario?"

"Maybe he's being framed."

"Why? By who?"

I folded my hands, wondering how much to tell him. "Have you spoken to Deirdra Mills?"

"Who?"

"Deirdra Mills. She's a cook . . . or at least she was . . . at Branford Middle School."

He scribbled something in his notebook. I resisted kissing him; maybe he was just notating that I was a lunatic who should be locked away at the first possible opportunity. "Why do you mention her?"

"I paid her a visit," I admitted and glanced toward the door, half expecting Rivera to burst in and threaten to haul me off to the hoosegow if I didn't desist.

"Why?"

"She's a friend of Micky's. I thought maybe she could shed some light on the situation."

"Ms. McMullen, you really should let the authorities—"

"She's a photographer." The words spurted out before I could stop them.

"What does that have to do with the crimes perpetrated?"

"Ahh . . ." Good question. Especially if you didn't know about the damning pictures Lavonn had found. "Maybe she photographed Lieberman doing something illegal. He threatened her and . . . Micky found out. Confronted him."

"So you think Goldenstone *did* shoot him."

"No." But I kind of made it sound like that. "Micky wouldn't hurt anyone. Not unless he was trying to save someone else, at least."

"And you think he was trying to save Ms. Mills?"

I shrugged. "I think she's involved somehow."

"Okay," he said and closed his notebook. "I'll speak to her."

"Really?" I said and barely refrained from dying of shock.

Twenty-three

"Giving birth. Like doing the splits over Mount Doom."
—Brainy Laney Butterfield

"How's it going?"

I propped my bare feet onto the couch cushion and considered a half dozen politically correct answers. Laney, after all, had recently pushed a watermelon-sized primate out of an orifice better suited for a zucchini-sized marsupial; maybe a true friend would try not to burden her with mundane problems like the fact that, according to Rivera, I was probably going to spend the rest of my natural life yoked to a woman named Squash.

"Fine," I said, grasping feebly for that true-friend status.

"What's wrong?"

"Nothing's wrong. Why would you think something was wrong?"

"Because in Macadoodle world, 'fine' generally precedes a cataclysmic disaster of biblical proportions."

I scowled, considered arguing, then sighed in surrender. "Why aren't *you* ever fine?"

"What are you talking about?"

"I mean, somehow you manage to be a movie star while simultaneously creating a human being out of hickory twigs, or whatever the hell it is you eat, without so much as popping a zit."

She laughed. "What's going on, Mac?"

I felt myself wilt. I was exhausted from trying to keep my problems to myself for more than thirty seconds. "Dad's sick."

"What?"

"Dad . . ." I cleared my throat. I might not be Ms. Stoicism, but I was not going to sob like a sleepy infant. Laney already had one of those and probably didn't need another one right out of the gate. "They think it might be cancer."

"Oh no! Poor Connie."

"Huh?"

"Your Mom must be worried sick."

"Mom?" I was pretty sure Laney had, long ago, gotten the memo that my mother, while appearing to be human, was actually nothing of the sort. Constance Iris McMullen was a twisted concoction of dried pasta noodles and guilt-inducing gamma rays.

"She thinks the world of Glen."

"Are we thinking of the same Connie McMullen?"

"You know she's human, right?"

"Of course," I lied.

"Has he started treatment yet?"

"Treatment?" I was beginning to sound a little daft, even to my own ears.

"Chemo? Radiation? What regimen are they planning?"

190

I was silent for a moment.

"Haven't they decided yet?"

"I'm not sure."

"He's not going to decline treatment, is he?"

"Decline—no! Of course not." A hard-wired zap of panic sizzled through me. "Why would he? Why would he do that?"

"I'm just asking, honey," she soothed. "What did he say?"

The panic melded with guilt, serving up a quixotic blend in my already volatile gut. After Officer Lawson's departure and Rivera's smoking exodus, I had finished off the cobbler, followed it up with a pint of Mad Mocha ice cream, and continued my gluttonous rampage at the In-N-Out on my way home. Luckily, or unluckily, depending on how one feels about my continued survival, my refrigerator was stocked with nothing but rabbit fare. "He said he had a load-and-go at the convention center. What the hell's a load-and-go?"

There was a moment of quietude as she considered this. "Your dad's a first responder?"

"No. Pete."

"But you've spoken to Glen, right?"

I let silence pulse for a beat. "I've been really busy, Laney. Did I tell you—"

"Mac!"

I actually jumped a little, then held my breath.

"Hang up."

"What?"

"Hang up the phone right now and call him."

"Dad?"

She sighed. "He's human, too, Mac."

I winced, remembering a dozen painful father-daughter encounters that suggested otherwise. "I know," I said, but to tell the truth I wasn't absolutely positive. One didn't want to jump to hasty conclusions concerning one's antecedents.

"And a pretty good guy."

"Dad?" I said again, voice weaker.

"I'm going to feed the baby. Call me after you've talked to him."

"Dad," I repeated.

She sighed as she disconnected.

I sat in silence for a moment, knowing she was right. I should call my parents. And I would. Of course I would; it was the right thing to do. But my toenail polish was chipped. What kind of degenerate would converse with her progenitors when she was in desperate need of a pedicure and couldn't remember where she had put her Passionate Pink . . .

Shikoku growled. Harley jumped.

My door swung open. I squawked as I twisted toward it. Lavonn Blount stepped inside.

"What the hell—" My voice was a couple octaves higher than a startled chicken's.

"What do you know?"

"How did you—"

"Tell me the truth."

"What do you mean, what do I know?"

Her eyes were dark and predatory. It wasn't too long ago that I had been sure she was a drug addict and a lunatic. That was before I realized she was a prelaw student and an informant for the cops. Now I found I was inordinately confused and run-of-the-mill terrified.

"What did Mick talk about in his sessions?" she growled.

"Lavonn, my information regarding clients is confidential. You know that. And you can't just"—I flapped a hand vaguely toward my traitorous front door—"barge into my house like a—"

"Listen!" She punctuated the word with a stab of her forefinger. "It's driving me insane. I got two boys who think Mick is God's gift to the world. You gonna let them find out the hard way that he's a fucking perv with a hard-on for kids?"

My stomach roiled at the thought. Shikoku growled again, just a little rumble of warning, gaze glued on Lavonn. Behind her, Harley cowered like the coward he was. But I loved that coward. Loved him like a child. If Lavonn felt half such intensity for her kids, I had to do what I could to keep them safe.

Memories rolled like thunder through my mind: mentors who'd tried to gut me with fillet knives, grandfatherly old men attempting to poison me, innocuous strangers taking potshots from the sidewalk. "I've misjudged a few people in the past," I admitted.

She scowled, waiting.

"But I'm sure . . . I *know* Micky Goldenstone has no perverse inclinations toward children."

She narrowed her lethal eyes. "Cross your fucking heart?"

I exhaled carefully. "Cross my fucking heart."

"Then somebody messed with those pictures. Someone's trying to frame him."

"Who? Why?"

"I don't know. You're the shrink."

"Psychologist," I said.

"And shrinks are supposed to understand people, right?"

"I'm a psychologist," I repeated.

"And they're not?"

I took a deep breath. "Does Micky have enemies?"

"You're his shrink!" She was beginning to sound agitated again. Shikoku twitched an ear.

"Psycholo—" I began, but she spoke over me.

"What about Daphne?"

I shook my head, floundering. "Daphne?"

"The food freak he was doing."

"Deirdra Mills? The school's cook?" I made sure I sounded surprised. Her photographic talents put her on the suspects list as far as I was concerned, but I had no desire to point Lavonn in that direction. "I thought they were just friends."

She shrugged. "Maybe that's what he thought, too. Only she didn't agree."

"So she frames him for child pornography because he's not in love with her? A little harsh, don't you think?"

"Life *is* harsh."

She had a point, but I shook my head. "It's just too . . . weird."

"Life's also weird."

Another excellent verity.

"Maybe she was doing Mick and Lieberman got jealous."

"You think she was dating both of them?"

"Why not?"

"She's a really attractive woman."

"So?"

"I've seen Lieberman."

"Maybe he was hotter when he was alive." I huffed at her irreverence but she was already moving on. "You know why she lost her former job?"

"What? No. What job?"

"Place called the Bistro. She was banging her boss's old

man," she said and sauntered toward the kitchen.

"How do you know that?"

"Micky must have told me," she said, and opening my refrigerator, scowled at the contents. "Why is there a damned meadow in your fridge?"

I winced at the fields of fresh spinach, the bouquets of kale. "I'm trying to eat healthier."

"Since when?" Last time she'd been in my house, she had eaten (without permission, I might add) her weight in high-sucrose cereal and Rocky Road ice cream.

"Since . . . it's none of your business," I said and shut the fridge, barely missing her nose. "How do you know so much about Micky's social life?"

"I'm his friend. Thought maybe you were, too." She eyed me. "So?"

"So what?"

"Are you or ain't you?"

I hesitated a second. According to the board of psychology, clients and friends are supposed to be kind of mutually exclusive. "Listen, the police have probably already proven his innocence."

She snorted. "Yeah, 'cause that's what they do with brothers with a past. You should check her out."

"What? Who?"

"That Daphne chick. Take a look at her PC."

"How would I—"

"You got skills, don't you?"

"Absolutely not." I wasn't exactly sure if I was refusing to investigate a woman Lavonn thought I had never met or declaring myself without skills. Regardless, Lavonne chuckled.

"You got any friends who do?"

"I'm kind of short on them, too," I said, but even as the words left my mouth, I was thinking of a height-challenged geekster who owed me about ten thousand favors. For one thing, I had introduced him to the most amazing woman in the world. For another, I hadn't killed him . . . yet.

"Sometimes short friends are the most effective kind," she said and turned toward the door.

"What does that mean?" I asked, and wondered a little manically if she, too, knew J.D. Solberg.

She shrugged as she turned the lock on my door and stepped onto my stoop. "Successful shrink like you should have a better security system," she said and left.

Twenty-four

"You're an idiot."
—Glen McMcMullen, upon being told that true happiness was
having a large, boisterous family underfoot

I called Mom that evening, but she didn't answer. I was relieved. And worried. And irritated. And indignant. And ashamed. Conventional wisdom suggests the human animal is capable of feeling four emotions. But I managed to experience about 117 of the little bastards that night. Each one was crazier than the last, spinning through me like mice on a roller coaster until I fell, exhausted, into bed.

Still, I slept restlessly. Harlequin, on the other hand, was as relaxed as a corpse . . . if corpses snore and take up most of the available mattress. Shikoku curled up on the floor near my brass footboard, nose pointed toward the front door.

I awoke with a huff of fear when I heard her rise to her feet, then jerked upright when the hallway light popped on.

Before I could scream or pass out or pull out my

unregistered spumante, Hiro Danshov stepped into the doorway of my bedroom, face impassive, dark-caramel hair pulled back in his silly-ass man bun.

My first word to him was something like, "Ffttwht!" delivered in a high, screeching tone recognized by any species on the planet as mind-boggling terror.

He raised one unimpressed brow. "Had I known you were so *pas bien fait* of your own survival, I would not have put such effort into your education."

"Wha . . . " I barely managed to breathe out that much. Shikoku strolled forward to touch her nose to her master's hand. He gave her a nod. She sat with a smile, seeming content. "What the hell are you doing here?"

"What do you know of Goldenstone?"

I shook my head, doing my best to orient, to think, to calm my queasy bladder. "Micky? Why do you care?"

His lips tilted, a minimalist's version of an actual expression. "I've no wish to see my training go to waste, *wuwei hua.*"

"Training!" I found, to my relief, that my sense of outrage was still fully functional. "Daily beatings is more like it, you sadistic degenerate. How can you even . . . " A toxic thought flew into my brain, stilling my tongue for a second. "What do you mean . . . 'go to waste'?"

He shrugged, the barest lift of one deceptively proficient shoulder. "You do not plan to allow him to kill you, do you?"

"Kill me? Micky? He wouldn't . . . " I made a *pff*ing sound, then cut it short. Mostly because I ran out of saliva. "Would he?"

"What of the woman?"

"What woman?" I was already beyond the weirdness of

finding him in the doorway of my bedroom, since the weirdness of discussing my own demise seemed so much more significant.

"She is his son's aunt. Is she not?"

"Lavonn?"

He gave me a single nod as if he was happy to learn I wasn't entirely brain-dead. "Are you not going to invite me to a cup of tea?"

"Tea?"

"I believe that is the socially accepted intercourse between two adults. Yes?"

"Inter . . . intercourse?"

"So to speak."

"At . . . " I blinked at the clock beside my bed. "Three in the morning?"

"It is six o'clock somewhere."

"And?"

"I will brew the tea," he said and turned away.

It seemed as if I had little choice but to follow. The floor felt cool against my feet, the air strangely soft against my bare legs.

Danshov opened a cupboard and drew out a tin I had never seen before in my life. "Where did that come from?"

He nodded toward a chair. "Sit."

I didn't. "Listen, you can't just break into my house whenever you want."

He was already running water into a kettle I was certain I didn't own.

"Or bring me teapots."

"I think you may be mistaken. Have you considered she might be responsible?"

I shook my head and wondered hopefully if I was sleeping. I glanced down at my legs. They sported two days worth of stubble. Firm proof of reality. "Responsible for what?"

"Lieberman's death. Goldenstone's injuries."

"That's crazy."

He put the kettle on the stove. "Does she seem the forgiving sort to you?"

His question gave me a moment's pause. On more than one occasion, I had considered the possibility that Lavonn Blount might, at any given moment, eat me alive. But I was not above lying. "Yes."

He settled his leaner-than-reasonable hips against my counter. It was bare . . . except for a toaster, three dirty plates, my current romance novel boasting a kilt-wearing Scot with really great abs, and a million breadcrumbs . . . in case I got lost in L.A. and needed to find my way home. "So she would not harm another?"

"Why would she?"

He ignored the question. "Even if Mr. Goldenstone acted dishonorably?"

Did he know about the photographs? And if so, how? "She's trying to prove his innocence. I believe that means she thinks him quite—"

"Have you not wondered how she broke into Lieberman's house so easily?"

"You broke into *my*—"

"Surely you have considered that she might wish ill on—"

"Will you quit interrupting—"

"The man who raped her sister."

I considered feigning ignorance. Instead, I sat abruptly, plopping, sans grace, into the nearest chair. "How do you know that?" I asked, but he had turned back toward the stove and was dipping a previously unseen orb into the boiling water.

"It is common knowledge."

"To who?"

"Whom."

I scowled, experiencing some vertigo and a little bit of out-of-body craziness. "Did you wake me at three in the morning just to correct my grammar?"

"You were not sleeping well regardless."

"How long were you watching me?" My voice was a little squawky on the vowels.

"Neither have you been meditating. Or eating your greens."

"Greens." I nodded vaguely at his censorious tone. "Did you take my peanut butter?"

"It has been proven that saturated fats muddle the mind."

I pushed to my feet, fists clenched as I stepped toward him. "What the hell is wrong with you?"

He raised a brow and straightened. "Did you wish to engage in a bout with me, Ms. O'Tara?"

His use of the ridiculously fictional name I'd adopted during my exodus from L.A. just made me madder. But even though he only exceeded my height by a few inches, I had learned, to my chagrin and never-ending throbbing muscles, not to underestimate him. He was made of barbwire and bamboo; I, of ice cream and overcooked fettuccini noodles.

"Or perhaps you have decided to allow your lieutenant to protect you." Reaching out, he grasped the fleshy portion of my upper arm. "You grow soft again."

"I do not." I swatted at his hand, but he caught mine.

Either I was as slow as a concussed tortoise or he was lightning fast. Past evidence suggested equal likeliness on both counts.

"You do not wish to be caught unprepared."

I tried to snatch my hand away but failed. I curled my lip. "Let me go," I growled, but he merely lowered his hotter-than-hell gaze to my fist and caressed my fingers. They fell open, revealing my palm.

"You have an interesting heart line."

"What?" There was something dreadfully disturbing about his touch. Maybe it was the fact that I had never been entirely sure whether he wanted to kill me or kiss me. That'll put a damper on a relationship, let me tell you.

"Here," he said and touched a fingertip, feather soft, to my palm. "It begins just under your middle finger. Are you aware of the meaning?"

I suppressed a shiver and allowed my other four digits to curl in slightly, letting the tall one stand alone. "I could venture a guess."

Laughter lit his eyes, but he didn't bother to interrogate further. "A long line means you are content with love."

"I am," I breathed, but the words came out kind of raspy.

An almost negligible shake of his head. "Yours indicates that you are *selfish* in love."

"You're full of—"

"It undulates here," he said and smoothed his finger, light as air, across my skin.

I did my best not to squirm, or pass out, or burst into spontaneous orgasm.

"Suggesting you have had many lovers."

I tried to pull away. Really, I did, but perhaps all I managed to do was to tug myself closer to his rock-hard chest.

"While the intersection here . . . " To my horror, he leaned forward and kissed my palm. My knees buckled. I fortified all joints and several sphincters, but not before he raised his knock-'em-dead eyes to mine. "Suggests you are easily wounded."

"Let me go," I breathed.

"Ahh, your life line." He narrowed his eyes. "A swooping downward curve. You are strong," he conceded.

"Damn skippy," I breathed, hoping to hell he didn't feel my hand tremble.

"It is good." He nodded. "For you will need that strength for the Things."

"Nice to know," I said. "Now if you'll just . . . " I paused, heart knocking hard on my ribs. "Wait! What things?"

He turned my hand, swept two fingertips almost absently across my knuckles, and released me.

"They have opened an eating establishment in the Valley."

"Who did? What are you talking about? What valley?" But I knew. Not so much in my heart but in my quivering gut. Oh yeah, I knew. The Neanderthal brothers I had dubbed Thing One and Thing Two, the pair of twins I had met just a few months earlier, had arrived in the City of Angels. "Why? Why! Why would they come here?"

He smiled a little. "Perhaps because you gave them the strength to break the ties that bound them to the trauma of their past."

But I hadn't meant to do that. Okay, I had *kind* of meant to do that. I mean, just because they were philandering barbarians with the collective intellect of a cotton swab didn't mean they didn't have the right to pursue happiness. But they damn well could pursue it somewhere else.

"And I believe they miss you."

"You're crazy," I huffed.

"Is that your professional opinion?"

"Professional and personal," I said.

His eyes laughed. "It is doing quite well."

My skittering mind tried to patch together this information, but its veracity seemed doubtful. "They have a restaurant? And health services hasn't shut them down?" Their business in the numbfuck backwoods, where I had waitressed for them (don't ask), had been what one might call early E. coli, but even I had to admit it was tasty E. coli.

He shrugged. "They have an excellent chef."

I stared at him, felt my jaw drop, my lungs collapse. "You're cooking for them?"

"The marsala bok choy is a favorite."

"But . . ." I waved desperately with my newly freed hand. "Why?"

He shrugged. "Fresh ingredients is an important aspect."

"I meant why are they *here*? Why are *you* here?"

His eyes sparked blue diamonds. His lips curved enigmatically. "Sleep well," he said and bowed shallowly.

I watched him head toward my door, where he stopped, turned. "And Christina . . ."

I felt numb, a little out of body.

"Tell your lieutenant you are surely worth a better security system."

Twenty-five

"I can always tell if Holly's pissed 'cause she gets real quiet . . . or real loud . . . or tries to kill me."
—Peter John McMullen, who is about as intuitive as your average husband

I didn't sleep for the rest of the night. Maybe it was because I was now aware that the herculean Things were within shouting distance. Maybe it was because I was wondering who would be next to breach the sanctity of my home. And maybe it was because my hormones were fired up like a Hell's Kitchen all-you-can-eat barbeque.

So instead of enjoying the sweet bliss of slumber, I returned to my research regarding Marvin Lieberman: He had been a coach and a science teacher at Branford Middle School for the past three years. Before that, he'd been employed as an educator at a trio of different institutions. He'd been married twice and divorced just as many times, had two grown children, and according to Lavonn, kept vomit-worthy pics on his computer. I couldn't help but wonder what else he had done. In my experience, once a pervert, a hundred times a pervert.

I waited until 6:42 to call Rivera.

"What's wrong?" His voice was midnight rough, morning ready.

"Why does everyone assume there's something wrong when I call them?"

"It's six thirty in the morning."

"Six forty-two." I have no idea why I delighted in correcting him.

"You're not usually up for another four hours."

"Am too."

"If you have a nine o'clock appointment. In which case, you roll out of the sack at eight thirty." I could hear his bed rustle and imagined him there, dark, hard, ever ready, kind of like the bunny but hell-and-gone sexier. "What's wrong?" he asked again.

I considered continuing down the "everything's great" path, but it looked too rocky. "I was thinking about Micky."

"So you called me?"

"Do you know anything?"

"Pretty broad question."

"About his condition."

"Last I heard, he was still unconscious."

I nodded, worry and abject curiosity sloshing through me in equal measures, but I quelled them by searching the fridge for edibles. And by *edible*, I mean something that couldn't be found in an alpine meadow. Spotting a plastic carton of sugar-infused yogurt amidst the greenery, I snagged it. "What about Lieberman?"

"Far as I know, he's still dead."

"You always this funny in the morning?"

"You could move in and find out."

The carton dropped from my fingers and splattered onto the floor. "What did you say?"

"I said, yes, I am."

I shook my head. But truth to tell, I wasn't prepared to tackle the can of worms he had just peeled open. Or that I *thought* he'd peeled open. Had he really suggested that I move in with him? It seemed unlikely. Sometimes my imagination is far richer than reality. That could be proven by a NyQuil-induced dream I had once experienced, featuring Rivera, a shower, and some X-rated dialogue that only I and that crazy-ass sandman had heard.

I had no idea where to go from there. I floundered for a second, but finally managed to stumble forward.

"What are they saying about Micky?"

"'They' being the LAPD?"

"Yeah."

"Probably that he's guilty as hell."

"What? No. Why?"

"Probably because he *is* as guilty as hell."

"You don't know that!"

"Lieberman's dead. Goldenstone was at the scene with the murder weapon."

"You don't know that either."

"His prints were on the gun."

I paused. "Are you sure?"

"Yeah."

"Were there other prints?"

"No."

"So we've no way of knowing who shot Micky."

"Do you have any idea how often a shooter turns the gun on himself when he comes to his senses?"

"Micky wouldn't do that. Not when his son needs him. It's inconceivable."

"Goldenstone was at the scene of the crime with the murder weapon."

"That doesn't mean anything."

"Is that your expert opinion, Christina McMullen, PhD?"

"Micky didn't kill him."

"How about deal in pornography? Did he do that?"

I fell into stunned silence. Did he know about the pictures? Did he know I did?

"What are you talking about?"

"You tell me," he rumbled.

"How can I tell you what you're talking about?" I forced a laugh. "If you're uncertain, I sure as hell—"

"What do you know about him and Lieberman?"

"What about them?" The question was breathy.

"Forensics found kiddie pictures on Lieberman's PC."

"What kind of kiddie pictures?" I was waiting for the next shoe to drop, waiting for him to tell me about the images of Micky. He didn't.

"We think he was selling pornography."

What about the pics Lavonn had mentioned? Hadn't he seen them? Was he toying with me? Had Lavonn deleted them? Or lied about the whole thing? But why would she do that?

"No comment?" Rivera asked.

"Maybe Micky found out about the pictures," I said. "Maybe he went to Lieberman to make him stop."

"And maybe he was in partnership with him."

"Not possible."

"Like your illustrious friend and all-around good guy David Hawkins wasn't a fucking lunatic who would try to kill you with a fillet knife."

I winced at the memory. "You gotta admit, that was a long shot."

There was a pause and then he chuckled. "Jesus, McMullen." He sounded tired, but it probably wasn't my fault. I mean, it was 6:43 in the morning. By rights, I should still be dreaming about hard men in hot showers. "Stay out of it."

"I *am* staying out of it."

"Oh, that's right. What did Officer Lawson say? Oh yeah, that you were a seemingly intelligent and caring therapist who staunchly supported the idea that Micky Goldenstone was incapable of any heinous crimes."

"Seemingly intelligent?"

"Yeah, that's what made him less than credible for me too."

"Six forty-four," I said, "and you're still hilarious."

"I'm thinking of doing stand-up."

"Really." My tone sounded dry even to me.

"Well, part of me is already auditioning." The bed rustled again.

My ovaries sat up and begged like a lapdog, but I scolded them fiercely and ended the call.

After some silent debate, I pulled on a pair of shorts, clipped a leash onto Harlequin's collar, and headed for the front door. If I was awake at such an ungodly hour, I might as well prolong the torture. Harley pattered doggedly (get it?) toward the door. I glanced at Shikoku.

"You coming?" I asked. I was not the boss of Shikoku. That much had been established long ago. But neither was she a dog that had to be bossed. In fact, I wasn't entirely sure she was a dog at all. Instead, she might have been some kind of furry spy. A self-disciplined furry spy.

Once on the street, I stretched three times, did a couple half-hearted arm swings, and headed up Opus Street.

Running is good for my brain. Don't get me wrong, I detest exercise with every fiber of my being, but the sheer agony of making my legs move step after step seems to convince my mind to check out, allowing it to go elsewhere.

So while the dogs trotted leisurely beside me, I panted onto Grapevine Avenue, mind spinning. The truth was, I wasn't positive that Micky was innocent regarding Lieberman's death. But I was sure, gut-level certain, that he would not, in any way, harm a child.

True, I had made mistakes in the past. I had believed, in fact, that my former client, Andrew Bomstad, was impotent. Until he chased me around my desk sporting a woody that would make a summer squash blush with inadequacy.

So I wasn't exactly infallible. But Micky and I had been through a lot together. Rage, guilt, redemption, and the eventual adoption of a son he hadn't known he'd sired. A son who brought him hope and happiness and enough frustration to have him grinding his teeth at every session.

So maybe that frustration had gotten to him. Maybe it had pushed him over the edge, prodded him into some sort of altercation with Marvin Lieberman. But child pornography? I couldn't fathom it.

I cried uncle after a mile and a half, turned, still jogging listlessly, at the stop light on Oro Vista, and shambled back home. By the time I reached my front door, I was wheezing like an asthmatic. I re-armed the apparently worthless security system, then stumbled into the kitchen to inhale a glass of water. Minutes later, I punched J.D. Solberg's number into my cell.

"Hello?" He sounded awake, chipper, and happy as a clam, though honestly, I'm not entirely sure we can correctly calibrate the emotional state of the crustacean population.

"Solberg?" I hadn't expected him to answer right off the bat and was still wheezing softly.

"Is this a lewd call? 'Cause if it is, I'm gonna have to tell you right now, I'm spoken for."

"What happened to your caller ID?" My voice was still a little raspy, but I managed to push out the words.

"Babykins?"

"Don't call me that."

He laughed. "ID's not working 'cause I'm testing out caller holographic, but I'm having a little trouble capturing the interference pattern between the beams of coherent light, which makes—"

"I need a favor."

There was a pause, long, painful, and wary, then, "Hey, I'd love to help you out, Chrissy, but I'm going through a tunnel right now. Why don't you call me back when—"

"No, you're not, and no, I won't." I had used that tired trick too many times on my mother to be fooled. I ignored the quick kick of guilt associated with familial entanglements and hurried on. "It's no big deal. I just want you to check out some guy's emails."

"Invasion of privacy? I don't think so. I'm a family man now and—"

"And who gave you that family?"

"Ummm, Angel?"

Okay, valid point. Still . . . "But who introduced you to Angel . . . Laney?"

"You did."

"That's right. You don't want me to unintroduce her, do you?"

"Unintro—"

"Or tell her about the vacuum cleaner?"

"I got no idea what you're talking—"

"I bet the paramedics do."

"Whose email?" Funny thing. He already sounded kind of tired.

Twenty-six

"If being a mother were easy, fathers would do it."
— Every mother that's ever lived

"Mom!" I said the word like a five-year-old in the throes of bogeyman terrors.

"Christina?" She sounded cheery and mildly surprised.

"Yeah, Mom, it's me."

"Well, hi, honey. It's good to hear from you. How's everything in L.A.?"

I scowled as a guy in a red convertible zipped past me on the right shoulder. I wasn't entirely sure, but I thought he had a pot-bellied pig riding shotgun. Either that or I was delusional, which seemed fairly likely considering my mother sounded not only normal but *happy*.

"It's fine."

"Nice weather, I suppose?"

My parents still lived on the outskirts of Chicago, where I had grown up. One great thing about the Midwest: you can always discuss the weather. Technically, I suppose you can do the same in L.A., but it lacks the gut-wrenching angst. In the great state of Illinois, you can get blistering hot and freeze-your-ass cold on the same day of the week. In Los Angeles, meteorologists are about as necessary as banana hammocks.

"Seventy-five and sunny," I said.

"Weren't you the smart one to move there?"

"What?" Surprise almost sent me crashing into the bumper of the BMW ahead of me.

"But you always were so bright."

"Mom?" I said, and wondered wildly what she'd done with my *real* mother. "What's going on?"

"What do you mean?"

"I mean about . . . " Her lack of bitterness. Her weird normalcy. "About Dad. Pete said he's got . . . " My voice broke, surprising me with its weakness. Five cars zipped past on my left. "Pete said he's not feeling well."

"That's ridiculous. Your dad's fine."

"He said it might be—"

"He's playing golf with Ralph Carrington. You remember Ralph, don't you? Say, it was really nice to hear from you, honey, but someone's at the door. We'll talk later," she said and hung up.

I sat in numb rejection, mouth open until a pair of teenagers pulled up beside me. The girl in the passenger seat flapped a limp hand against her chest in an age-old mocking gesture. Maybe it was because I was driving thirty miles an hour below the posted speed limit. Or it might have been my slack-jawed expression. But who was she to judge? Her mother probably hadn't just hung up on her. Her world had probably not been turned upside down by news of her father's mortality. I narrowed my eyes and refrained from flipping the little twit the bird, accelerated, and tried to think.

The truth dawned on me in slow increments: Dad wasn't sick. Which meant that Pete had lied to me. But that shouldn't surprise me. He had lied a million times in the past. Had lied about everything from what was on our dinner plates to how babies were made. But I wouldn't stoop to his level. He might be mired in sophomoric stupidity, but I could rise above.

I called him next.

"Hey, sis, how's it hangin'?"

"You're a fucktard," I said.

There was only a momentary pause. "About average, I take it?"

"I actually believed you."

"Really?" He sounded mildly surprised, borderline euphoric. "About what?"

"Dad! I just talked to Mom."

"Seriously?"

"Yes, you miserable vomitus mass. She said—"

"It seriously took you that long to call them?"

I paused to fill my lungs with blasting oxygen, but he spoke before I could singe his ears with my vitriol.

"Shit! If my daughter's as hard-assed as you when she's an old maid, I'll slit my wrists."

"Well, then I certainly hope she's . . . " I stopped myself just short of saying something truly awful. "The point isn't that I'm a hard-ass," I said, guilt making inroads into the rage. "The point is that you're a lying sack of—"

"Did you talk to Dad?"

I inhaled. "He was playing golf. Playing *golf!*"

There was a pause, then, "Any idea what the weather's like

215

here in the Heartland, Chris?"

I glanced at the thermometer on my dash. Seventy-five degrees exactly.

"It's thirty-seven degrees here," he said. "With a nice brisk wind off the lake. Even if he liked golf, which he doesn't, he'd have to be a fucking polar bear to be out in this."

"But Mom said . . . "

"Whatever she could to keep you from worrying?"

"No!" I made a *pffsh*ing noise. "She wouldn't do that." He didn't argue, which was simply confusing. I mean, Peter John McMullen had probably exited the womb arguing. "Why would she do that?"

He sighed, deep and long suffering. "You really need to hear this?"

"Hear *what?*"

"That you're successful. That you actually have a career, a *life* that she doesn't want to mess up."

I pulled the phone from my ear to scowl at it for a moment. "Tell me the truth, has Schaumberg been invaded by aliens or something?"

He chuckled. "Believe me, Crazy, it surprises me as much to say it as it does for you to hear it."

"Yeah but . . . you *did* say it, right?"

"Jesus, what's wrong with you?"

"Nothing! What's wrong with—"

"Why can't you just take a simple compliment from me?"

"Uh, lack of experience?"

"I guess maybe I was kind of an ass."

"*Kind* of an ass? You told LeRoy Lanquist that I was having sex with Victoria Munson in the girls' bathroom."

He chuckled. "Yeah, I did."

"And that I wanted it filmed."

"Oh God." He sighed happily. "Who knew he'd bring the whole damn video team along to see you taking a—"

"I hate you," I said.

"No, you don't."

"I do," I argued. "I actually do. In fact, I hate you more than—"

"How do you feel about Dad?"

The question stopped me dead in my verbal tracks. In theory, I might have once hated my father, too. But reality seemed to be a different story.

"Tell me the truth," I said. "Is he sick or what?"

There was a pause. If I tried really hard I could imagine him gazing out the window of his two-story fixer-upper. In that deep imagination, he looked intelligent and far seeing. No one ever said I was too firmly grounded in reality. "I don't know," he said finally.

"You don't know? You said he had cancer and now you don't know? You're worse than a fucktard. You're a—"

"Holly saw a black Lincoln parked at St. Al's three days in a row."

"The medical center?"

"Yeah."

I waited in silence. So did he.

"That's it?" I snapped finally. "That's your entire reason for making me believe Dad was at death's door? Do you have any idea how many black Lincolns are registered in the state of Illinois?"

"It had a bumper sticker that said *Shut Up and Speak English.*"

"So?" I asked, but we both knew Dad's longstanding

distaste for anything un-American. "Lots of people—"

"It was his."

I considered arguing the point, but I could already feel my IQ dropping and didn't want to risk extending the conversation. "Maybe he was just . . . in for a hangnail or something."

"Dad?"

"Yeah."

"Remember when he fell off the ladder while cleaning the gutters?"

I did remember. Claire Brannigan, from three doors down, had called the cops to complain about his language.

"Broke his arm in two places," he added.

The memory made me feel a little queasy. The ensuing emotion that might have been homesickness made me even more nauseated. Christina McMullen, PhD, did not get homesick. "So?"

"Refused to go to the doctor till Mom threatened to hide his beer."

"Nobody ever said the McMullens were normal."

"Nobody never said we weren't tough, either."

No. No one had. Not without suffering the consequences, at any rate. All of which were undoubtedly swift and juvenile, but probably also fairly creative.

"Still, maybe you're right," he said. "Just because he doesn't go in for multiple fractures or when passing kidney stones the size of ostrich eggs, doesn't mean he won't make an appointment for a tummy ache."

"I hate you," I said again and hung up.

Five minutes later, I was on the phone with Laney's husband again.

"Jesus, Chrissy, what do you want now? My firstborn?"

"He looks like you."

"So?"

"So no," I said, and immediately regretted it. I hadn't called to insult him. It was just so hard to break pattern. "Listen, J.D., I need you to do something else for me."

"Does it involve sensitive explosives or lethal poisons of any kind?"

"Of course not. Why would it?"

"I assume you're trying to get me killed."

I didn't admit that in the good old days, before I believed that my best friend in the world could actually have feelings for a height-challenged geek with an irritating-as-hell sense of humor, I *had* actually deliberated about hiring a nice hit man. "I'm not trying to get you killed."

"What do you want?"

I considered buttering him up a little. But the truth was, J.D. Solberg had always been greasy enough. "I need some medical records."

"What?"

"You heard me."

"Goldenstone's?"

I cleared my throat. "No."

"Lieberman's?"

"My dad's."

There was a confused pause. "You can't just ask him?"

"No."

"Ever thought of finding a good psychologist?" he asked and hung up before I could think of a real snappy comeback.

219

Twenty-seven

"I am neither a night owl nor an early bird. I'm more like a perpetually exhausted cuckoo."
      —Elaine Butterfield, shortly after the birth of baby Mac

"Horseback riding." Rose sat on my client couch, looking simultaneously prim and sassy.

"I beg your pardon?" I said.

"I'm thinking of taking up horseback riding."

"May I ask why?"

"You're the therapist."

"Okay. Why?"

"Because Amy about blew a gasket when I mentioned skydiving."

I didn't bother asking if she'd told her daughter about the gigolo.

"I believe she thinks I'm trying to kill myself."

"Are you?"

She considered that for an instant. "Have you ever

watched someone you care about die, Christina?"

I controlled the wince always brought on by talk of death, banned the thought of my father's bumper sticker showing up at St. Alexius Medical Center, and did my best to keep my expression placid, if not intelligent. "No, I haven't."

"Health professionals often use terms like *dignified* and *peaceful* and *going to a better place*. But they're full of doo-doo," she said. "There's nothing dignified about dying."

"You never told me how Orvill passed."

"Was I supposed to?"

"If you want to."

She considered for a second. "Are you familiar with ALS?"

"I know a little."

"It begins so quietly. Like nothing at all. A tremor. A bobble." She looked distant, lost in the past. "Orvill was always clumsy. Those big feet of his." The wisp of a smile lifted her lips. "We used to laugh about it. It was how we met. A group of us kids were down by the lake. We lived in Minnesota then. They have ten thousand of them, you know. Lakes, that is. We were playing by the water, being foolish. Like you do when you're young . . . before the world washes away your silly."

"How old were you?"

"Sixteen. Just. I wore my hair like Marilyn Monroe." She laughed, touched her wispy white curls with bent fingers. "We all did. Mine was red then. Ginger, maybe. Amy, when she was little, called it allburnt. Orvill said it was the first thing he noticed about me. He had just screwed up his nerve to come talk to me. Came marching across the sand before his courage petered out, and fell flat on his face on somebody's leftover sandcastle. He looked so pathetic lying there, like a spanked puppy. I didn't know if I should help him up or offer him a Milk-Bone." She exhaled slowly, softly. "He wasn't handsome or rich or any of those things that people seem to think are important these days. But he was . . . " She thought for a moment. "*Kind* doesn't seem like a big enough word somehow." I watched her. Her face in that moment looked as young as a child's, as radiant as a saint's. "He was the one who was good with words. Always had so many of them. I think I fell in love with him before sunset. How could I not? He said being with me made him feel like you do just when your snow sled first tilts downhill. Before it even begins racing toward the bottom. Like you want to laugh and scream and hold on for dear life."

"How long has he been gone?"

"Three years now."

"I'm sorry," I said, and I was. So very sorry. Because she had lost the man of her dreams. And maybe a little bit because I hadn't found mine.

"I'm not trying to die, Christina," she said. "I'm trying to *live*."

Was Micky? I wondered, sitting very still as I watched him from the discomfort of Alhambra Medical Center's guest chair. In repose, he looked Tibetan-monk restful and movie-star handsome. Was he trying to live? Or would he just as soon check out? I had learned about his thoughts of suicide early in our sessions together. But I had no reason to believe he still entertained such horrid ideas. I believed, in fact, that he had embraced life. Was looking forward to the future.

Had I missed something?

"Isn't he a fine-looking boy?"

I rose with a start. Esse Goldenstone, better known as Grams by those who dared to know her at all, stood in the doorway of the hospital room. She looked like an animated garden gnome as she hobbled into the room, cane tapping rhythmically.

"Isn't he?" she demanded.

"Yes," I admitted. "He is."

"Always was. Always was too pretty for his own good. Even when his ears was sticking out like a dairy cow's. His momma, my Sadie, she tacked them down with duct tape."

I had heard the story before. Grams pivoted slowly, lowered herself laboriously into the remaining chair that stood in the corner.

"What you doing here?" she asked.

I sat again, but cautiously now. "I just came by to see how he was doing."

"You don't have a phone?"

"Oh, yes," I said and began digging in my purse for my cell. "Did you want to use—"

She flapped a gnarled hand at me. "Why didn't you just call and ask?"

"Oh. I guess . . . " I stilled my motions, glanced at Micky again. "I wanted to see him."

"You believe it?" she asked.

I shifted my attention back to her. "Believe what?"

"That he's a pervert?"

"I . . . " My lips kept moving, but I couldn't seem to force out any words that would make me sound more intelligent than the ventriloquist's dummy I was clearly trying to mimic.

"You think he's a child molester like Lavonn says?"

Holy rat's ass, had Lavonn actually spewed those words in

the presence of a woman who could, I was sure, kill a pachyderm with a glance?

She stomped the cane. "Do you?"

"I . . . It's not . . . I don't . . . " I began, blundering wildly, but she took pity on me and spoke.

"He's not!" she said. Her tone was absolutely even, entirely certain. "Don't get me wrong. I'm no sentimentalist. I see his faults. See them clear as morning. He's hotheaded." She glanced at him, voice softening ever so slightly. "Violent, even. I used to blame his mother, his friends, myself. But blame just makes me tired."

I nodded. It was the most intelligent thing I'd done all day.

"Still . . . " She pinned me with her beady, bird-bright gaze. "I'm gonna blame *you* if he doesn't make it."

"What? Me!" I stood abruptly, launching myself from the discomfort of the plastic chair. "How can you think this is my—"

"You're his therapist, aren't you?"

"Yes, but—"

"Paid to figure things out?"

"That's not exactly true." Or anywhere near fair. "I simply help the client ascertain which areas of his or her life should be—"

"You're not an idiot."

"I . . . " Paused, cautious. Generally when people say something like that, it's followed by a big ass *but*. "Thank you?"

"My Michael likes you. Respects you even."

"Well, I—"

"And he'll know."

"Know what?"

"If you give up on him. He'll know and he won't bother coming back."

"I don't think—" I began, but she rose to her feet with surprising verve.

"Get out of here now."

"What?"

"You get out of here and figure out what's really going on."

"Listen . . . " I huffed my outrage. "I'm sorry about what happened to Micky. Extremely sorry, but—"

"Go!" she ordered, jabbing me with her cane.

For a second, I actually considered arguing. But I like to think I'm not completely brain-dead.

j

I was justifiably miffed on the way home from the hospital. I mean, Micky's situation wasn't my fault. And I wasn't taking the blame. In fact, I was relinquishing the reins, letting the police handle the investigation. Believing that justice would . . .

"Oh for fuck's sake!" I swore and turned toward Branford Middle School, Micky's current place of employment.

Twenty-eight

"Hey, Math, I'm tired of finding your X. Face it, dude, she's gone."
  —Michael McMullen, always better at humor than arithmetic

"Principal Heyd will see you now," the receptionist said.

I'd been waiting for forty-five minutes in an anteroom that smelled like day-old tuna casserole and boredom. A boy in the torturous throes of puberty sat hunched in the corner, trying to look defiant while sweating like a Clydesdale. I would have felt sorry for him if I'd had a lobotomy and couldn't remember teenage boys. In my opinion, they generally deserve to be sautéed in olive oil and served on toast points.

As for myself, I stifled a little shiver as I stepped into the principal's office. I don't know what other people's reactions to such places are, but they made my liver want to crawl into my spleen and die.

"Ms. McMullen." A man rose from behind his desk. Atop that desk was a brass plaque that read *Benjamin Heyd*. Principal Heyd was tall, dark, and good-looking enough to make my endocrine system consider possibilities other than death. "Ms. Pauly said you have information regarding Michael Goldenstone that you wished to share."

"Oh." I gotta tell you, he threw me. In my experience, principals were wizened little nuns who looked like Yoda but lacked the intrinsic charm. "Well . . ." I cleared my throat. It was starting to close up, and I found that I wanted quite badly to declare in loud and possibly sophomoric tones that it wasn't my fault. Toby Uberman, that wart-faced turd blossom, was to blame. "Yes."

He motioned toward the chair opposite his own with an elegant hand. I sat, trying to look dignified, but I was starting to sweat a little myself. He raised his brows. His complexion was something between dark chocolate and caramel. Two of my all-time favorite concoctions. "Please, proceed."

"He was shot."

His brows remained where they were, somewhere in the northern hemisphere. "I'm aware of that, Ms. McMullen."

My right knee was starting to bounce and I could feel acne boiling like lava beneath my skin. "It wasn't my fault."

He stared at me for a full five seconds, then steepled his fingers and leaned back in his chair. "Tell me, Ms. McMullen, were you, by chance, raised Catholic?"

"Maybe." My voice had lost the intelligent adult tone I had hoped for and was sliding rapidly toward belligerent schoolgirl.

"Educated by nuns, perhaps?"

I nodded, wondering how he knew. In retrospect, it was probably the rivulet of sweat making a causeway from my hairline to my cleavage. Which was, by the by, well hidden. I like to think I'm not a complete idiot.

"How's the recovery coming along?" he asked and smiled.

It was just the corner of a grin, but it was killer.

I felt the knot in my stomach ease up a little. "About as well as can be expected."

"You don't want to let those expectations get too lofty."

"It's a mortal sin," I admitted.

"Is it?"

"Isn't everything?"

"I attended Sacred Heart."

"And survived," I deduced.

He chuckled. "Even decided to work in the field of education."

"Tell me the truth: did they brainwash you? Torture you until you agreed to their fiendish ways?"

"Actually . . . " He shrugged, a casual lift of well-defined shoulders. "I wanted to change the system. Be a more approachable educator."

"I assume approachable educators still employ bamboo slivers."

He cocked his handsome head.

"The kid in the waiting room looked like he might die of anxiety before you ever get a chance to approach him."

"Ahh," he said and sighed. "Alex Traynor."

"What'd he do?"

"What didn't he do?"

"Superglue his sister's underwear to her ear?" My brother, Pete, had been a particularly big fan of adhesives of all sorts.

"What?"

"Never mind. About Micky . . . "

He sobered. "What about him?"

I had to step carefully here. There was no reason to believe Principal Heyd knew anything about the alleged pictures. And even less reason to *want* him to know. "Have you heard anything from the police about what may have happened?"

He rose to his full height, which was pretty full. He was built like an athlete, long and hard and pretty as a postcard. "Can I ask how you know Mr. Goldenstone?"

"I'm a friend." I agonized for a moment before continuing. "And his therapist."

"He needed a therapist?"

I felt my hackles rise. "Doesn't everyone?"

"Maybe. Probably. I won't ask why," he said, shoving a hand into the pocket of his fitted trousers. They stretched tight across his crotch. Not that I noticed. "I respect your profession and therefore your need for discretion, but if you can shed any light on the situation, I would be grateful. Personally and professionally."

"I assume you found someone to replace him until he recovers?"

He shook his head. "You can't replace a good teacher, Ms. McMullen. You can only hope to muddle along without them until they return."

"He's good at what he does?"

"The kids not only respect him, they like him. Everybody likes him."

I nodded, unsurprised. Micky had experienced enough tough times to make him tough, enough empathy to make him empathetic. "Except Marv Lieberman."

He shoved his other hand in his pocket. The stiletto-edged crease that bisected his thighs made me suspect he was married, despite the absence of a ring. "Did *you* know of any animosity between the two of them?"

I considered refusing to answer, but the truth was so

convenient. "No."

"Me either. Well . . . " He shook his head. "I knew they weren't BFFs. There was some tension."

"Why?"

"Mr. Lieberman could be kind of rough on the kids. Typical gym coach, I suppose. Micky was more flexible with the students."

I couldn't help but notice that Lieberman was a "Mr." while Micky was not. "Can you tell me why Mr. Lieberman has worked for four different schools in the past ten years?"

He didn't look surprised that I knew. "I wondered that, too, of course."

"But you saw no reason to inquire about the situation?"

He gave me a look that could have quashed a chunk of petrified rock. Luckily, I'm not as sensitive as a rock and remained unquashed.

"I did inquire, only to learn that he had some family issues."

"Such as?"

"The death of his parents, which meant he no longer felt the need to live in Seward, Nebraska. And later, the dissolution of a marriage. After which he moved again."

I didn't mention that only explained two of the jobs and then only halfway. "So there haven't been any complaints against him?"

I watched him closely, but if he was sweating, he hid it better than the kid in the waiting room . . . and me.

"Nothing out of the ordinary."

"What's *in* the ordinary?"

"Are you telling me you never complained about a teacher, Ms. McMullen?"

"Not so anyone listened." But then maybe "she's a raisin-faced gargoyle" just wasn't something the powers that be were going to take seriously.

He smiled grimly. "We try to listen here at Branford. There were no serious allegations."

"Did Micky have other enemies that you know of?"

He thought for a moment, brow handsomely furrowed. "None that I can think of."

"Any particular friends?"

"Paige Ellery, I suppose."

"What kind of friends are they?"

He scowled as if considering his answer but finally he shrugged. "They look after each other's kids from time to time. I have no reason to believe there was any more to their relationship than that."

I filed that away for the time being. "Who else?"

"He and Deirdra seemed a little . . . flirtatious for a while."

"Deirdra?" I said the name as if I hadn't scoured her Facebook page, interrogated her in person.

"She works in the cafeteria. Or at least, she *did*. I'm told she's taken the whole thing pretty hard. Hasn't come back to work since it happened."

So she still hadn't returned, even though she needed the money. "Who else is Micky friends with?"

"Ms. Cross collaborated with him on exams periodically, and he might have socialized some with Ms. Haven. Mr. Goldenstone is quite popular with the female persuasion," he said and paused. "I hope you didn't think you were the only woman he was interested in."

"I'm here in a professional capacity," I said.

"Exclusively?"

"Yes."

"Great," he said, and gave me a knock-'em-dead smile. "You busy this weekend?"

Twenty-nine

"Of course I'm a feminist. Do I look stupid . . . or male?"
　　　　　　　　　　　　　　　　—Ms. Sharon Cross

Why would Handsome Heyd ask me out? And why . . . dear God, why would I say yes? I mean, okay, he was attractive enough, if you were into that tall-dark-and-handsome thing, which, let's face it, everyone in the known universe is. But he was the principal of the school. The principal whom I had questioned about his decisions regarding Lieberman.

But I had little enough time to obsess about our upcoming date, because, surprisingly, I had been offered a spontaneous interview with one of Micky's coworkers. Sharon Cross, Branford's resident English teacher, was the other woman in the picture I had obsessed about on Lieberman's Facebook page.

"Why are you here?" she asked when I took a seat across the desk from her.

If any of Holy Name's nuns had tipped the scales at a cool

three hundred pounds, Sharon Cross would have been perfect for that lauded institution.

I refrained from shuffling my feet like a naughty third grader. "I was hoping you could shed some light on Micky Goldenstone's situation."

"Why?"

"He's my . . . " I refrained from saying "client." The idea of people receiving therapy tended to scare other people out of their mental health. "Friend," I said.

"What kind of friend?" she asked and caught me with her narrowed eyes.

I straightened my spine, pretty sure I could hear it creak under the pressure. "I don't see how that pertains to this situation."

"Sex pertains to every situation," she said, and rising with laborious difficulty, crossed to shut the door. I felt a moment of panic before remembering that not only was I an adult, I could probably exit the room before she managed a U-turn. "Michael has enough trouble with women here at *school*."

Against the wall, a fleet of depressing novels were aligned like Marines in their dress blues. Faulkner, Salinger, Golding, Tolstoy. Not a mostly naked Scotsman to be seen. Ms. Cross was either gay or masochistic. "Which means?"

"Half the female staff here are single," she said and sighed heavily as she sat again. "After his arrival, the other half wished they were."

"You disapprove?"

"Of women flaunting themselves to every man with a decent-looking face and a couple of brain cells that manage to flutter up from below decks? Yes."

"How about the men?"

"They can objectify themselves if they so desire," she said and cast her gaze back to the papers on her desk, but I thought I saw a glint of something in her eye. Humor maybe. Or irritation. Or murderous intent. I had no way of knowing.

"Did he have trouble with them, too?"

"Well . . ." She glanced up. "Supposedly one of them shot him. So you tell me."

"Lieberman?"

Her woolly-bear eyebrows rose dramatically. "You know of someone else who tried to kill him?"

Actually, I did, but now didn't seem the time to share that news. "Why would he bear Micky ill will?" I was pretty sure old Tolstoy would have been proud of my phraseology.

Ms. Cross, however, seemed unimpressed. Taking an inkpad from the middle drawer of her desk, she stamped the letter D in bright red on the top-most paper, then shuffled it aside and settled back to stare at me. "Why are you here, Ms. McMullen? PhD."

"I didn't flaunt myself, if that's what you're thinking."

She said nothing. I refrained from fidgeting, but sometimes silence makes me long to chatter like a mynah bird. "We're friends. Nothing more. Well . . ." I did fidget now. "I'm also his counselor."

"Legal or emotional?"

"I'm a licensed psychologist."

She laughed. "As opposed to what? A recreational psychologist?"

Sometimes dignity is damned hard to hang on to, but I curled my fingers into its shorthairs. "Why would Lieberman shoot Michael Goldenstone?" Or vice versa.

"My guess? Because society allows . . . even encourages . . .

men to act on their baser instincts instead of demanding that they behave as civilized human beings."

Watching her, I tried to think of the antonym of misogynist. But I couldn't come up with it. Was that sexist? "Had the two of them had disputes in the past?"

"Don't all men?"

"About what?"

"Guess."

"Flaunting women?"

"You really do have a PhD, don't you?"

"Which women in particular?"

"I like to believe females are the more evolved of the genders, but you don't always make it easy."

I ignored her use of pronouns. "What about Paige Ellery?"

"What about her?" she asked, then skimmed the top paper on her desk and marked it with another sanguine D.

"In your opinion, could she have been involved?"

She shrugged. "Anything's possible, I suppose," she said, casually destroying another student's hope for a decent grade in English. "But it seems unlikely, seeing as she just hatched her third or so kid."

"When was that?"

She stared at me. "Let me check my records where I document the birth of every child ever born."

I gave her high scores for sarcasm. "Any idea where she'd be?"

"Northridge hospital, maybe."

I had no idea where that was. "How about Deirdra Mills?"

"How about her?"

"Do you know her?"

"I've visited the lunch room a time or two."

"And?"

"The word 'bimbo' was not coined without reason."

"Were she and Micky seeing each other?"

"This is going to surprise you, but I have a few things to occupy my time besides following the exploits of an oversexed woman with the IQ of a pomegranate."

So mean, but not entirely wrong. "Brooke Haven?"

"She supports the possibility, however remote, that some artists might actually have a functioning brain."

"She's an artist."

"Digital, graphic . . . " She shrugged, already looking bored with the subject. "At least before the bloodletting."

I gave her a head tilt.

"Region-wide cuts." She snorted. "So what if kids can't spell *cat* when they graduate to the eighth grade?"

"They've eliminated language classes?"

"Always the next thing after the arts, which were gutted. Luckily, the gladiator sports remain intact."

"So Lieberman's job wasn't in jeopardy?"

"He might have taken a pay cut."

"But the football program is still in place?"

"How would we survive without our little warriors battling over a pigskin?"

"I take it you don't care much for organized sports."

"Boys have enough difficulty evolving into civilized beings without us insisting that they become gladiators for the entertainment of the masses."

"You don't think they're predisposed to battle?"

"If you're asking if I think they're inherently assholes, yes. I do. But for a few endless months, it's my unfortunate responsibility not only to protect them but to teach them." She banged out another blood-red D, raised her squinty eyes to mine. "And I take my responsibility seriously."

"How about Coach Lieberman? How did you feel about him?"

She rested her smiting stamp to watch me. "Marvin Lieberman was a rutting philistine with the morals of a satyr and the mental capacity of a snail. The world is a better place without him." She smiled. The expression looked strangely beatific on her tuber-like features. "May he rest in peace."

Thirty

"Reality is merely an illusion, albeit a very persistent one."

—Albert Einstein

I tried to return to my office after my meetings with Cross and Heyd. Told myself that would be the smart thing to do. Return to L.A. Counseling, check in with Shirley, maybe even catch up on paperwork.

Instead, I used my GPS's voice-activated capabilities. Although, in my defense, I felt kind of silly doing so. "Morab?"

"Yes, my lovely." His smoky tenor purred from the vicinity of my dashboard. "With what can I assist you this day?"

"I need to get to the hospital in Northridge."

Worry infused his voice. "I pray you are not feeling unwell."

"No." I cleared my throat and glanced sheepishly out my side window, but no one seemed to be observing my conversation with a virtual love slave. "I'm fine. I just want to visit . . . a friend."

"Ahh, such is your kind spirit. Northridge Medical is on the boulevard called Roscoe. It shall be my greatest pleasure to guide you there."

Twenty minutes later, I stood in the lobby of Farr Tower. Labor and Delivery was on the fifth floor. I rode the elevator up, but what now? It was possible, I supposed, that a person who had just pushed a human being out of her bottom wouldn't care to be accused of homicide, but the doors were already opening.

I stepped out, feeling oddly guilty.

"Can I help you?" The woman behind the reception desk smiled.

I managed to do the same. "Yes. I'm here to see Paige Ellery."

She checked her screen. "Room five twenty-one. You'll need to sign in and fill out a name tag."

I did so. In a minute I arrived at the appropriate room . . . and strode past.

What was I doing here? I couldn't interrogate this poor woman. She was a new mother. New mothers didn't commit homicide.

On the other hand . . .

"Hello." A nurse in monochromatic green passed me.

"Hi," I said and amped up my speed as though I had somewhere to go. My mind was skittering; when Lieberman was killed, Paige had not yet given birth. And who was more likely to commit murder than someone hopped up on estrogen while waddling around with an extraneous forty pounds hanging from her midsection?

Making sure no one was watching, I reversed my course. Thirty feet ahead, a door opened. The nurse from moments before stepped into the hall.

"Can I help you?" she asked and secured the top button of her smock.

She'd changed her shirt from a V-neck to a button-up. "Oh. Yes. Ah . . . " I put a hand to my stomach, which, thanks to the craziness of my evolving plans, felt a little queasy. "Fish tacos . . . they never agree with me."

She raised a brow.

"Is there a restroom nearby?"

"Oh, sure, just round the corner," she said and left me to my insanity.

In a minute, I was hiding in a bathroom stall while trying to talk myself down from crazy. But the memory of Micky unconscious and alone spurred me on.

I stepped out of the restroom with newfound determination. The hallway was empty. Heart thumping, I glanced toward the door through which the green-clad nurse had exited. The plaque read *Women's Changing Room. Employees Only.*

Voices issued from around the corner behind me. I goose-stepped to the watercolor that hung nearby and examined it as if it held the meaning of life.

Two women passed me, chatting amicably.

I exhaled heavily. This was certifiable behavior. I couldn't . . .

But just then the changing room door opened, and suddenly my feet were moving, dragging me forward like an unwilling captive. I stepped into the doorway just as a nurse stepped out. We bumped, shoulders, elbows, thighs.

"Oh! Sorry!"

"No. No. My fault," I countered and sidling around her, scurried inside.

The room was blessedly empty. Just me, my insanity, and shelves of folded scrubs. I closed my eyes, ready to bail. Laughter boomed from the hallway, drawing nearer.

Grabbing the closest garment, I yanked it over my head, and was already exiting when a women wheeled in a cart loaded with supplies.

"How you doing?" she asked, still smiling.

"Good. Good. I'm good," I rambled and dashed out.

A remaining modicum of good sense declared that I should make a plan. Should stop. Should think. But why start now?

My palm felt sweaty against the plastic plaque that identified room 521.

"Hello." I felt sick to my stomach but stepped up to the computer monitor near the end of the bed that filled most of the room.

Paige Ellery glanced up. She was sitting cross-legged in bed. She looked good. Hair brushed, nails lacquered an arresting shade of red. "Hi."

"How are you feeling?" I asked and pretended to fiddle with the keyboard.

"Good. This is the first time in six years that I've had time to polish my fingernails." She wiggled them at me.

I tried to give her the kind of bland, patronizing smile of which doctors everywhere are capable. "Very nice. Is this an okay time to answer a few questions?"

"Sure. I guess, but listen, I was wondering if you have any of that strawberry-swirl cheesecake you had last time I was here."

I glanced at her. She wasn't exactly acting like a murderer. In fact, she was acting suspiciously like a woman who had just given birth and wanted, rather desperately, to enjoy every minute of her time alone before returning to full-time teaching and overtime parenting. "I'm afraid you'll have to check with ahh . . . food services about that."

"Oh, I thought you were with food services." She scowled at me. "Blue for cafeteria. Purple for surgeons. Green for baby nurses . . . "

Panic sprinted through me. "Oh!" I glanced at my purloined shirt. "Is this blue?"

She raised her brows at me. "Ahh, yeah."

I laughed. It sounded like the croak of a dying seal. "Don't tell my husband. He swears I'm color blind. Sorry. I should have introduced myself. I'm . . . " Not a nurse; they did all the work. Not janitorial; I'd probably be required to clean a toilet or something. "Doctor . . . " I swallowed and scanned the room, desperately searching for inspiration: blood pressure cuff, sink, rolling dresser crammed with flowers, plastic cups, tissues. "Kleenex."

"Dr. Kleenex?" Her eyes made perfect circles as her brows shot upward. "Really?"

"Yes. Crazy. I know." Believe me.

"I thought I'd met the entire OB staff. But I would have remembered Dr. Kleenex."

I chuckled. Please kill me. "I'm new. Just . . . gathering some stats today . . . for research. Collecting information regarding . . . " Why was I here? Why? Why? Why? "The days immediately preceding delivery. To determine how subsequent births change the landscape of a pregnancy." Dear God, make

243

me stop. "So this is your . . . third baby?"

"Fifth."

Holy shit! Really? Why? "And when was that exactly?"

"About ten minutes after I showed up at the front desk. You guys need to expedite the check-in process for women in labor."

"I'll be sure to make a note of that. So you delivered . . ." I took a stab in the dark. "Yesterday?"

"At 7:25 p.m.!" She sounded a little panicked. Why? I watched her. "So I can spend the night, right?"

"Ahh . . . " What was she afraid of? "I guess you'll have to clear that with your attending—"

"You're not going to send me home tonight, are you? It's my turn to feed the horde."

"What?"

"Mondays, Wednesdays, and Fridays, I cook. Tuesdays, Thursdays, and Saturdays, it's up to Tom. Sundays, they're with my mother-in-law . . . God bless her." She paused, looking winded. "Please don't send me home yet."

"I'm sure they won't—"

"I'm not feeling the best anyway."

"I'm sorry to—"

She coughed. "Kind of weak."

"I'll make certain someone checks your . . . "

"You want to make sure I'm up to caring for the new baby, right?"

"We won't let you go home until you're well rested," I lied.

"Really?" She sounded breathy with hope, causing guilt to almost overwhelm the panic in my system.

"Of course. Now if we could just get back to this survey. It's fairly extensive, I'm afraid, but the sooner done, the sooner you can rest." I tapped a few keys as if I had some idea what I was doing. "So how were you feeling one week ago . . . say . . . on Sunday?"

"Like I've felt for the last month. Gassy. Angry. Hungry. Wait!" She paused, thinking. "Sunday's the day I checked in."

I glanced up sharply. "Checked in?"

"Yeah. Contractions started about nine at night. I was so excited. Tom's mom had to keep the kids overnight. I was sure I was going to get out of Monday night dinner, too. But then my uterus just . . . " She shook her head, looking crestfallen. "It just gave up. We had mac and cheese. Again."

"So let me get this straight. You were here . . . in the hospital . . . last Sunday night."

"Yeah. I had the chicken Alfredo and two pieces of that swirly cheesecake." She sighed. "It was fantastic."

"Well . . . " As alibis went, hers was top shelf. "I guess that's all I need." I firmly tapped a key as if shutting down a program. "Thank you for your time."

"We're done?"

"Yes, and I've got to run. Thanks again for—"

"You're going to tell them not to send me home, right? I have a cough. Maybe a fever. And my stitches itch!" She threw back her blankets, baring her lower half. I shrunk back as my gaze skittered to her bottom. "Probably infected. Maybe you could take a look," she suggested, but I was already bolting out the door, stomach heaving.

Thirty-one

"Relax, will you? You're all crazy. It's not a competition."
—Chrissy McMullen to her adolescent brothers

"Did you talk to Glen?" Laney asked. I could hear baby Mac cooing in the background. Or maybe it was her husband. Being in Laney's proximity tends to make males gibber like infants, regardless of age.

"He was golfing," I said and stroked Harley's ear. He sighed happily, stretched tree-limb legs over the armrest of the couch, and settled his snout on my thigh.

"Does one punt or chip in snowdrifts?" she asked.

"Why would Mom lie?"

"Isn't it the McMullen go-to form of self-defense?"

"Do you think he's really sick?"

"I think you should go find out."

"You mean . . ." I felt my stomach cramp. "Go to Schaumberg?"

"Yes."

"In person?"

"Unless you have a clone you could send."

"Hasn't Solberg invented some sort of hologram or something?"

"Honey?" She raised her voice slightly.

"Yes, angel face?" He was wheezing a little when he answered. Probably because he had dashed in from another county when he heard her murmur his name. To say that J.D. Solberg is smitten is like saying the pope wears a funny hat.

"How's that interactive hologram coming along?"

"Oh baby, I'm almost there," he said, then oozed a stream of technobabble so intense I felt nerdy just listening to it.

"Did you get that?" she asked.

"Holy f—foly," I said.

I could hear her grin. "Yes, I think you should go there in person."

"But . . . you've met my family."

"They're not that bad."

"They are," I argued. "They really are."

"Your dad's sick."

"Maybe. Or maybe" —I dropped my voice to a conspiratorial murmur—"it's a diabolical hoax."

"With what goal in mind?"

"To convince me to return to Illinois."

"If they want to see you badly enough to construct such an elaborate ruse, you should go there anyway."

"Maybe they plan to steal my brain," I whispered.

"You think?"

"Yeah. Until they steal my brain."

She laughed. I took that opportunity to change the subject.

"How's the farm search going?"

"I quit searching."

"Because you realized that raising a kid, being a superstar, and tolerating Solberg is challenging enough for one lifetime?"

"Well, that and because I already *bought* a farm."

"What?" I straightened abruptly enough to startle Harlequin. But then, Harley was once startled by clouds.

"I bought a farm!"

"You're kidding me!"

"It's gorgeous, Mac," she gushed. "Amazing."

I remained silent, dumbstruck, and something else I hadn't quite figured out.

"Mac?"

"That's fantastic! I'm so happy for you."

"What's wrong?"

"Nothing. Will Solberg keep his mansion?"

"I haven't told him yet."

"What? Why?"

"Well . . . I don't know how he'll feel about it. He's not exactly a country boy."

"Or a real live boy."

"You're right," she said, and sighed lustily. "He's all man."

"Excuse me," I said, and made a gagging noise. She laughed even though my heart wasn't fully into the retching. How could it be? Laney had just made one of the biggest decisions of her life without my advice. On the other hand, she deserved to have castles and hot tubs and equestrian swimming pools big enough to sail a yacht in. It was about time she started acting like the princess goddess she truly was.

"When are you going to come see it?" she asked.

"I'm not sure."

"What are you doing tomorrow afternoon?"

"How do you know it's not a whom?"

There was a quizzical silence. I scowled. The Laney I knew from Holy Name, the girl with the ugly pigtails and the orthodontic headgear, would have known exactly what I was talking about, but I didn't show my disillusionment.

"As in whom am I doing," I explained.

She ignored me, which, actually, was pretty standard Laney. "Mac, please don't do anything stupid."

"What are you talking about? I'm not going to."

"So you don't have Jeen ferreting out privileged information?"

"Psstt." I made an air-leaving-a-hose noise. "What makes you think that?"

"He shut the door of his office."

"Wow?" I cleverly made it sound like a question.

"And when I asked what he was working on, his ears turned pink."

"A sure sign that he's been out in the sun for more than twenty seconds."

"And a guilty conscience."

I gasped. "Maybe he's having an affair."

She didn't even bother to consider that possibility. What would it be like to be so secure that you wouldn't even pause to think about it? "He's working on something he promised not to tell me about, isn't he?"

"That's ridiculous."

"Should I call him in here again and ask him to explain himself."

"Are you trying to break his mind?"

"Listen, I'm not going to ask again that you refrain from doing . . . whatever it is you're trying to do. Just . . . please be careful."

"I will be. I am."

She sighed, slow and long suffering. "Any idea what's going on with Micky?"

I didn't want to disturb her, but I was desperate for her input. Laney is not only stunningly beautiful, she has one of the most agile minds in the known universe. No one said life's fair. "I guess Lavonn's been doing some . . . investigating."

"Lavonn Blount."

"Yeah."

"And?"

"She found some photographs of . . . of Micky and . . . some kids."

"What kind of photographs?" Her voice was low, as if she dreaded the answer.

"Pornographic."

"No." She breathed the word.

"I just . . . " I closed my eyes, shutting out the world for a second. "I can't believe he'd do such a thing."

"Because you don't *want* to believe or because it's beneath his moral capacity?"

I thought about that for a moment, remembering my last conversation with him. His worry, his hope, his smile. "Because of the sequoias," I said.

"What about them?"

"He said he was planning a trip to King's Canyon with Jamel."

"Okay."

"When he first came to see me he was riddled with guilt. Periodically suicidal."

She thought about that for a moment. "So if he was

involved with child pornography the remorse would kill him . . . literally."

"He sure wouldn't be planning a vacation with his kid." I shook my head. "He's not perfect. Not by a long shot. But I can't believe he's guilty of something this heinous."

"Then he isn't."

"What?"

"You're a good judge of character, Mac."

I considered that for a second. "You must have forgotten about my first hundred or so boyfriends."

"Wouldn't that be nice," she said.

Thirty-two

"You don't need a Do Not Disturb *sign. You need a* Disturbed as Hell. Save Yourself *sign."*

  —Chrissy McMullen, upon finding her brother James
  mysteriously hanging from an ankle in their parents' garage

"How was your first gig?" I asked.

Jeremy Jones was a budding musician, Ozzy Osbourne–dark and David Bowie–scrawny. His parents had sent him to me because of suspected homosexuality, about which they were "extremely evolved," and other issues, which were a little more vague.

"Play any George Strait? *Amarillo by Morning,* maybe? *All My Exes?*"

He snorted. It was as jovial as he ever got.

I settled into my chair and let the accustomed silence sift between us. "Your solos go all right?"

"I guess."

"And your vocalist . . . did she get over her bronchitis?"

"She was okay," he said, but there was something in his tone that suggested a little more than okay.

I let it slide . . . for now. "What about your parents? Did they show up?"

His lips tightened. I waited. Waiting, as it turns out, is one of my most effective tools. I lifted an eyebrow, my second favorite implement, but he said nothing. My arsenal was just about empty.

"No."

I analyzed the tone, the body language, the expression. "Did you tell them about it?"

His foot, shod in a laced black boot, bounced twice. "No."

"Hard for them to support you, then."

"Like they would anyway."

I shrugged, trying to hold on to the jovial Jeremy for as long as possible. "If they wouldn't anyway, why not tell them?"

He didn't answer.

"Were you more afraid they'd come or that they wouldn't?"

Still nothing.

"Or both?"

"I don't care what they do."

Right. And I was a flyweight boxer with cauliflower ears and a storied past. But enough about me; I was losing him. I could see him sliding into the abyss of his own self-involvement.

I reached for a lifeline: shock and awe. "Why not tell them the truth?" I asked.

"I told you, they wouldn't have come anyhow."

"Not that."

He scowled his question.

"That you're straight," I said and watched his eyebrows shoot into the blond roots of his ebony hair.

"Hi." Principal Heyd stepped out of his SUV. He looked cool, intelligent and well-dressed.

I felt hot, dumb as a chunk of coal, and raggedy, though I had dressed carefully. My classy ensemble consisted of a secondhand Dior suit and painfully cute caged heels. I closed the door of my Saturn cautiously behind me. It was daylight, we were in the parking lot of a trendy new restaurant, and Heyd didn't seem to be armed with anything deadlier than a killer smile. But a girl can't be too careful. Someone once tried to murder me in a car wash. No kidding.

"Hi," I said.

"Thanks for coming."

"Thanks for asking me," I said, but I wasn't really all that appreciative. In fact, I was about two seconds from jumping back into my little automobile and screaming toward home.

He motioned toward the restaurant. "I've heard good things about this place."

I nodded but didn't take my eyes off him. One never knows when her current date is going to pull a cannon from the pocket of his extremely well-fitted khakis.

"Are you okay?" He was beginning to look concerned. Perhaps it was my silence, or maybe I looked like I was about to stab him in the eye with my keys and make a run for it.

"Yes, of course," I said.

"Good. After you."

After *me*? *After* me? My skin crawled as I turned my back. But I braced myself and headed toward the restaurant. He opened the door and ushered me through. Inside, the walls were paneled with corrugated metal, mismatched boards, and aging timbers. But I barely noticed the rustic ambiance. My attention was still focused on the dagger that was probably going to be stabbed between my shoulder blades at any given moment.

"Welcome to the Holler," someone said. "Where . . . " The salutation halted. "Scarlet?"

I snapped my head to the left. A giant in single-strapped overalls was staring at me. Memories stormed in. Memories of backbreaking labor and come-ons lame enough to make a grown woman weep. I opened my mouth to speak, but he had already wrapped me in a hug that threatened breakage and possible dismemberment.

"Love bucket!" He swung me around like the proverbial sack of feed, then set me on my feet before I could knee him in the groin. "Look at you." He pushed me to arm's length, which was a considerable distance, and scanned me, heels to hair. "Ain't you the swanky one! What you doin' here?"

"I . . . " Couldn't seem to fish a single thought out of my scattered brain, much less parlay that thought into some semblance of articulation. "How . . . "

"Me and Rom bought us a place here in the big city."

"Romulus is here, too?"

He grinned. "Since you helped us work out our differences, we're like brothers."

"You *are* brothers." I sounded weak. Weak and pale and just about ready to pass out.

"Wait till I tell Momma."

God save me! I glanced around. Momma Hughes, aka Big Bess, was the approximate size of a tank but not quite as cuddly.

"She'll be tickled pink."

"I . . . please don't bother her."

He laughed, that deep-throated chuckle I remembered. "You don't need to worry. She ain't so protective as she once was. She's got herself a beau."

"A . . . " I shook my head. The truth was, I had never been entirely certain what species she claimed as her own.

"Fact is . . . " He paused. I caught my breath, waiting for the hammer to fall, and found that he was flushed, blushing like a debutant. "I sorta have a special someone my own self." He nodded to the left. A thirty-something demigod with dark hair and smoldering eyes nodded back.

"Holy hell," I breathed. Back in the original holler, I had suggested that he consider the possibility that he might be batting for the home team. I hadn't, however, expected the captain of the home team to look like a dark-haired Thor.

"But here I am yappin' your ear off and you're probably hungry enough to sauté a skunk. Come on in. Come in. You, too." He ushered Principal Heyd in behind me. "Best table in the house," he said and motioned us toward a fenced-off area that looked as if it might be a mud pit.

"Is that a . . . "

"Mud pit? Yeah." He chuckled. "I thought it was kinda low class, but Graham"—he glanced toward the demigod again—"said you couldn't go too far in L.A. Wanna try it?"

"I—"

"Just ribbin' ya, love monkey. You look good enough to eat," he said and winked. I winced. While schlepping meals at the Home Place, I had been somewhat concerned that the oversized twins might actually be cannibals. "What can I get you to drink? It's on the house. Anything you want. A Pigpen, maybe? Or a Slick Crick?"

I asked for an ice water. My date did the same, after which we sat in dumbfounded silence for a trio of seconds before speaking at once.

"So you—"

"It's a long story!"

He stared at me, lips twitching. "But an interesting one, I bet."

"No! Nope." I fiddled with the bent tines of a tarnished fork laid on the burlap tablecloth. "Boring, really. Boring as beans."

"Really?"

"Just your average, everyday . . . " I shook my head, feeling a little woozy as I motioned vaguely at the swinging door through which Remus had disappeared. "We're just . . . friends . . . casual friends."

"I see."

"Howdy." We glanced up at the woman carrying colorful drinks on a battered wooden tray. I have no idea what they were. But it was a moot point; her ensemble snagged my attention. She was dressed in a sleeveless plaid shirt and a camouflage skirt barely big enough to stick on a postcard. "How y'all doin' today?"

Heyd grinned. "Excellent. How are you?"

"Happy as a pig in a puddle. I brought you some drinks."

"We didn't order any—" I began, but she interrupted.

"They're on the house. A Salty Stallion for the gentleman."

I shook my head, but Heyd was already reaching for the sunset-colored beverage.

"Thank you.

"And a Frisky Filly for the little lady."

"Please kill . . . " I began, but at that second I realized the similarity between her outfit and the ensemble I had worn while waitressing at the Home Place just months before. I felt myself pale.

"Compliments of Re," she tittered.

I managed a thank-you.

"No problem a'tall. You need anything . . . anything at all, you just say yahoo," she said and swiveled away, blond curls bouncing against half-bared boobs.

"Yahoo," Heyd said.

She twisted back with a smile.

"Just practicing," he said.

She giggled and left. I kind of hoped I'd die before the appetizers arrived.

"I'll pay you," Heyd said.

I turned my dazed attention toward my date.

"For even an abridged version of the story."

"It's nothing. Really."

"There was a giant at the door who called you *love bucket.* Pardon me for saying so, but I actually think that might be the definition of a story."

"You say potato . . . " I took a sip of my drink. It was fantastic. "I say potahto."

"Really?"

"No. No one says potahto."

He chuckled. "At least tell me why he called you Scarlet."

I drank again, fortifying.

"Let me get you started," he said. "You're Christina McMullen, compassionate psychologist to the denizens of Eagle Rock and friend to the Amazon Queen."

"How did you—"

"I'm pretty good on the Internet. Have to be to stay ahead of the kids. You are, by all accounts . . . well . . . " He waggled his head. "*Almost* all accounts, an excellent therapist."

"Almost all—"

"But what you're really good at is solving crimes."

"What? No!" I actually reared back. "What are you talking about?"

"Come on. You think your exploits haven't made the news?"

"What exploits? No. News? That's crazy."

He settled back in his chair, expression somber, if a bit pitying. "I'm not going to hurt you, Christina. You can trust me. You know that, don't you?"

"Of course. Yes." I drank again, feeling frantic and a little lightheaded. "Why wouldn't I?"

"Because your life has been compromised by a number of people in your past."

I neither denied nor confirmed.

"It's one of the reasons I wanted to meet with you."

I raised my gaze to his, breath held.

"I'm hoping you can help me figure out this Lieberman-Micky mess."

"Help how?"

He shrugged. "What do you think happened?"

"You know the situation better than I do."

"Maybe I thought I did. Now . . . " He exhaled heavily, wiped the moisture from the Salty Stallion with his thumb. The digit looked broad and capable. "Dammit!" The expletive shocked me. Honest to God, I thought principals were not only legally prohibited from cursing, but physically incapable. "What a clusterfuck. Do you think Micky killed him?"

I said nothing.

"Is he capable of such a thing?"

I stared at him, remembering the Micky who had sometimes paced my office like a panther, angry, frustrated, and volatile as nitroglycerin. "I think . . . " I cleared my throat. "Most of us are capable of violence in the right circumstances."

His face remained expressionless, then he glanced away, watching as our waitress served another table. "I suppose I shouldn't expect anything else from you. I mean, your profession necessitates confidentiality. And hey . . . " His shoulders rose and fell. "Maybe I deserve to lose my job."

I froze, straw almost to my lips. "You're going to get fired?"

"I hired them, right? So I'm responsible for their actions."

I didn't agree. But I didn't entirely disagree. "Did you check their credentials?"

"Of course. I mean, Mr. Lieberman had changed jobs a few time, and I knew he was strict, but the field of education isn't for weaklings. Kids these days . . . *some* kids . . . aren't getting enough structure at home. They've got to learn to toe the line somewhere."

"There wasn't anything in his past that worried you?"

He sighed. "A somewhat messy divorce, but nothing that would lead me to expect something like *this*."

"What about Micky?"

He stared at me, jaw set, then glanced away again. "They're going to scream racial bias."

"What?"

"I'm black. He's black." He shrugged and drank. "But I didn't hire him because of it."

"Why *did* you hire him?"

"Any number of reasons. He was great with the kids, not too soft, not too strict. He's intelligent, insightful, humorous, and . . . "

I waited. He didn't speak. "And black?"

"Is that so bad?" He leaned forward abruptly. "I mean, half my classroom is filled with kids who look like me . . . who look like him. Is it so terrible to find them a role model with a similar skin tone?"

"No."

He pinned me with his eyes, then exhaled heavily and settled back against the distressed rungs of his chair. "If I tell you something, will you swear to keep it confidential?"

"I don't know if I can—"

"Unless you're indicted. If you're legally bound, I'll understand of course."

My stomach twisted. "Okay."

"He's been accused of sexual misconduct."

I didn't admit that I was already privy to that information. "No. Micky?"

He nodded.

"There must be some mistake."

"About being assaulted?" He raised haunted eyes to mine. "Can you be wrong about something like that?"

I tried to assure myself that I wasn't personally involved in this. But I was. Micky was not only a client, he was a friend. I took another sip of my Frisky Filly. "So you believe in the veracity of the accusation?"

"Experts seem to agree that it's unlikely for an individual, especially an underage individual, to lie about such a thing."

Oh God. "So she, or he . . . was a minor?"

"A student, yes."

"Male or female?"

He was silent a second. "The accusation was anonymous."

"Have y'all made a decision?"

We glanced up in unison. Our waitress beamed at us.

"I'm sorry," Heyd said. "We haven't had a chance to look at our menus yet."

"Well, don't you worry none. I was told to give you the queen-bee treatment. You just yahoo when you're ready. I'll be here quicker than a squirrel with the squirts," she said and hustled away, rear end waggling.

Heyd turned back to me. His eyes were still worried, but the corners of his lips lifted the slightest degree. "It's a little more . . . rustic here than I expected. I hope you're not insulted."

"Insulted?"

"My mother would be appalled if she knew I had brought a sophisticated woman like you to a joint like this."

"Oh. Well, thank you," I said and picked an imaginary speck of lint from the lapel of my jacket. "But I enjoy seeing the more . . . primitive side of life now and—"

"What the fuck?"

I turned to my left with a snap. Sure enough, speaking of primitive . . . Lieutenant Jack Rivera stood not four feet from our table, growling like a wolverine.

Thirty-three

"You ask me, every parent-teacher conference should come with a shot of tequila and a bottle of Advil."
—Principal Heyd, after a few too many tequilas and not enough Advil

"Rivera! How—" I rasped, but true to social norms, he interrupted me.

"What are you doing here?"

Anger zapped me like a blowtorch at his barbaric tone, but I remembered that sophistication comment and held onto the rage with clawing fingernails. "Hand . . . *Ben,*" I corrected, "this is Jack Rivera. Rivera, Benjamin Heyd."

Rivera seared me with his eyes for another eternity, then snapped his attention to Handsome Heyd. "If you have additional information, you should be talking to the officer in charge of the investigation."

"What?" I said and turned from one to the other.

"I'm afraid the officer in charge hasn't been forthcoming

with a plethora of helpful facts," Heyd said.

"What's going on?" I asked.

"The investigation is ongoing," Rivera snarled.

"So I'm supposed to wait patiently while one of my teachers is buried and the other catatonic?"

"You know each other?" My grip on the anger was beginning to slip a little. Maybe Heyd heard it in my voice, because he actually deigned to respond.

"Lieutenant Rivera here was good enough to visit my office a few days ago."

"And Heyd was foolish enough to ignore my advice completely."

"Ms. McMullen's record for solving crimes is quite extraordinary," Heyd said.

"Ms. McMullen's record—" Rivera began, but someone interrupted him. It was about damned time.

"Perhaps it is not that *her* record is so impressive," crooned a voice. "But that yours is so lacking, Lieutenant."

I glanced right and felt my heart strike my ribs like a Chinese gong. Hiro Jonovich Danshov stood beside our table. He was dressed in an unimposing loose-weave shirt and drawstring pants. His burnt-amber hair was pulled back into a sissy-ass man bun. But he still looked *GQ* sophisticated, Navy SEAL tough. How he managed that might have something to do with a pact he'd made with the devil years before. Or his sea-storm eyes.

"Stay out of this, Danshov," Rivera snarled.

"While I recognize the wisdom in such a suggestion," Hiro agreed, "I fear I cannot."

"The hell you can't."

He spread his artist's hands. "For this is my

establishment."

"Yours!" Rivera laughed. "From what I hear, you're nothing more than a short-order cook."

Danshov smiled, slowly, dangerously. "Nevertheless, I will not have you disturbing my customers." He shifted his kill-me-now gaze to mine. Something shivered up from below decks. "You are well, Ms. O'Tara?"

"Yes, I um . . . " Okay, Hiro Danshov and I have a past checkered with a couple of kisses and colored with a thousand bruises, but there was something about him. Something that made men growl and women purr. I contained that purr and the girlish giggle that threatened to follow. "I'm fine."

He held me bound in his gaze for an endless moment, then nodded once, as if in complete agreement. "Indeed," he said.

And, God help me, that's when it happened. That's when I let that regrettable, puerile giggle escape. Maybe it was the stress of the situation. Maybe it was the Frisky Filly. And maybe, God forgive me, it was simply a girlish impulse caused by swimming in a vat of unfettered testosterone.

Whatever the reason, Danshov glided toward me, Heyd stared wide-eyed, and Rivera, that territorial caveman, stepped close and grabbed the front of Danshov's shirt in both hands.

"Stay the hell away from her!" he growled.

Danshov lifted his eyes to Rivera's. Their gazes struck, amber on quicksilver. "I only wish to see to her well-being."

"Her well-being? Is that what you call it when you beat the hell out of a woman?"

"Still, you underestimate her," Danshov said and shifted his gaze back to mine. "I see fire where you see but embers."

"Touch her again and you won't be seeing anything for a

week!" Rivera vowed and shoved him.

Danshov stepped away, then twisted and kicked, striking with his heel. Rivera took the impact on his chest, stumbled backward, then charged.

A woman gasped. A man yelled. Patrons scattered. A chair crashed to the floor.

Someone grabbed my arm, tugging me from the melee, but I barely noticed. The combatants faced off, circling each other like baited bears.

"Hey, sweet cakes, you okay?"

I turned vaguely, still held in a steely grip. Romulus, previously known as Thing One, seemed to be speaking to me but grinning at the combatants, giant left hand clenching and unclenching.

"What?" My mind felt murky. Danshov was speeding toward Rivera, performing a flying dropkick, but the lieutenant caught his leg. They hit the floor together.

Rom grinned. "Listen, firecracker, maybe you should git while the gittin's good."

"Good?" I echoed vaguely.

Patrons were dashing toward the door like potheads at the sound of police sirens.

"There's a clear path through the kitchen," Rom said and turned toward my half-forgotten date. "Take her through there and out the back, will ya?"

"Oh." Heyd seemed as surprised to be called into service as I was to find him still there. "Right. Thank you."

Rom nodded, lowered his head, and waded into the brawl.

Heyd was already steering me toward the rear of the building. Behind us, pandemonium reigned. In a matter of moments, however, we were standing safely near my car.

"Well . . . " Principal Heyd glanced toward the restaurant and grinned crookedly. "That was . . . " He paused, apparently short on euphemisms for *weirder than shit*. "Is your life always this . . . interesting?"

I shook my head, ready to lie, to assure him that my days generally lazed along as boring as wood shavings, but I couldn't quite muster such a whopper. "Yeah. Actually, pretty much just like this."

He chuckled, glanced toward the restaurant, then turned back to me again. "Ms. O'Tara?"

"What?" The question sounded kind of . . . misty to my ears, as if I'd been swaddled in wet cotton and left in the sun to dry.

"He, ahhh . . . the good-looking Bruce Lee guy . . . he called you Ms. O'Tara."

"Did he?"

"Yes."

"Oh."

He shrugged. "Any particular reason."

"No. Uh uh. I don't think so."

"It's not . . . a pseudonym or something?"

I turned toward him, a modicum of reality finally slivering through the insanity. "I don't know . . . I didn't think . . . I mean, I knew he was around. 'Cause, you know, he said . . .and anyway, who else would shove bushels of kale into my refrigerator like . . . But Rivera, he's . . . And the Things . . . " My voice drifted away. I glanced toward the restaurant again.

"Yeah," Heyd said. "I have no idea what you're talking about."

I exhaled heavily and forced my mind back to the present. "Consider yourself lucky," I said. Popping the Saturn's locks with hands that were just slightly unsteady, I slid behind the steering wheel and left the insanity behind.

Thirty-four

"Evidence is fairly conclusive that the principle purpose of female breasts is to make men act like idiots."
—Gertrude Nelson (aka Athena), premed student and topless Vegas performer

It took a good fifteen minutes before my mind was working full-steam again. By then I was almost home. I pulled out my smartphone when it rang, saw the number, and debated ignoring it. But who was I to eschew a good-looking man with an actual IQ?

"Benjamin?"

"Ms. Sweet Cakes?"

I considered sliding under my seat in shame, but since traffic on the 5 was zipping along at an unprecedented twenty miles per hour, I thought it best to remain upright. "Listen, Ben . . . I hope those . . . gentlemen . . . at the restaurant didn't . . . sully my reputation. I mean, I hardly even know them."

"So casual acquaintances call you 'firecracker'?"

I ground my teeth, loosed my grip on the steering wheel long enough to flip off the motorist who had just cut me off, and felt a little better.

"And passing strangers stop by to warn you against getting involved?"

I cleared my throat and ignored the sarcasm. "Well, no, I have been . . . familiar . . . with Lieutenant Rivera for quite some time."

"Familiar?"

"It's a long story."

"I'd love to hear it."

"I'm pretty sure you're mistaken."

He laughed. "Can I see you again?"

The word *why* galloped through my mind, but I lassoed it. Maybe he just liked me. Maybe he didn't plan to murder me in my sleep. Perhaps he didn't even hope to hold me hostage until I surrendered whatever information he might be looking for. Stranger things have happened. Maybe. "My schedule is pretty tight," I said.

"It *does* look like a full-time job."

I puzzled over that for a second. "What does?"

"Fighting off all those gallants who are battling for your attention."

"I think you may have misinterpreted the situation, Mr. Heyd."

"I'm pretty sure I've got it nailed . . . Ms. Love Bucket," he said, then sobered. "I keep expecting to wake up and find out it was all a horrible mistake. That my educators are all well, that the police aren't knocking on my door."

"Rivera can seem a little intimidating."

He paused a second. "You're diplomatic, too?"

"What?"

"I would have said he was bat-shit crazy."

Once home, I parked the Saturn in its usual spot on Opus and hurried inside. It wasn't that I was nervous, exactly. But there had been no attempts on my life in several weeks and I was hoping to extend that fortuitous trend.

It was Saturday afternoon. I intended to clean my toilet, tidy up the house, and go for a run. But Harley's longing glance at his empty bowl convinced me to shop for groceries (his and mine), after which I consumed a goodly portion of those groceries (mine only) and fell onto the couch into a post-consumptive coma.

The dreams that followed involved a corpulent me tied to a giant chocolate-chip tree. A half dozen man-beasts cavorted in the campfire light in varying states of dishabille.

I felt disoriented and Goodyear-blimpish when the phone rang.

"How's it going?" Elaine's voice was upbeat.

"Good." I tried to make mine the same. I may have managed muzzy. I tugged my feet out from under Harley's bony rear end. The left foot was entirely numb. "Fantastic."

"Yeah?"

"Absolutely."

"Well, you've always liked to have men act like battling baboons over you."

I considered that while trying to slap feeling back into my toes. "Tell me the truth, are you spying on me?"

She neglected to answer. I didn't know if that was a yes or a no. "Are you okay?"

"I think so."

"What's up?"

Not my self-image. The man-beasts had seemed more interested in the chocolate-chip tree than in me. "Has Solberg learned anything yet?"

"So I was right. He is checking into something for you."

"Have you ever been wrong?"

"Several times."

I refrained from begging her to share one of those instances just to inflate my flagging self-esteem. "What does he know?"

"You should talk to him about that."

"Do I have to?"

"Come to dinner tonight."

"At Solberg's place?" I knew my tone was sketchy. I also knew that I shouldn't call it *Solberg's* place. His ungodly union with Laney, after all, made it her house, too. But I had never quite been able to reconcile her earthy goodness with the chrome curiosity he called home sweet home. I wasn't sure, however, she'd fit into a turreted estate that was still expecting an attack from the redcoats either.

"Six o'clock."

"Okay," I agreed, and tried to pretend that the cavorting man-beasts of my dreams had been more disturbing than arousing.

Thirty-five

"I didn't say I was still angry, I said if he ever gets trampled by a crash of rhinoceroses, I hope someone's got a camcorder handy."
—Cindy Peichel, zookeeper and environmentalist, who might not be entirely over her fiancé's infidelity

"Babykins!" Solberg crowed.

What is it about me that makes men feel the need to label me with idiotic monikers? "Geekster," I said and tried not to limp as I stepped inside, but there was something about the ultramodern monstrosity he called home that made my most recent injuries throb.

"How's life in the psycho world?"

"I don't know. How is it?"

He heehawed a laugh. So nice to be able to slide seamlessly into my former life. "Angel's waiting for you." He generally referred to Laney as *angel*. It was just one of the 4,047 things about him that irritated me most.

Laney, on the other hand, I had loved since the day she

decked Sam Shinder for trying to peek at her Wonder Woman undies. She stood now in the middle of a space-age kitchen, elbow deep in something that looked like green brains. Laney's smart, talented, and disgustingly pretty, but her homemade concoctions can make even a consummate eater like myself take a kinder view of fasting.

"Whatcha making there, Lane?" I asked and set a box of organic chocolates on the counter.

"Linguine and kale with lemongrass sauce."

"Looks yummy."

She laughed. "You okay?"

"Yup. Where's Mac?"

"Sleeping. I think you're good luck. This is the first time in forty days and forty nights."

"No wonder you look so awful," I said and tried not to be jealous of the bushels of strawberry-flax hair, the nonexistent waist, the perfectly rounded hips. She was, if I wasn't mistaken, back in the jeans she had worn in high school. If there was a God in heaven, surely she would have cellulite growing like cauliflowers on her thighs.

"Thanks for taking time out of your busy schedule to see me."

I snorted.

She grinned. "It's gotta be rough fighting off all those besotted knights."

Her statement was terribly close to something Principal Heyd had said. "Who have you been talking to?" I asked and took an organic carrot from the ceramic bowl next to my candy.

"Baby Mac mostly," she said. "And then it's generally begging him to sleep."

I took a seat at the counter. It was made of some sort of space-age Plexiglas. Triangular lights hung over a stainless-steel table. "So you haven't spoken to anyone at Branford?"

The oven timer dinged. Probably announcing the doneness of some inedible concoction made of sea asparagus that's been previously regurgitated by beluga whales.

"I've got to make the salad. Jeen, why don't you tell her what you've found?"

Oh good, we were having salad in addition to green brains. Plus, I got to spend time with the geektard.

"Okee doke. Come into my parlor," he said.

The invitation was as creepy as hell, but I was no longer worried about my virtue where he was concerned. Since meeting Laney, other women had ceased to exist in Solberg's world. Megan Fox could don a purple bustier with fishnet stockings and sit on his face. He'd do nothing more scandalous than claw his way free and scamper home like a balding spider monkey.

Unlike the remainder of the house, his office was cluttered with notes, pictures, and unidentified gadgets. It was also state-of-the-art. I had been inside that hallowed sanctum once before while trying to ascertain if anyone in the world might be delusional enough to want to kidnap him. Another long story.

"It took some time and my particular brand of genius," he said, settling his bony ass into the chair behind his keyboard. "But I achieved my objective."

"You got Dad's medical information?"

"Oh . . ." He glanced up. "No."

"Why not?"

"I didn't . . . " He shrugged. "It didn't seem right. If you're worried about your father you should talk to him in person."

I narrowed my eyes. "You told Laney about it, didn't you?"

"No!"

"And she told you not to do it."

"Please don't tell her about the vacuum cleaner."

I considered doing just that, but he looked too pathetic to torture. "What've you got?"

Gratitude lit up his face, making him look almost human for a second. "I gained access to a certain something."

I paused for a moment, trying to decipher, then, "You hacked into Micky's emails?"

"Hacked!" He jerked back as if slapped. Considering the barf-worthy come-ons he'd dished out for the past couple decades, I'm sure he's had plenty of experience. "No. Not hacked. Don't say *hacked. Hacked* can get you two to ten in San Quentin. Let's just say I . . . paid a visit."

"Whatever. What did you learn?"

"Invasion of privacy can have serious consequences also."

"I take it you didn't read the emails?"

"What emails?" he asked, expression terrified.

I rolled my eyes. "Bring them up," I said.

"If you go down for intrusion of solitude—"

"I'll say you had nothing to do with it. That I learned everything I know from a YouTube video."

He gave me a dubious look, but a moment later I was alone in his office. I skimmed Micky's correspondence. Most were innocuous: notes to fellow teachers about classes; a long, winding thread concerning an upcoming school dance. According to Sharon Cross, English teacher and misanthrope, Missy Moore could get a little handsy with the boys. Tyrone Clarity was especially prone to her advances. They should watch her like the proverbial bird of prey.

There were a few correspondences with Deirdra Mills. Flirty, lighthearted notes that might have sounded completely harmless if I hadn't met her. Hadn't seen the angst in her eyes. One message was particularly interesting: *Hey, I'm thinking about hiking at Fryman this weekend. Wanna come? I could pack a picnic. Maybe take some shots of the canyon and stuff. You could even keep your clothes on this time if you really wanted to.*

She ended it with a little smiley face, but I wasn't laughing. No matter how I thought about it, I had to conclude that she had taken nude pics of Micky. Could she have, later, photoshopped those images to make him appear guilty of child molestation?

I had no answers. Only more questions as I skimmed other missives.

The first sign of trouble began with a note from Lieberman. It was short and pithy: *If I go down, you go down, stonehead. Don't forget that.*

I winced. It would be so easy to believe the two of them had been selling naked kid pictures together. So easy, if I didn't know Micky. If I hadn't looked into the soulful depths of his eyes on a hundred heart-rending occasions.

Admittedly, he might be guilty of any number of crimes, even murder if he'd felt Lieberman was threatening him or someone else. But child pornography? No way.

So what could Micky go down for? And why the term *stonehead?*

The notes between them were few and far between, but the tension seemed to be escalating. I read on, desperately searching, until my gaze bumped across a note from Lavonn. It was neither short nor pithy. Instead, it was a soulful and filled with nostalgia.

Hey, Mick, I'm sorry about last night. I shouldn't have said the things I did. But Jesus, you're a teacher, you should have known Taye wasn't big enough for that stupid zip-line thing. He could have gotten seriously hurt. Still, now that I've had some time to cool off, I regret getting so wigged out. He had a great time. Good clean fun. Not like for us, huh?

It was different back in the day. We were all a little crazy. A lot desperate. Fighting for our lives, really. Even then, you were the best of us. At least that's what Keneasha thought. I know it's whacked, but sometimes I'm still mad as hell at her. She had everything: looks, brains, personality. I was jealous. All the boys liked her. But now I think maybe if you two had gotten together things would be different.

Anyway, it was just a bloody knee, right? Sorry for the things I said. Hope to see you again soon.

L.

I scowled at the monitor, realizing her note had been sent three weeks before Lieberman had been shot to death in his foyer. Back in October, she had still believed her children were safe with Micky. I skimmed the remainder of Micky's emails. There were only 147. Compared to the zillions waiting on my own PC, it seemed like a pretty low number. Clicking over to his trash bin, I skimmed that, too. At least a half dozen women seemed to be interested in him on a personal level. But I could find no reason to believe any of them wished him ill. Neither could I find anything incriminating in his Sent box.

"How's it going?" Laney stood in the doorway, looking glamorous in faded jeans and a tattered T.

"All right, I guess."

"Learn anything?"

"Yeah, Missy Moore can get kind of handsy with Tyrone

during the school dances."

"Anything else?"

"The other boys might not be safe from her either."

"Hmmff," she said and leaned one shoulder against the doorjamb. "If early promiscuity is any indicator, Missy might make a pretty good psychologist someday."

I called Officer Lawson's cell phone on my way home that night. He answered in a moment.

"Hello?"

"Hi. This is Christina."

There was a pause.

"Christina McMullen."

"Oh, yeah, hi."

An inauspicious beginning, but I forged ahead. "I was wondering if you've learned anything."

"About?"

Was he serious? "Micky Goldenstone's case."

"Oh." He cleared his throat. "There is no case."

"*What?*"

"It's just what it appears to be?"

"Which is?"

"A murder-slash-attempted suicide."

I gritted my teeth, reminding myself to remain civil. "You don't have a problem with the fact that a person attempting suicide would shoot himself in the ribs."

"Listen, Ms. McMullen, I appreciate your concern, but I can't discuss this with you."

"It's because of Rivera isn't it? He told you not to talk to me."

"Try to put this behind you. I realize Mr. Goldenstone is

your client and you want to believe the best about him, but sometimes—"

"Did you even talk to Deirdra?"

A moment of silence, then, "She is not involved in this."

"So you spoke to her?"

"Yes."

"And?"

"Like I said, I'm not at liberty to discuss—"

"She's guilty." I'm not sure how those exact words flew from my mouth, but they were gone, escaped into the ether. Too late to draw them back.

"Her alibi was corroborated by more than one individual." His tone had gone frosty.

"Maybe they were lying."

"They weren't."

"How do you—"

"I heard you could be a pain in the ass."

"So you *did* talk to Rivera," I said, but he had already hung up.

Thirty-six

"Sometimes it is the size of the dog in the fight."
—Micky Goldenstone, who's been called Pit Bull . . . and who
is hung like a horse

"What'd you do with the photos?" I asked.

Lavonn was silent on the other end of the line for a moment then, "What photos?"

"You know what I'm talking about."

"What if I don't?"

"I'm not saying Micky's guilty, Lavonn."

"Kinda sounds like it."

"Maybe you're right. Maybe he's being framed."

There was a long pause fraught with a butt-load of angst. "Yeah. And maybe he's guilty as hell."

"What?" I felt a touch of vertigo from her about-face. "This was your conjecture."

"It's these fucking pictures!" she snarled. "I can't get them out of brain. Out of my . . . " She exhaled shakily.

"So you still have them."

"I wanted to get rid of them. Planned to. But . . . Jesus . . . it's him. It's Mick. Sure as sin."

"What are you going to do?"

She exhaled noisily. "Wouldn't that Jacobs chick have an orgasm if she got them in the mail?"

"What? What Jacobs . . . " I began, but her meaning struck me like a bomb. Kirsten Jacobs was one of those blond goddesses that the television stations manufacture in a back room somewhere and present as regular human beings. "The news anchor? You're not serious."

"If he touched my boys . . . " Her voice had gone flat, a feral blend of weepy and deadly. "If he touched them he deserves worse than a media shitstorm."

"Lavonn, what happened? You used to believe in him. Used to trust him."

"It ain't like I was planning to have his babies or something."

For a second. I almost admitted the truth . . . that judging from the things she'd said, not to mention her email to him, she was kind of hoping to do just that. That she not only trusted him but admired him. That she had allowed her children to spend time with him. But I remembered her temper and her woman-eating dog just in time.

"You liked him," I said. "You can't deny that."

"Yeah, well, just because a brother's hot doesn't mean he's not a douche."

True that. In fact, I could get that little maxim embroidered on a pillow, but I stayed my course. "It doesn't mean he *is* either."

"I see you've still got a thing for him."

I didn't bother to address that but let my mind spin. "Do you know anything about Sharon Cross?"

"Who?"

Apparently, not much, I thought. "The English teacher at Branford Middle School. She didn't seem to lose any sleep over Lieberman's death," I explained. "I don't think she was too crazy about Micky either. In fact, men in general seem to kind of piss her off."

"You think she could have shot them?"

I remembered Cross's heft, her cynicism, her disregard for people in general. "I don't know," I said. It seemed unlikely at best, but I had no one else to pin it on. No one but Micky himself.

"You got any sort of reason she might want to off them, besides the fact that they got balls?"

"She said it's her job to keep the kids safe. Maybe she found out about the pictures, too."

"Okay, so she somehow gets Mick to Lieberman's house . . . *with his gun* . . . shoots both of them, then tosses the murder weapon in the bushes?"

"I admit . . . " I began, then paused, thoughts whirring. "How do you know they found the gun in the bushes?"

"You spend every evening watching *Wheel of Fortune* or what?"

"No," I said and didn't bother telling her about the unlikely amount of time I've spent with *Walker*. "Why?"

"Jacobs did a whole segment on violence in the school system."

I didn't comment.

"No shit? You don't watch the news?"

"Life's depressing enough without it," I said and glanced

through my window to the Al Sadrs'. Their lights were off. They were probably floating in dreamland. I wished I were so lucky. "If there was some sort of child-pornography thing going . . ." I paused, took a breath. "Who would be most damaged by it?"

"Besides the kids?"

"Maybe I should have asked who would be the angriest? Angry enough to kill?"

She exhaled quietly. "I was wondering when you were going to decide it was me who shot them."

"What? I haven't decided—"

"I knew about Mick's gun. Knew where he kept it. In a safe in his closet. He showed it to me. Gave me the combination . . . in case something happened to him."

I could hear myself breathing in the silence.

"What kind was it?"

"How the hell would I know? You think I actually shot him? Killed Lieberman? Tossed the gun?"

"I . . ."

"Well, I didn't!"

My head was spinning. "Okay."

She huffed a breath. "You were right. I liked Mick. Kind of thought everybody did. But maybe it's time we faced the truth."

"Which is?"

"That he's not the guy we thought he was. That . . ." Her voice broke. "Nothing good ever came out of the 'hood."

"You did."

"I'm as messed up as anybody."

"You helped take down Andrews." She had, in fact, lived with the man who had designed a deadly little drug called

Intensity. Had, in the end, helped bring him to justice. But I wasn't entirely sure she had always been on the side of the law during that fiasco.

"I didn't have much choice."

"You took in your sister's son." To me, that was the ultimate sacrifice. I could barely manage an extra dog. "And you're a good mother."

"Yeah, well . . . " She cleared her throat. "They're monsters. But they're all I got."

They're all I got.

Hours later, those words still haunted me. Micky was all Jamel had. What would happen to him if his father was convicted of murder?

I owed it to them both to do all I could to prove his innocence.

Knowing the 5 would be a logjam of fire-breathing motorists I took an alternative route to Van Nuys. Once outside Deirdra's ugly apartment building, I sat in my Saturn for a moment, trying to come up with a decent plan of action. But in the end, I simply marched up to the intercom and hit the buzzer.

"You're early." She sounded bright and happy, entirely changed from the woman I had spoken to just a few days before.

"Deirdra?"

"Who is this?"

Probably a little late to take an alias. "Christina McMullen."

Silence stretched between us. "I'm really sorry about Micky, but I told you everything I know."

"No, you didn't."

"What?" The cheerfulness in her voice had been replaced by a breathless caution.

"I need to speak to you."

"If you don't go away, I'm going to call the cops."

"If you don't talk to me, *I'm* going to call the cops." And say what? I was completely blowing smoke . . . and stunned when the door buzzed. I hauled it open and hurried down the hall before she could change her mind. When she let me in, I saw that her makeup was impeccable, her hair a long, sexy sweep of ebony. But more importantly, she didn't seem to be holding any weapons with which she intended to kill me.

Still, my heart was pounding as I stepped inside and glanced around.

Boxes were stacked on every available surface, some taped shut, some spilling contents from the top.

I caught her gaze. "You're moving?"

"Listen, I don't know what happened between Micky and . . . " Her voice broke. "And Marv."

"I do."

"What?"

I took a deep breath and leapt. "I know about the photographs."

"Oh Jesus!" She clasped her hands over her mouth and stumbled backward.

"You took the pictures, didn't you?"

She shook her head, lacquered nails gleaming in the overhead lights.

"You needed money and you—"

"I'm sorry! I'm so sorry!" she cried and dropped to her knees. "We were just . . . we were just fooling around. It was so hot. Perfect for skinny-dipping. And it was such a pretty shot with the white caps breaking against his thighs. He's got great thighs." She wiped her cheek with the back of her hand, smearing mascara all the way to her ear. "I didn't intend to show it to Marv, but he was losing interest, so I thought maybe if he believed Micky and I had a thing going he'd pay more attention. Maybe finally get around to proposing. I didn't think . . . I didn't think they'd *kill* each other over me," she said and sobbed like a brokenhearted child.

I watched her, brows raised, mind spinning, and when the sobs turned to hiccups, I tottered into her bathroom, released the roll of toilet paper from its confines, and handed it to her. She mopped her face and looked up through soaked lashes.

"I always thought it would be cool to have men duel over me. Romantic, you know? But it's not cool. It's horrible."

"So . . ." I took a breath, trying to think. "You believe they fought because they were both in love with you."

"Yeah. I mean . . ." She blinked, eyes wide and innocent. "Sure . . . why else?"

"The pictures you took of Micky, did you give them to anyone?"

"Like, what do you mean, print them up or something?"

"Or email them. Did anyone else have access to them?"

"No. That'd be weird."

"Uh huh. Could I see them?"

"The nudies of Micky?"

"Yes."

She raised her chin and narrowed her eyes. "If I show them to you, will you promise not to tell my boyfriend about . . . any of this?"

"You have a boyfriend?"

Maybe my surprised tone offended her, because she

287

stiffened a little. "It's a new relationship. Just met him a couple days ago. But with Marv gone . . . " She sniffled, shook her head. "He's been so great. I don't want him to think I'm . . . you know . . . a runaround."

A *runaround*? "He won't find out from me."

"Okay," she said and, taking a deep breath, pattered out of the room. I followed her. Retrieving a camera from the dresser, she turned it on, flipped through images, and handed it to me. There were fourteen shots of Micky. My first thought was . . . well . . . *wow!* My second was that every single picture was full frontal; there was no way any of them could have been altered enough to work in the picture I had seen of him with a child.

"Is this all you have?" I asked.

"What?"

"Did you take any other nude photos of him?"

"Isn't that enough?"

I shook my head, entirely at a loss.

"Hey, baby . . . " A voice sounded from the living area.

We turned in unison.

"You ready to get moved in with the long arm of the law?" Officer Lawson stepped into the doorway.

"Pumpkin!" Deirdra's voice broke as she flung herself into his arms.

He hugged her close, expression perplexed until his gaze fell on me. Then his brows bunched. "What's going on?"

"I have no idea," I said and, taking advantage of the fact that he was tied up in his soon-to-be live-in's embrace, scurried from the apartment.

I called my parents that evening. But no one answered.

Guilt spurred me. I was a terrible daughter. Laney contacted her family regularly. Of course, her father hadn't habitually ignored or embarrassed her, but maybe that was no excuse. I should be able to forgive. I should be like Brooke Haven . . . who, according to Rivera, spoke to her mother even when entertaining guests. Brooke, insightful, cute, perky Brooke. I hated cute, perky women. Insightfulness just added insult to injury. But perhaps it was that very insightfulness that could help me figure out this whole mess.

I thought about that during my commute the next morning. Considered it while I stood in line at the Jitter Bean to order caramel coffee with extra caramel. It wasn't that I was avoiding Tony at Sunrise Coffee . . . exactly. But maybe Elaine was right; maybe I had enough weird men in my life for a while. What with the dark lieutenant battling the fridge-stocking Hiro and Handsome Heyd being, well, handsome, I had a lot on my mind. Not least of which was my current client.

"So have you tried horseback riding?" I asked.

Rose smiled sheepishly from the couch. "Not yet," she said. I wasn't surprised. Oftentimes, my office is where people come to talk about things they'll never do.

"Well, it's nice to explore the possibilities without committing to anything too dangerous."

"But I *do* have an appointment for my first jump."

"What?"

"I've decided to go solo."

"You're going skydiving? Alone?" I couldn't help but be surprised. I was almost fifty years her junior and didn't intend to jump out of a plane anytime soon. Judging by past experiences, someone might push me, but if they did, I planned to do my damnedest to pull them out with me.

"Ultimate Rush L.A."

"I see. Well, I hope they know what they're doing."

"You know what they say."

I shook my head.

"If at first you don't succeed, skydiving's not for you."

I laughed.

"And . . . " She sighed, looking thoughtful. "In the end, you're more likely to regret the things you *didn't* do than the things you did."

"Do you think that's true?"

"I don't know. But I intend to find out."

I sat alone in my office, considering that as Shirley ran out to get us some lunch.

Maybe Rose was right. Maybe it's the things we don't do that we'll regret the most. In which case, I should have asked Shirley to get me a big-ass order of fettuccine Alfredo with breadsticks instead of a cobb salad with dressing on the side.

The front bell dinged. My stomach rumbled. But before I reached my door, it popped open.

I lurched back, right hand already searching my desktop for an impromptu weapon as my visitor stepped inside.

"Angie! What are you doing here?"

Angela Grapier, my favorite green-haired pixie client, stared at me, expression somber. "Dad picked me up after class."

"What?" I asked, heart still pounding in my chest.

She eyed me for a second, then closed the door behind her and settled onto the edge of my couch. "He took me to Punjab Palace."

I swallowed, knowing where this was headed. "I've heard

the naan is excellent—"

"He hates Indian food."

"Well, some people find it a little spicy for—"

"You called him, didn't you?"

"What?"

"You called him. Told him I was thinking about doing Granger. Told him . . . " Her eyes teared up. She wiped her nose with the back of her hand. "He said Abby was his fault."

I shook my head, trying to keep up.

"Said if he'd paid more attention to her maybe she wouldn't have gotten involved with Creole. Maybe she wouldn't have gotten hooked on drugs. Said maybe she knew . . . had known all along . . . that I was his favorite."

I exhaled, drowning in my own guilt. I hadn't meant to cast the blame on him. I had only wanted him to think . . . to see what ignoring his only remaining daughter might cost him. "Angie—"

"He's so sad."

"I'm sorry."

"He wants to . . . " She drilled me with her eyes. "He wants to see you with me. Like a father-daughter counseling thing."

"Okay," I said, cautious.

"I should report you!" she said, jerking to her feet.

I remained silent, unable to argue.

"You had no right to call him!" Her hands were fisted, her teeth clenched. "It's supposed to be confidential. What I tell you is supposed to be just between us."

"You're right," I said.

"I should report you," she repeated and exhaled heavily, hands flexing. "But I guess I'll just . . . thank you," she said and left.

It took me a while to get my bearings after Angie's departure.

I ate my unwanted salad in solitude, stared at the wall for ten minutes, then dialed Brooke Haven's number.

I still didn't know if calling William Grapier was regrettable or laudable. Nevertheless, there was a buttload of other things I *did* regret. So, according to Rose Ungar's theory, I could really regret the things I left undone.

"Hello?"

"Ms. Haven?" I was surprised she picked up, thinking instead that the call would go to voicemail.

"Yes?"

"This is Christina McMullen."

"Who?"

Apparently, I hadn't made a big impression on her the night of Lieberman's death. "Christina McMullen, Micky's friend."

She didn't respond.

"The psychologist?" I said it like a question. Which was stupid. I *am* a psychologist, dammit.

"Oh, yes, of course, I'm sorry. There's just so much going on . . . projects due, my mother . . . " She let the sentence run into nothingness. "What can I do for you?"

I opened my mouth to speak before realizing I had no idea where I wanted to go. Every question I considered sounded foolish. "Your ahhh . . . your mother's all right, I hope."

"Her arthritis is flaring up again. She's got to have another eye exam, and . . . " She chuckled. "I bet you're sorry you asked."

"You're a good daughter," I said and felt another attack of

gnawing guilt.

She sighed. "You think so?"

"I do."

"Thanks. Have you learned anything more about Michael?"

"That's what I wanted to talk to you about."

"Oh no!" She hissed a breath. "Something happened. What is it? Is he gone? Is he—"

"No. He's fine. Well . . ." I stopped, shook my head. "He's not fine. I just . . . No," I said, making my voice firm finally. "As far as I know, his condition remains the same."

At least that's what the nurse had said when I'd called on the previous night. Guilt doubled in volume. I should have gotten an update that morning.

"Well that's . . . hopeful . . . maybe."

I nodded, not quite sure how to continue. "I was wondering if I could come by tonight."

"Come by?"

"I just have a few concerns . . . about Micky."

"Concerns? Surely you don't think Michael's guilty of any wrongdoing."

"You're certain he's not?"

"Yes. Of course. He's a great guy. Everybody loves him."

"Everybody except Mr. Lieberman?"

She paused. "I would have never believed Marv would do such a thing."

"But you do now?"

"I don't know what else to believe."

The rest of the day flew by.

"You going to see Ms. Butterfield's ranch tomorrow?"

"What? Elaine's? I didn't plan to. Why?" I glanced across the case file I'd been updating. Shirley stood in the doorway, ten-gallon purse slung over her shoulder like a fast-draw's gun belt.

"You don't have any appointments until two o'clock."

"Great. We can both sleep in." We had made a few changes in our communications system recently so that Shirley could take office calls at home.

"And spend the morning listening to Dion obsess about that girl that don't have the sense of a flea? No thanks. So, you going?"

"Going to what?"

She narrowed her eyes at me and stepped into my office. "What's up with the two of you?"

"What do you mean? Nothing's up."

"If my best friend in the world bought a zillion-dollar place in the Hills, I'd throw a party and invite God himself."

"Well . . . " Guilt again. "I've been busy."

"Friends are important."

"I know that."

"Then you going to go see her new place?"

"Yes," I said. "Now will you get out of here before you miss your bus?"

"All right." She snugged her purse closer to her bosom. A mugger would have to be a lunatic to try to snatch that thing. Not that the City of Angels is in short supply of lunatics. "I'll see you tomorrow, then."

"Good night."

"And you better have details about every piglet."

I laughed as I juxtaposed that image with the reality of the estate I had seen a few days before. "I don't think it's that kind of farm. But I'll make sure to take notes."

It only took me a few minutes to finish updating my records. I was just filing the card when the door jingled. I turned, already nervous.

"Hey." Brooke Haven smiled, but the expression was a little shaky. "I was just filling a prescription for Mom and realized I wasn't going to make it home before our appointment, so I thought I'd just drop in."

"Oh."

"I hope you don't mind."

"No, of course not. Is everything all right?"

"Yes," she said and started to cry.

On the sidewalk outside, a coffee-bearing pedestrian glanced through the glass door, brows raised.

"What's wrong?" I asked.

"Nothing. I . . . " She shook her head. "Listen, I'm sorry. I'm going to take off before . . . "

"No, please." Another passerby glanced in. "Why don't we talk in my office."

"I don't want to bother you. I mean . . . " She hiccupped a laugh. "Talk about a busman's holiday."

"It's no problem. Really," I said and ushered her toward the back.

She sank onto my couch, looking small and lost and as cute as a duckling. "I'm fine, really."

"Yeah, well . . . " I forced a smile. "I didn't want my neighbors to think I was torturing you in here."

"Sorry."

I shook my head. "Is it your mother?"

She inhaled long and deep, dropping her head back a little as she did so. Not a blemish spoiled the pert perfection of her face. "It's everything. My mom, my job, my . . . boyfriend."

There was something about the way she said the last word that made my stomach drop. "Boyfriend?"

"Tell me the truth. Is there . . . " She glanced away, then pursed her lips as if fortifying herself for the truth. "Was there something between you and Michael?"

"What?"

"Michael and I"—she laughed without humor—"we were going to get married."

Thirty-seven

"Yeah, I saw the speed-limit sign. I just didn't know there was a dumb-ass cop hiding behind it."
—James McMullen, shortly before being incarcerated by said dumb-ass cop

"You and Micky?" I didn't mean to sound shocked, but I *was* shocked. Maybe in the back of my mind, I had half believed Lavonn's assertion that Micky had a thing for *me*.

And what about Lavonn? She was crazy about him, whether she admitted it or not.

"We hadn't set a date or anything. I mean . . . " Haven drew in a breath. "We didn't want anyone to know about us. Office romances . . . so many things can go wrong, and he'd been kind of a player . . . before me." She bobbed a shrug, still adorable even with mascara smeared below her eyes like Rocket, the high-tech raccoon. "He wanted to keep it quiet so we didn't make anyone uncomfortable. At least, that's what I believed. But now, I don't know. Maybe everything he told me was a lie."

I wanted to assure her it was not. But perhaps it would be wiser to let her talk. Clearly there were things going on that I knew nothing about. "What makes you doubt?"

"Well . . . he shot Marv!"

"Are you sure of that?"

"No! God, no. But why was he there?" She paused, expression pained, seeming to think I might actually have an answer.

I didn't. "Maybe there's a good explanation."

"Do you think so?" Her voice was breathy with hope, soft with uncertainty. "I just . . . It's driving me mad. Not knowing. One minute, I'm sure he's the sweet, thoughtful guy I thought he was, then . . . "

"Then what?"

She remained silent. Seconds ticked away.

"Brooke?"

"Nothing. It's just hard, that's all. Waiting. Not knowing if he'll ever wake up. I just wish we hadn't . . . I wish my last minutes with him hadn't been so malicious."

"What are you talking about?"

"We argued."

"Everyone argues."

"Not us. And it was so stupid. Sophomoric. But I still hoped he'd come to my party." She shook her head. "It was just a little get-together. A couple of friends. He called it my junk-food jubilee. You know, between Halloween and Thanksgiving. But he said he'd come. When he didn't show up, I never dreamed he'd gone to Marv's instead."

"What'd you fight about?"

"It was stupid. Just one of those idiotic misunderstanding:

that gets out of hand. I know that now. I'm sure of it."

"Sure of what?"

She shook her head.

"If you know something—"

"I don't. Honestly. It's just . . . "

"What?"

A dozen emotions twisted her face before she finally spoke. "Have you ever heard of Rohypnol?"

I felt my stomach drop. "The date-rape drug?"

"It's . . . maybe it's been called that, but it's a . . . it's a very effective sleep aid."

And I was a prima ballerina with mile-long legs and a tutu. "What about it?"

"I saw some. In his shaving kit."

"When was that?"

"Just . . . " She exhaled heavily. "A couple weeks ago. I asked him about it. He said he was having trouble relaxing."

"But you don't think that's true."

"I did. I believed him. But then I found out about . . . I learned some things. Disturbing things."

"About what?"

"About Jamel."

Our gazes met and locked. My guts cramped. "What about him?"

"Michael's relationship with the boy's mother . . . it wasn't . . . consensual."

I shook my head, playing dumb . . . or maybe just being dumb.

"You must have known," she said. "You're his therapist."

I neither denied nor confirmed. "Where did you get that information?"

299

She smiled. It looked hollow. "That's the worst part."

I waited, doubtful.

"I heard it from Jamel's aunt."

"Lavonn?"

"Yes." She popped up, paced the room. "I was at Michael's house, napping. Jamel was at a sleepover. I'd spent half the day writing grants for our moribund art program and the other half playing babysitter for a classroom of . . . " She shook her head as if none of it mattered. "When I woke up, I could hear Michael conversing with someone. It was obviously a serious conversation. I didn't want to interrupt."

"What'd she say?"

She clasped and unclasped her hands. "That she knew he'd forced her sister. That she knew everything."

Holy hell! Why hadn't Lavonn told me? Why hadn't Micky? My mind was spinning, but I nodded, ever unruffled. "What happened then?"

"Micky admitted it. Said he should be incarcerated . . . or worse. That there wasn't a punishment bad enough."

"What'd Lavonn do?"

Brooke shook her head. "It was amazing. *She* was amazing."

I waited, breath held.

"She forgave him. Absolved him of guilt."

Thirty-eight

"What's with the monthly bloodbath? I mean, seriously, why can't my ovaries just send me a text? Be like . . . Hey, girl, you're not preggers. Rock on.*"*

—Angela Grapier, who has lots of other great ideas, too

"Hey." Rivera's voice rumbled quietly through my overstimulated system, reverberating through every quivering fiber. It's not that I missed him. But being in danger is like being in estrus: the closer I get to the breaking point, the more attractive the proverbial he-man becomes. And I was in danger. I didn't exactly know why yet, but I could feel impending doom like a tickle on the soles of my feet. Hence my call to the dark lieutenant.

"Hello," I said but wasn't sure how to follow up on that auspicious salutation. So I cleared my throat. "You okay?"

"Why wouldn't I be?"

I huffed a gust of disbelief, irritation already mounting. "I believe there was a *disturbance* at a local restaurant."

He said nothing.

"A rustic place."

Silence.

"A mud pit. Scrambling patrons. A martial arts expert flying at you feet first. Ring any bells?"

"It's good to hear your voice."

I felt the irritation drain away. Felt other emotions seep in. "Yeah." I cleared my throat and decided to give honesty a try. How bad could it be? "Yours, too."

Silence lay between us, ticking quietly.

"What kind of trouble are you in?"

"I'm not in trouble," I said. So much for that honesty thing. It clearly wasn't for me.

Another silence, punctuated now with tired disbelief. "Just a quiet night at home with the dogs?"

"Pretty much."

"Good. Put Harley on the line."

"What?"

"I just want to say hello."

I fidgeted in the seat of my little Saturn. "He's, ahh, busy right now."

"Working on algebraic equations again?"

I forced a laugh. "Hammering out his thesis."

"Well, I won't take too much of his time. Put him on the phone."

For a moment, I actually considered trying to replicate Harley's signature growling bark, but impersonating a Great Dane seemed wrong. Even to me. "Listen . . . " I began, then stalled, brain freezing.

"I am," Rivera said. "But I'm not hearing my boy."

So he knew. Absolutely knew I was lying. "I *was* at home

with the dogs," I said.

"Yeah? Where are you now?"

"Meeting a friend . . . for dinner."

"Male or female?"

I considered telling him it was none of his concern but found that I wanted, quite desperately, for it to be *someone's* concern. "Female. She's . . ." I tightened my fingers on the steering wheel. "She's going through kind of a rough patch."

"A rough patch," he said and chuckled. "Where are you meeting her?"

"I need you to stay out of this, Rivera."

"That why you called me? To tell me to stay out of it?"

I winced. The man made a valid point. "Well . . . I need you to stay out of it unless . . . you know."

"Once your body's found washed up on Venice Beach, it'll be a little late, don't you think?"

Fear struck me like a mallet, throbbing in my fingertips. But I fought it back, wrestled it into submission. "She won't hurt me."

There was a moment of silence, then, "Yeah, because Blount is such a mild-mannered little thing. That's what Albertson thought anyway . . . right before she put a slug between his eyes."

"Albertson was dirty," I reminded him.

"Right," he agreed. "Unlike Blount, who's clean as a saint's underwear."

"She won't hurt . . ." I began, before catching myself. "I didn't say it was Lavonn."

"Where are you meeting her?"

"I'll tell you," I said, "if you promise not to interfere unless . . ." I paused, trying to catch my breath.

"Where?" I could hear the engine of his Jeep purr to life, felt relief and worry race each other to my tingling extremities.

"I can't tell you until I have your promise."

"How about why? Care to share that?"

I wasn't sure how much to reveal, but I had to tell someone. Had to talk it through, hear it said. "I think . . . I guess she knows about Micky."

I could hear him shift into gear. "What about him?"

"He, ahhh . . . when he was just a teenager, young, scared, neglected—"

"Dammit, McMullen, spit it the hell out!"

"He raped Lavonn's sister."

He swore, quietly but with a considerable amount of sentiment. "And Blount knows about it?"

"I guess so."

"So you think she shot Goldenstone."

"Maybe she just . . . just orchestrated it somehow." I exhaled heavily, not wanting to believe. "She would have reason to be angry."

"You think?"

Despite the circumstances, I didn't like his tone. "Listen, Rivera, this has been a hell of a—"

"What about Lieberman?"

"What?"

"How does he tie in?"

"They hated each other. Him and Micky. Had kind of a vendetta. I think . . . Maybe Lavonn used their mutual hatred."

"This is still the woman who won't hurt you, right?"

I winced.

"How'd she get the two of them into a showdown?"

I remained mute. I'd like to say it was an intelligent silence but the truth was I was too scared to conjure up enough saliva to speak.

"You don't think she did," he concluded. "You think she shot them herself. Lieberman, then Goldenstone. Shot them, wiped down the murder weapon, planted Mick's prints, and threw the piece into the bushes."

Terror ticked through me. "It's sounds so . . . so cold when you say it."

"Stop your fucking car."

"I can't."

"Why the hell . . . " He paused, drew a steadying breath. "What's your end game?"

"If she did it she'll talk to me. Tell me the truth."

"'Cause you're BFFs."

"Because she's basically a good person. We can resolve this peacefully. Before anyone else gets hurt."

"Are you honestly that delusional? Murderers—"

"She'll want to get it off her chest. Clear her conscience."

"Are you out of your mind? Pull over right now! That's an order, McMullen."

"She told me she knew where Micky kept his gun."

"And that's supposed to make me feel better. Holy Christ—"

"I'll call you when we're done talking. Tell you what I learned. I just wanted to . . . " My voice broke. I was going to say I wanted to give him the facts, but there was so much more than that. "I guess I just wanted to hear your voice."

"Chrissy, please, don't do this. Come on, just stop for a minute. Think things through."

"You're a . . . You're as irritating as a toothache. But I guess I've kind of missed you."

"At least tell me where you're going."

"Goodbye, Lieutenant."

"McMullen!" he roared, but I was already shutting down my phone.

Thirty-nine

"I just want the chance to prove that if I win the lotto I'll still be the same humble, smoking-hot guy I've always been."
— Peter McMullen, the number one reason Chrissy still has
nightmares involving adhesives

Lucky's Sports Bar butted up against a scruffy hillside, but its parking lot was well lit, its clientele boisterous.

Lavonn was already seated when I arrived.

The hostess, wearing a bicolored skirt the size of a hangnail and a skin-tight top emblazoned with the word *Tigers*, set menus on the table. "Your umpire will be with you in a minute." Her voice was cheery. Her pigtails bobbed with enthusiasm as she bounced away.

"You shitting me?" Lavonn asked, apparently unimpressed by the staff's level of perkiness.

"Thanks for meeting me," I said and slid into the booth across from her.

She eyed me, gaze hard. "What's going on?"

"I, ah . . . "

"Hey, team!"

I glanced up, startled. Our waiter, short, animated, and dressed in stripes generally associated with sporting events and African mammals, slid a loaf of pumpernickel bread onto the table. A knife had been thrust into the center up to its hilt. "What's the game plan?"

"Um," I said and considered the possibility that I should have chosen a restaurant with a little less *atmosphere*. But at decision-making time I'd been most concerned about finding a busy, well-lit venue that would reduce my chances of being killed. Now I wondered if Lavonn might off me just for exposing her to such an eye-jabbing level of pep.

"We've got Coke products, iced tea, a hall-of-fame selection of alcoholic beverages, and . . . Hold on . . . " He studied me, long-lashed eyes snapping with bonhomie. "You look like an iced-coffee kind of player to me."

I shook my head, trying to get my bearings. "I don't need any—"

"Maybe with caramel and a winning portion of whipped cream?"

"Thanks, but . . . Oh, okay," I said, coming to my senses long enough to remember I'd sell my soul for caramel sauce drizzled on high-calorie dairy products.

"And you?" He turned his mile-wide smile on Lavonn. "You look like you'd like—"

"Get me a water."

"Okay, but we've got—"

"I just want some damned water."

"You're the coach," he said and, still grinning, hurried off I couldn't help noticing that he looked just as good leaving a he had facing us.

"Once you're done ogling the dude, maybe you can tell me what this is about."

I turned back toward Lavonn with a jolt. "I wasn't ogling."

"Sure," she said. "Why am I here?"

"Well..." I shifted a little in my chair. "We're friends, right?"

She raised a brow a quarter of an inch and remained silent.

I refrained from clearing my throat. "Anyway, I thought maybe it was time to put all our cards on the table."

"What cards are those?"

"Time to be completely honest."

"About?"

Our drinks arrived. I took a slug of my caffeinated caramel. Not bad. "Micky."

She scowled, suddenly intense. "What do you know?"

"Nothing! I mean..."

"Did he wake up?"

"As far as I'm aware, he's still the same."

She pinned me with her hard-ass gaze. "I'm paying a babysitter fifteen dollars an hour to hear that nothing's changed? You said this was important. You said..." She caught her breath, eyes going wide. "You know something. Shit! You know who shot him."

I shook my head. "No. I don't."

"Then why here? Why bring me to this hokey, overpriced shithole if you don't have any more inform—" She stopped abruptly. "Fuck you!" she rasped, half rising.

"Lavonn!" I grabbed her arm at the same instant she snatched the knife from the pumpernickel.

I hissed a breath. The blade was inches from my face.

"Fuck you to hell!" she gritted.

"I've called the cops." My voice quavered like a scared castrato's.

"Yeah?" Around us, the other patrons merrily swilled their drinks and masticated their meals. "And what did you tell them, *friend?*"

I swallowed while I still could. While my heart continued to beat, while my bladder remained strong. "I know you know, Lavonn."

"Do you? And what do I know?"

It took everything I had to force out the next words. "That Micky raped your sister."

She said nothing.

"That's why you went to Lieberman's." My voice was no more than a whisper now. "You knew the feud between him and Micky was escalating. Knew he was going there. You followed him to exact justice."

Her hand trembled. Her face crumpled. The knife clattered to the table.

"Tell me the truth," I pleaded. "I'll do my best to help you. Be a witness on your behalf. If you plead temporary insanity . . . "

She laughed. Softly at first, then louder. Around the room, every customer turned to stare. Sure, now they were awake.

I squirmed. She was sounding a little maniacal.

"You think I'm crazy?" She laughed again, then tilted her head back and sighed. "Maybe I am. Maybe that's why I forgave him."

"No one can blame you for . . . " I paused, froze. "Wait? What? You forgave him?"

"I knew." She said the words softly. "Knew years ago

310

Down deep. Didn't want to believe it. Not Mick. Not . . . "
She glanced away. "He was the best of us. If he could do
something so heinous, so fucking awful . . . " Her wince
looked painful. "You know the worst part though? The most
confusing part?"

I winced, drowning in uncertainty.

"I can't forgive myself for forgiving him."

I tried to conjure up some kind of intelligent response.
Nothing.

"She was my sister. Blood kin. I should want him to burn
in hell."

"But you don't?"

She gritted her teeth, glanced away. "I couldn't take the
guilt anymore. Not with Kaneasha's boy under my roof. I went
to Mick's house. Got the gun out of his safe. His own gun. Put
it in his face. Told him I was gonna kill him."

"And?" My voice was almost soundless.

"He said I should do it. That he deserved it. Deserved
worse."

"Holy hell."

She drew a deep breath, leaned back in his seat. "He didn't
tell you that?"

"No. I . . . no. So . . . you didn't . . . " I shrugged.

"Why would I have risked my neck sneaking into
Lieberman's house if I wanted to see Mick go down?"

Fair question. "To plant evidence suggesting his guilt?"

She cocked her head at me.

"Evidence they haven't found yet but . . . Dammit. I'm
back to square one."

"Sucks to be you." She rose to her feet.

I stood with her. "Are the pictures real?"

"You think I did that sick shit?"

I shook my head, floundering.

"Why would I do that?"

"To make Micky pay for his sins."

She snorted. "I'm going home. Got to say goodbye to my kids before the cops show up." She pivoted away.

"Wait. Lavonn!" I stumbled after her, ricocheted off a waiter wearing a hockey mask. But she was already out of sight.

Forty

"Till death do us part? Don't tempt me."
—Pete McMullen's third wife, who was tempted on more than
one occasion

"Lavonn!" I raced out of the restaurant. She was nowhere to
be seen. I tore around the corner and slowed to a walk,
breathing hard.

"Keep moving." The words came from behind me. Quiet.
Spiked with unquestionable resolve.

I questioned anyway. "What?"

"Keep walking." The voice seemed disembodied,
unrecognizable. I shifted my eyes to the left, but the cold steel
of a gun muzzle prevented me from turning my head. "I won't
hurt you," she said and prodded me forward.

"Who are . . . " I began, but answers suddenly clicked in
my head. "Haven."

"Get going."

I stumbled into the scruffy woods that bridged the gap

between the hillside and the parking lot.

"Michael said you were smart." Her voice was civil, well modulated, chatty.

"You shot him."

"Talked about you like you were God's gift to the universe," she said and shoved me forward.

I stumbled, caught a branch, and turned, heart thumping as I backed away. "You killed Lieberman."

"But how would I have done that, Christina? Riddle me that. I was hosting a party." She smiled. It was picture perfect even in the uncertain light. "There all night. We watched *Scary Movie*. I had guests who swear it's true."

I shook my head.

"Lou wanted to see the second in the series, but those girls just can't hold their liquor," she said and paused as if waiting for me to catch up. Finally, I did.

"Rohypnol," I hissed. "You drugged them. Used the same stuff you used on the kids. The same stuff you said you saw in Micky's shaving kit. The stuff you used to make the porn with Lieberman."

"It wasn't porn."

"They were naked," I said, feeling my stomach roil. "Naked twelve-year-olds."

"It's art."

"Wh . . ." I breathed but wasn't quite able to finish the word.

"Marv was just taking nudies. Making a few bucks on the side. His programs were cut, too. Not that they shouldn't be. Gladiator sports. Who cares? But the arts!" There was passion in her voice. Passion and insanity. "The arts can't be compromised. They're the foundation of civilization. The cornerstone of society."

I watched her in breathless wonder. "So you were just . . . expressing your artistry?"

"That's right."

"With naked kids."

"You're just as pedantic as the rest of them, aren't you? People didn't understand Picasso either. Even Michael. Thought maybe he'd be a little more enlightened. But he wasn't."

"He knew about you. That's why you shot him."

"You give him too much credit." She scoffed. "As did I, actually. But he was getting suspicious about Marv and I couldn't trust Lieberman not to implicate me."

I watched her, mind spinning. "You were there when Lavonn threatened Micky, knew where he kept his gun. So you took it, planning to kill both of them."

"I gave you that whole sad story about me and Micky. About how it broke my heart when I saw the Rohypnol. You should have believed me. Should have told the cops."

"But it was a lie."

She shrugged, smiled. "You can't say I didn't try to help you out, Christina. You had every opportunity to lay the blame elsewhere. First on Micky, then on Ms. Blount. But you failed repeatedly. I should have known. Shrinks," she scoffed and shook her head. "Willing to sacrifice your career for a little slap-and-tickle with your client. You didn't even tell the cops about my beautiful photographs."

"You planted them on Lieberman's PC," I said. "Set up the shot, superimposed Micky onto the picture."

"I wish you could see the ones I've created of you. They're even better."

"What?"

"I'm going to have to have a reason for Ms. Blount to kill you."

"I—"

"It's because you were in the porn ring, too, if you're wondering. She'll shoot you. Then, overcome by guilt, she'll take her own life. Tragic."

I shook my head. "I'm not going to die!"

"A bullet to the frontal lobe is fairly lethal."

"But . . . No! You said you wouldn't hurt me." I was starting to babble. "You promised."

"And you believed me?"

I nodded, rapid fire, scared out of my mind.

"Jesus, pedantic and gullible," she said and aimed.

That's when I ducked. The branch I'd been holding sprang forward, striking her in the chest. She stumbled back, fighting for balance, but I didn't give her a chance to regain her footing. I leapt. The gun exploded in my ear. I tackled her. She fought like a mad thing. But I was fueled with rage, caramelized caffeine, and a double shot of terror.

Hiro had taught me well; one head butt to the forehead and that bitch was out cold.

Forty-one

"When a woman says, "Do whatever you want," do not, for the love of God, do whatever you want."
—Glen McMullen, trying, rather hopelessly, to educate his
sons

I felt kind of surreal as I applied my makeup. I mean, seriously, someone had just tried to kill me a few days before and now I was worrying about whether or not my eye shadow matched my gown. My hand shook a little. But I steadied it and moved on to the mascara. I looked pretty good . . . for someone who had just been attacked by a nut-job with an art degree and a grudge.

My cell rang. I answered it with my right hand while holding my towel in place with my left.

"Are you sure you're okay?" Laney's voice was still laced with worry. She'd wanted to visit after hearing about my ruckus with Haven, but I'd said it wasn't necessary. Baby Mac had a cold; she should take care of him.

"I'm fine," I said.

"Positive?"

"Yeah."

"Okay." She exhaled as if forcing herself to believe. "Then come help me at the farm tomorrow."

"With what? Can't count all the bedrooms alone?"

"I want to start cleaning out the barns."

"What?" I had seen the barns. They were neater than my bathroom. "What are you talking about?"

"The barns. They're filled with . . . everything. Mr. Foster didn't like to get rid of stuff."

"Who the hell is Mr. Foster?"

"The former owner."

"I thought it belonged to Gable's grandkid or something."

"The ranch in Santa Clarita? You thought I bought that monstrosity?"

"Well . . . yeah."

She laughed. "My place is a little more . . . early hoarder than English castle. But you should see the land. It's amazing. Surrounded by the mountains. Once I get it weeded and cleaned up and fenced and . . . everything . . . I can start taking in animals."

"Animals?"

"Sick ones, lame ones, old ones." She sighed. "I don't know. Maybe I'll start a therapeutic riding program or have some kind of interactive farm for city kids or . . . The possibilities are endless . . . if you'll help me."

I was almost giddy by the time I hung up the phone. Brainy Laney Butterfield was back. Or maybe she had never left. Maybe it was my own neuroses that fueled my insecurities that made me believe she had changed, had outgrown me.

I laughed when Harley pranced into the bathroom carrying his leash, fondled his ears, then let the dogs out (literally, not musically) to romp in the fenced yard.

In a minute, I was shimmying into the low-backed gown Rivera affectionately calls my "mermaid getup." It boasted a single broad strap and a dangerously low back with a pendant seated very near the base of my spine. The garment was a little snugger than was necessarily required by law. But it was the kind of dress that would make a corpse look good. And luckily, I was not yet in that category.

"I trained you better."

I spun toward the voice, simultaneously jerking my hands up in self-defense. But as luck would have it, mermaid gowns are not designed for really effective kung fu action. My big toe, carefully polished and stylishly bedazzled, got stuck in the hem. I tottered sideways with a squawk. Someone caught me, put me back on my feet.

I pushed away, breathing hard. Hiro Danshov shook his head as he backed away. There was a bruise on his forehead, a laceration on his left ear.

"I trained you to be alert."

"Are you kidding me right now?"

He raised one laconic brow.

"You sneak into my house like a demented"—I waved a fluttering hand—"ninja. Again. And tell me I should notice when you sneak into my house?"

"Vigilance is its own reward."

"I don't even know what that means."

"Then you must listen to your inner voice, *wuwei hua.*"

I rolled my eyes. He'd called me that on more than one occasion. According to Laney, it meant *fearless flower.* But I suspected it had another meaning . . . like *dork*.

"My inner voice?" I shook my head. I was trying to understand, but what I really wanted was to kick him in the eye. Unfortunately, I had tried that sort of thing before, never with astounding success. "Why are you here?"

"I heard of the attack on your person."

I felt my hands shake again, but I steadied them against my thighs. It was like hugging a sequined seal. "And you wanted to give my attacker some pointers?"

A spark of humor shone in his quicksilver eyes. He stepped forward. "Apparently, it is you who needs additional education."

"You try any of your *Kung Fu Panda* moves on me and you'll"—I glanced around. The deadliest weapon in my immediate vicinity seemed to be a curling iron. I grabbed it— "spend the next week trying to get this thing out of your nostril."

It looked for a moment like he was struggling not to laugh. My blood rose to a soft boil. "You must not allow yourself to become overly distraught."

I stared at him. "Are we talking about the fact that a perky little art teacher tried to shoot me in the head to cover up the fact that she was making a tidy sum circulating child pornography?" Anger bubbled up a little hotter. I took a step toward him. "Or the fact that you keep scaring the bejesus out of me in my own house? Because I gotta tell you, both those things are always going to piss me off a little."

"Nevertheless, you should not let anger control you."

"Screw you!" I said and reached out to ward him off with the curling iron, but he grabbed my arms. We were face-to-face, so close I could feel his heat, could see the dark velvet flecks in his eyes.

I was breathing hard. I wasn't sure he was breathing at all. We were inches apart. His hand, that killer poet's hand, touched my waist. My head fell back a scant inch.

He skimmed my body, scorching on contact. I felt my sexual allure like a seldom-used superpower.

"You look good, *wuwei hua*."

"Look your fill, Danshov," I said. "'Cause that's all you're ever going to get."

Light blazed in his eyes. It might have been lust. But it could just as easily have been amusement. How the hell would I know?

"So this . . . " He nodded almost imperceptibly toward most of me. "Is for your undeserving lieutenant?" He skimmed his fingers, feather light, up my bare back. I stifled a shiver.

"It's for . . . " I began, but his hand was still wandering up my spine, performing some sort of forbidden voodoo. "Me." It was all I could do to push out that final word.

He smiled at the gust of air. "So you do not care about men?" He touched an erogenous zone I didn't know existed. But I managed to speak.

"That's right," I said, but I was already leaning in. His breath touched my lips. I trembled and prepared to fall.

"Even Mr. Goldenstone?" he asked.

I paused, scowled. "What?"

"Perhaps this dress is all that is needed to bring him fully into the light."

"I don't . . . " I hissed a breath and jerked back. "What do you know?"

He said nothing.

"Is he conscious?" I asked.

"Perhaps you would have the answer to that query if you were less concerned about the physical than the transcendent."

"I don't even know what that . . . " I shook my head. "I've got to get to the hospital," I said and backed shakily away. But at that moment, the doorbell rang.

I gasped like a horror-flick starlet.

He raised his brows. "That will be your lieutenant, I assume."

"Quick," I ordered, temporally insane, "under my bed." But, of course, this being my life, he was already heading toward the foyer.

"No!" I rasped as he opened the door.

"What the hell are you doing here?" Rivera's voice was low and hard.

Danshov's was smooth as glass. "Good evening, Gerald."

"Where's Chrissy?"

"You look well in your finery."

"If you've hurt her again I'll strangle you with your own fucking—"

"I'm fine!" I said and stepped into view.

Rivera's gaze snapped to me. Midnight passion fired in his eyes, highlighting the bruise on his cheek, the cut on his brow.

"Through no fault of your own," Danshov said, gaze riveted on the lieutenant's.

Rivera shifted his attention back to Danshov. "What the hell's that supposed to mean?"

"It seems even an unskilled officer of the law should have been able to save her from a hundred-pound educator."

"Well, to be fair, she was an artist, too," I said. If I was hoping to lighten the situation, I failed miserably. "Listen," added, "let's not point fingers. The fact is, I'm fine. Everything's fine. How about—"

"If you hadn't made her believe she was invincible, maybe she wouldn't take such dumb-ass risks," Rivera snarled.

"So like the police to blame the innocent."

Rivera lowered his head, eyes blazing above the perfect cut of his tuxedo. "I'm blaming *you*," he said. "And you're hell and gone from innocent."

"Hey!" I chirped. "Who wants to take me to the hospital to see—"

"And you are far from able to protect her."

"The hell I am."

"Care to attempt to prove that?"

"I'm leaving." I grasped my gown in one hand, my keys in the other, jiggled them madly.

They didn't even turn toward me. I was just closing the door as the first punch landed.

Forty-two

"If a witness testifies that he failed to notice a woman's attire, believe him. If he failed to notice the size of her boobs, assume he's a lying sack of shit."

—Officer Sheila Edwards, forensic science instructor

A blue-smocked nurse and a bespectacled doctor turned toward me as I stepped into Micky's hospital room. They examined my getup, brows raised in mutual surprise.

Behind them, Micky lifted his lips in a weak smile. "Hey, Doc," he said.

"Micky . . . " My voice sounded a little odd, kind of husky, kind of hopeful. "Good to see you back among the living."

"Or in heaven," he said and eyed the twin globes that had magically appeared above the décolletage of my coppery mermaid gown.

The doctor, a pudgy woman with a nest of greying hair gave me the stink eye. "Mr. Goldenstone needs to rest."

"Okay."

"He just regained consciousness a few hours ago," she said and headed toward the door. "Overexertion could do irreparable damage."

"Or fix him right up," the nurse murmured, giving me a conspiratorial wink as she passed me.

I opened my mouth to refute both suppositions, but the door was already closing, leaving us alone.

"This for me?" Micky asked.

I turned toward him. "What?"

He skimmed my body, starting at my collarbone and working his way down. "If you're trying to make me decide life's worth living, you're on the right track."

"Oh . . . " I cleared my throat. "I was planning to attend a function."

"Does it involve clamshells and singing crabs?"

I cocked my head at him, wondering if he was still a little loopy in the noodle.

"Jamel's a big Ariel fan." He tilted his head. "Hell, who isn't?"

"Have you seen him yet?"

"Lavonn brought him by," he said and glanced toward the window. "Kid cried like a baby." He cleared his throat, eyes suspiciously bright. "Boy's got to toughen up or he'll get eaten alive."

"Lavonn'll take care of him until you're out of the hospital. She's like a grizzly on steroids."

"I owe her big."

"She's good people," I said and felt guilty for all the things I had thought about her minutes before I almost became dead.

"Then there's you," he said, fixing his gaze on me.

"What about me?"

"I heard it was you saved my ass . . . again."

"Who told you that?"

"Your lieutenant."

"Rivera?"

"How many lieutenants you got?"

I remembered Rivera charging Danshov and felt my ire rise. "He talked to you?" And didn't bother to inform me that Micky was conscious?

"Gotta tell you, his was not the first face I wanted to see." His gaze was warm on mine. "But it was nice to know he believed my story."

I watched him in silence for a moment, letting relief seep into my bones. "What is your story exactly?"

He inhaled, glanced toward the window. The tears had been replaced by anger. "Lieberman . . . We'd been at odds for months. I didn't like the way he treated the kids. He found out that I'd smoked some weed in the past. Called me *stonehead*." He scowled. "Man was a grade A ass. Knew that from the start. But I didn't think he was a fucking pervert. Not until a couple days ago, when . . . " He paused, exhaled. "*Weeks* ago now, I guess," he corrected. "I saw him and Brooke talking in the hallway. She looked upset. When I asked her about it, she said it was nothing, but she . . . damn, she has those big doe eyes. We'd dated some and I thought . . . " He shook his head. "I thought Lieberman was poaching. Went to his office to confront him. There was a picture on his laptop. I didn't get a good look at it before he slammed the screen shut. But I could see there was a lot of skin. Told him he'd better straighten up."

"So you knew about the pictures?"

"Hell no. I thought it was your average, everyday kind o porn. Still, school boards get pretty wound up about that sor

326

of thing."

Everyday kind of porn. Holy hell. "Then what?"

"Then we kind of got into it. He shoved me. I shoved him back. That's when Ben showed up, told us to cut it out before we were both canned. We backed off. Fourth hour was just starting. Didn't see Lieberman for the rest of the day. Then after school, I get a phone call. It's him, says he wants to see me, to clear the air."

"So you went to his house?"

"Didn't know he was a whack-job. Truth is, though, he acted kind of chill. Said he was in the wrong. Shouldn't have been checking porn during school hours. I said damn straight and while he was at it he could stay the hell away from Brooke. That's about the time she walked in."

"You still had no idea she was involved?"

He shook his head. "She was acting strange. Funny, though, my first thought was that she must actually have a thing for him. Must have already been there when I arrived. I got pissed. Asked how the hell could she prefer him to me? She laughed. Said Lieberman was a better businessman than me. Knew how to market. Just didn't know shit about art. She didn't like to share the profits and now that I was here she wouldn't have to. I was confused as hell. And that was *before* she pulled out the gun."

"So she planned to kill you both. Make it look like you were partners in this porn thing."

"Guess so. Said the cops wouldn't look much further once they saw the pictures I'd given Lieberman." He shook his head. "Nothing was making sense."

I watched him, reading every nuance. "Did you see the pics?"

He shook his head. "Who were they?" A muscle bunched in his jaw. "Not my students." He sounded like he might be sick.

I shook my head, not knowing. "The kids weren't alone, Micky."

"Shit!" He jerked upright, fists clenched. "Was Lieberman with them? Was that sick fuck touching them?"

"You were," I said.

For a moment, I thought he'd explode, but he settled back against the pillows, body tense. "Brooke . . . " he said and dropped his head against the white linens and chuckled drily. "Digital art was her forte. Man, I can pick 'em, can't I?"

"Were you in love with her?"

"Love? No. But I . . . trusted her. She was there when Lavonn showed up. When she told me she knew about . . . about Kaneasha. About the rape. Brooke helped me through it, helped me handle the guilt, and I thought . . . " He shook his head. "Holy shit. She shot me. Left me for dead."

"Lucky you faint so easily," I said.

He grinned, but the expression was crooked. "Lucky I met you," he said and, reaching for my hand, tugged me gently down beside him. "Or I would have been gone a long time ago."

He'd been depressed then, sliding toward suicidal.

"I think you have a pretty strong will to live."

He raised my fingers to his lips, kissed them gently. Feelings shimmied up my arm. "Turns out I got a few good reasons not to check out."

"Then don't do anything stupid." We turned in tandem when Rivera spoke from the doorway.

His black tie was missing and his lapel was torn. His lef

cheekbone was scraped and starting to swell.

Micky raised his brows. "He with you?"

"No," I said, pissed.

"Yes," Rivera argued, just as pissed.

Micky grinned. "I'd like to believe you, man, but anyone escorting the doc here should at least have a triton."

"I've got a badge," Rivera said. "That'll have to do."

Micky laughed, kissed my fingers again, and released them before turning his attention toward Rivera. "Thought you were giving me a clean bill of innocence."

"There are a few things we still have to clear up. The gun used wasn't—"

"What are you people doing here?" The doctor was back, her expression thunderous.

Rivera glared at her. "I have additional questions that can't—"

"I told you earlier, he can't get excited at this time."

"But you let *her* in here?" he asked, nodding toward me.

"Get out," she said. "Both of you. Before I call security."

Rivera scowled at her, then at Micky. "We'll talk tomorrow."

"I'm not going anywhere."

Rivera put his hand on the bare skin of my back, just above that low-seated pendant. I didn't swat him away, but I didn't exactly French kiss him either. We reached the parking lot without comment, but my good-luck silence had run out by the time we stood beside my Saturn.

"What the hell was that about?" he asked.

I popped my locks and opened the driver's door. "Good night, Rivera."

"Wait!" he said and grabbed my arm.

I swung toward him with a snarl, but he had already released me, had already raised his hands in surrender. "Just . . . " He exhaled. His expression suggested frustration and a couple dozen other emotions I couldn't catalog. "What is he to you?"

"Who?" I felt my anger drift a little. "Micky?"

"For starters," he said.

I stared at his cheek. It was turning an arresting shade of puce. "Micky's a client."

He gritted his teeth. "That you repeatedly risk your damned life for?"

It was a good question. I mean, it wasn't like I wanted to get shot . . . again. "He's had a rough time of it."

"That's not your fault," he said.

"Isn't it?"

"No."

"I'm his therapist. I should have known . . . "

"What? That a middle-school art teacher was selling child porn on the Internet?"

"I should have suspected something the first time I met Brooke."

He raised a brow.

"Anyone with a house that clean has some kind of serious mental illness."

He snorted, but I was on a roll. "I should never have doubted Micky. And Lavonn . . . I thought . . . " I shook my head. "I mean, she's saved my life, and I was still more prepared to trust that skanky Haven chick than her."

"So you misjudged."

"About a hundred times."

"You? I almost let you get killed! Again. If that fucking

Danshov hadn't taught you to . . . " He glanced away, jaw bunching.

I snorted a laugh. "Holy shit, Rivera, are you feeling jealous that someone else's efforts saved my ass for once?"

"No." He deepened his scowl. "I'm feeling . . . guilty."

"Oh no. You can't highjack my guilt."

"And you can't be responsible for every ex-Skull who's shot by an art teacher."

"How many of those can there even be? But it's not that. Well, it's not just that."

"What then?"

"Everything's wrong."

"What's worse than being attacked by an art teacher?"

I felt my face contort and tried to contain the words, but they slipped out. "Dad . . . "

His brows dipped and rose in surprise. "What about him?"

"He's sick."

"What? Your father? I thought he was indestructible. Like Schwarzenegger . . . and Ho Hos."

I gave him a look that said, *Right?* But I spoke with more maturity. "They think it might be cancer."

"Why didn't you tell me?"

"I didn't think we were a 'we' anymore."

He scowled but didn't try too hard to work it out. "How's he doing?"

"That's just it." I cut my eyes toward the front entrance of the hospital. An elderly couple was hobbling inside, gnarled hands clasped. "I haven't talked to him."

"What?"

"I tried . . . kind of . . . but he didn't answer his . . . What are you doing?" I demanded as Rivera punched a number on his phone.

"Calling your father," he said and put the phone to his ear.

"You have my father on speed dial?"

"Connie? Yeah. Hi. I'm fine. Uh huh." He nodded. "She's fine, too."

"Why do you have my father on speed dial?" I was hissing the words.

"Well, someone's got to do it," he said and chuckled a little as he rubbed a bruise starting to bloom like sunrise on his neck. "Don't mention it. Yeah. Hey, is Glen there by chance? Chrissy wants to talk to him."

I did. Of course I did. He was sick and I was his daughter. His *only* daughter. But I seemed to be shaking my head and backing away. Rivera followed me, glowering as he thrust the phone into my hand.

"Hello." I could hear Dad's voice clear as a curse from the other end of the line. "Chrissy?"

I paused, mind short-circuiting. "Dad?"

"What's wrong?"

"Nothing. Nothing's wrong. I just . . . " My throat was closing up and my eyes were burning. "Are you okay?"

"Me? Sure. I'm fine."

"Quit coddling her, Glen." My mother's voice, always as sweet as lemon juice, was clear, too.

"Dad?"

Silence stretched between us, then, "I guess I got a little . . . a little lump is all."

"A lump?" My nose was starting to run. I wiped it with the back of my hand. "What kind of lump?"

"Something in my throat."

"It's on his larynx," Mom said.

I bumped backward, hitting the car with my coppery mermaid's ass. "Laryngeal . . ." I began but couldn't quite force the word *cancer* past my lips.

"It ain't nothing," Dad said.

"Nothing!" I hiccupped the word, unraveling like a skein of yarn. "What are you talking about? You could . . . It might be . . ." I wiped my nose again and straightened, searching for the strong me, the grown-up me. "Have you seen a specialist?"

"They don't know nothing."

I winced. "What'd they say?"

Another pause. "I got an okay chance."

"If he has the surgery," Mom countered.

"What do you mean? What do you mean, *if*?"

He remained silent.

"Dad! What does she mean, if?"

"I was shot in the head in 'Nam. Didn't go under the knife then, sure as hell ain't going to now."

My eyes flooded. "Daddy, you gotta do it. You just gotta."

"It's not . . ."

"Please, Dad. Please. For me?" I begged, and suddenly I was sobbing, crying full out. "*Please!*"

"Quit that, Pork Chop," he said. "Quit it now."

"She don't like to be called Pork Chop," Mom chided.

"What?" Dad sounded perplexed, slightly miffed. "You don't? Why not?"

"Please, Daddy," I said again.

"You don't like the name Pork Chop?"

I swiped my cheek with my knuckles. Rivera handed me a Kleenex, which I squeezed into a wad. "Not too much."

"How come?"

"It's just . . ." I shrugged, strangely unaware that he

couldn't see me. "Being referred to as pig meat doesn't seem very complimentary."

"What are you talking about? Pork chops with applesauce . . . ain't nothing better than that."

I sniffled, thinking. "That's why you gave me that name? Because it's your favorite?"

He cleared his throat, and when he spoke his tone was gruff. "Why'd you think?"

"I don't know. I guess . . . " I shrugged again. "It's not like I ever gave it much thought," I said and cut my eyes to Rivera.

He rolled his.

"So you'll . . . you'll get the surgery?" I asked.

"If that's what you want."

"It is," I said. "It really is."

"All right, well, I gotta go. The Bears are playing the Vikings," he said and hung up.

I blinked, lowered the phone, and stared at it.

Rivera took it from my hand. "You okay?"

"Yeah. No." I exhaled. "I don't . . . " I found his gaze in the near darkness. "Pork's his favorite."

"You didn't know that?"

"No, I mean, I'm not talking about dinner options."

He stared at me.

"I'm talking about *me*. I'm his favorite."

"That can't actually surprise you."

"What? Of course it can. It *does*. I mean, it's not like my brothers are much competition. But they're boys and athletes and . . . " I released another shaky breath. "I'm his *favorite*." I felt something lift in my chest. "I gotta tell Pete," I said and reached for his phone again, but he pulled it away.

"Give me that," I demanded.

"So you can tell your brother that you're your father's favorite?"

"Yeah!"

He raised a brow. I pursed my lips, fighting the old name-calling, hair-pulling Chrissy like mad.

"You're right. Of course you're right." I exhaled, smiled. "I should wait and tell him in person."

Rivera snorted. "You okay now?"

"I think so."

"Want to go to a ball?"

I studied him in the uncertain light. "Your tux is ripped."

"Yeah?"

I raised my arm. "I think I have snot on my wrist."

He took my hands in his. Our gazes met and fused. A little tremor of excitement shivered between us. "You must know the truth."

"What truth is that?"

He said nothing, midnight-secrets eyes hot on mine.

"Is someone else trying to kill me? Is that the truth? Or—"

"If you shaved your head and wore a cardboard box you'd still be the most captivating woman in the room."

"What?" I felt my cheeks heat up and lowered my gaze. "No. Really?" I snapped my attention back to his mesmerizing face. "No. You mean that?"

"Jesus, Chrissy, for a shrink you are completely clueless."

I tightened my fingers on his. "That's the nicest thing you've ever said to me. I mean, the captivating part, not the . . . " I shook my head and took a step toward him. "You really mean it?"

"You walk into the gala wearing this thing, I'll have to put a gun to half the men in the room just to keep them off you."

I slipped my hands up his chest. "And the other half?"

"The other half will need paddles."

I kissed the scar at the right corner of his mouth. "Paddles?"

His lips twitched. Other parts were not so subtle. "To jump-start their hearts."

"How about you?" I asked and pressed my coppery length up against him. "How's your heart doing?"

"I think it can stand the pressure," he said, sliding his hands past the low-seated pendant to tug me tight against him. "If we take it slow."

Discover More by Lois Greiman

Chrissy McMullen Mystery Series:
Unzipped
Unplugged
Unscrewed
Unmanned
One Hot Mess
Not One Clue
Uncorked
Unleashed
Unhinged

Hope Springs Series
Finding Home
Home Fires
Finally Home

Home in the Hills Series
Hearth Stone
Hearth Song

American Historical Romance:
Surrender My Heart
The Gambler
My Desperado

European Historical Romance:
Highland Wolf
Highland Flame
Highland Jewel
Highland Heroes Box Set
Highland Hawk

Highland Enchantment
Highland Scoundrel
The Lady and the Knight
Bewitching the Highlander
Tempting the Wolf
Taming the Barbarian
Seducing a Princess
The Princess Masquerade
The Princess and Her Pirate
An Accidental Seduction
The Fraser Bride
The MacGowan Betrothal
Warrior Bride
Beloved Beast

Paranormal Romance:
Charming the Devil
Seduced By Your Spell
Under Your Spell

Contemporary Romance
Counterfeit Cowgirl
His Bodyguard
From Caviar to Chaos

Young Adult
Mixing Magic (written with Tara Daun)

Children's
Buffalo Knees

Connect with Lois Greiman

There are lots of ways to get in touch with me. I'm on Twitter, but I don't tweet much. You can reach me on Facebook, where I have giveaways, random thoughts, and information on upcoming events. You can also subscribe to my newsletter. Newsletters are sent out quite infrequently, and your address will not shared with anyone else. If you need to get in touch with me directly, you can email me.

If all else fails, check out my Events page and come and meet me in person to get a book signed or just stop by to say 'Hey.'

About the Author

Lois Greiman is the *USA Today* bestselling author of over forty novels. She currently lives on a small Wisconsin farm with her family, some of whom are human.

http://www.loisgreiman.com

Made in the USA
Middletown, DE
27 February 2018